JAMES PATTERSON

& HOWARD ROUGHAN

KILLER INSTINCT

CENTURY

1 3 5 7 9 10 8 6 4 2

Century
20 Vauxhall Bridge Road
London SW1V 2SA

Century is part of the Penguin Random House group of companies
whose addresses can be found at global.penguinrandomhouse.com

Copyright © James Patterson 2019
Excerpt from *19th Christmas* © James Patterson 2019

First published by Century in 2019

www.penguin.co.uk

A CIP catalogue record for this book is available from the British Library.

ISBN 9781780899404
ISBN 9781780899411 (trade paperback edition)

Printed and bound in Great Britain by Clays Ltd, Elcograf S.p.A.

Penguin Random House is committed to a
sustainable future for our business, our readers
and our planet. This book is made from Forest
Stewardship Council® certified paper.

For Joe and Joan Garrett
&
in memory of Scott Edwin Garrett
(1964–2011)

PROLOGUE

BOTTOMS UP

ONE

PROFESSOR JAHAN Darvish nudged his thick black glasses along the bridge of his nose and stared into the minibar fridge of his swanky Manhattan hotel suite while doing his best to ignore the outrageous price list posted off to the side. *Twenty-eight dollars for one of these tiny little bottles of vodka? Seriously?*

But Darvish didn't really care. The flight down from Boston, the expensive hotel, each and every lavish meal—it was all on MIT's tab. Besides, it's not like the minibar charges were going to be itemized on the bill. For all that the university bean counters would know back in Cambridge he drank a bunch of Diet Cokes and cracked open that fancy jar of pistachios. Better yet, the pistachios *and* the tin of macadamia nuts. Maybe even a Red Bull, too. How else was he supposed to work late into the night preparing for his major speech at the nuclear symposium?

"Is everything okay over there, Professor?" she asked from the large armchair behind him.

Darvish smiled. He loved that she was calling him that.

Professor. Finally a woman who knew what really mattered in a man. Brains.

It was meant to be.

Normally he would've never introduced himself to her. Fear of rejection almost always got the better of his nerve. But there she was, sitting by herself at the bar earlier in the evening drinking a glass of pinot noir while reading a book—the same book he had just recently finished. *The Alchemist* by Paulo Coelho.

If that didn't make it fate, then the fact that they shared the same homeland, as they quickly discovered, surely did. It was incredible, thought Darvish. Only in America could he meet the Iranian girl of his dreams.

Her name was Sadira, and she was drop-dead gorgeous.

Better yet, she didn't care that he wasn't. Handsome, that is. As they talked about the plot of *The Alchemist* and moved on to discuss everything from politics and global warming to French cinema and Italian opera, she kept telling him how impressed she was by his mind. It apparently didn't matter to her that he was twenty pounds overweight and losing his hair, or that his striped tie didn't match his plaid shirt, which didn't match his rumpled brown suit. She saw past all that. Sadira saw the person *inside*.

"Yes. Everything is more than okay," said Darvish as he continued staring into the minibar fridge with its little bottles of liquor all lined up in a row. He tilted his head, pondering. "Just so many choices."

"I don't care, so long as it's strong," said Sadira. "If you can't already tell, I'm a little nervous."

Darvish turned around, raising a bushy eyebrow. Actually, no, he couldn't tell at all that she was nervous. Nor could he help himself. He just blurted it out. "*You're* nervous? I'm the one who should be nervous. I mean, you're—"

4

"Please don't say it," she said, cutting him off.

"Don't say what?"

"That I'm beautiful."

"But you are. You truly are," he said. "How could you not know that?"

"It's not that I don't know. It's that everyone..."

Her voice trailed off, and in the words left unsaid, Darvish understood exactly what she was telling him. Sadira wanted to be appreciated for more than just her looks. Of all things, Darvish felt guilty. A tad shallow, even.

"I understand," he said. He truly did. "And I'm sorry."

Darvish turned back to the minibar, grabbing two bourbons. Jim Beam. It suddenly didn't matter what he chose for them to drink. Quickly, he poured the little bottles into a couple of glasses next to the empty ice bucket. "Hope you like it neat."

"Neat is perfect," said Sadira, standing. "The way it should be."

She met him halfway across the carpet, her fingers gently grazing his as she reached for one of the glasses from his out-stretched hand.

Again, Darvish smiled. How could he not?

It was the way she was looking at him. The adulation in her eyes. She made him feel so alive. So powerful. Tonight, he was more than a professor at MIT. He was Superman. Invincible.

"What should we drink to?" asked Darvish.

Sadira didn't hesitate. *It was meant to be.* "To seeing each other for who we really are," she said.

TWO

—

DARVISH WATCHED as Sadira made quick work of her bourbon. Was she looking for liquid courage? Perhaps she truly was nervous, he thought.

"Shall we have another?" he asked.

"No, I've had enough," she said before producing a smile of her own. "At least as far as the drinking goes."

English wasn't Darvish's first language. Or even his second. After Persian and Arabic, English was actually a distant third. But he was still pretty sure that was a highly suggestive double entendre.

Sadira promptly handed Darvish her glass and cozied up to him, her head nestling against his shoulder. Her long, dark-brown hair smelled like lavender.

"Have you ever been tied up, Professor?" she asked.

Forget liquid courage. It was as if he'd slipped something into her drink. Only he hadn't.

Tied up? Darvish shuffled his feet awkwardly. "Only in traffic, I'm afraid."

Sadira began loosening his tie. "Are you afraid now?"

The professor was speechless. Aroused beyond belief, but still speechless. Sadira began to laugh.

"Oh, you should've seen your face just now!" she said, pointing. She was kidding. *Of course* she was kidding. She didn't really want to tie him up.

"You got me," said Darvish.

"Do I?" Sadira brushed her full lips against his before whispering softly in his ear. "Trust me, I want you to be able to use your hands with me."

She let go of his tie and turned toward the bed, motioning over her shoulder for him to follow.

Darvish took one step, however, and stopped. Something was happening.

The room had begun to move. It was spinning. Slowly at first, then faster and faster. He tried to focus, but his vision had gone blurry, as if there were Vaseline smeared on his glasses. He could barely see Sadira or anything else. He felt dizzy. Nauseated. His knees were beginning to wobble.

"Something's wrong," he said.

"No," said Sadira, reaching for her purse on the chair. She removed a pair of latex gloves, sliding them on. "Everything's going exactly as planned."

The combination of drugs she'd slipped into Darvish's drink at the bar while he was in the bathroom was finally kicking in—with a vengeance. Stronger versions of his prescribed Oxy-Contin and diclofenac, plus lots and lots of sildenafil, a.k.a. Viagra.

Darvish reached out for Sadira, the two empty glasses of bourbon slipping from his hands. "Help me," he begged. *"Help me…"*

The professor had about two minutes of consciousness left. Three, at most.

Sadira would indeed help him. To the bed, at least. That's where she needed the professor to be. After pulling down the covers and messing up the sheets a bit, she helped him lie down.

"Here," she said, propping up his head on the pillows. She wanted it to look as if he'd been watching TV.

So far, so good. But still so much to do.

Sadira thoroughly washed the glass she had drunk from, spic-and-span, before returning it to its place next to the ice bucket. Darvish's glass was then positioned on the bedside table next to him.

Keeping the gloves on, she grabbed the remote and ordered a movie. The hotel offered a selection of six pornos. The choice for Professor Darvish was a no-brainer. *Naughty College Co-eds.*

Ironically, while the minibar charges weren't itemized on the hotel bill, the movie selections were. Titles included.

Sadira checked on Darvish again. He was out cold, officially unconscious.

It was time to finish the job.

Unbuckling the professor's belt, she undid his trousers and pulled them down around his ankles. Next, she rolled him over onto his stomach and grabbed one of the little bottles of bourbon.

Those latex gloves weren't just for avoiding fingerprints.

"Bottoms up, Professor," Sadira whispered. Then she made the bottle disappear inside his rectum. Completely.

Because all perfect murders have one thing in common.

They never look like murder.

BOOK ONE

NOTHING IS SACRED, NO ONE IS SAFE

CHAPTER 1

THERE'S NOTHING quite like walking into a room packed with more than a hundred students and not a single one is happy to see you...

If I didn't know any better, I'd almost take it personally.

"Good morning, class," I began, "and welcome to your final exam in Abnormal Behavioral Analysis, otherwise known as Professor Dylan Reinhart messing with your impressionable minds for a little while in an effort to see if you actually learned anything this glorious spring semester. As legend correctly has it, I never give the same test twice, which means that all of you will be spared any repeat of a previous exam, including my personal all-time favorite, having everyone in the class write and perform an original rap song about Sigmund Freud's seduction theory."

I paused for a moment to allow for the inevitable objection from the brave, albeit delusional, student who thought he or she might finally be the one to appeal to my better judgment, whatever that was.

Sure enough, a hand shot up. It belonged to a young man, probably a sophomore, wearing a rugby shirt and a look of complete consternation.

"Yes, is there a question?" I asked.

He was sitting in the third row, and best I could tell, it had been three days since he last showered. Finals week at Yale is hell on personal hygiene.

"This isn't fair, Professor Reinhart," he announced.

I waited for him to continue and plead his case diligently, but that was all he had to offer. There was no rehearsed speech on how all the other professors give their students a study guide or at least explain what they should expect on the final.

"That's it?" I asked. "That's all you've got for me? *This isn't fair?*"

"I just think we should've had a chance to prepare for this test," he said. "The only thing you told us was that we all had to bring our cell phones."

"Yes, I see. Clearly a miscarriage of justice," I said. It was a little early in the morning for the full-on Reinhart sarcasm, but sometimes these kids left me no choice. I turned to the rest of the class. "With a show of hands, how many of you agree with your esteemed colleague here? How many think that what I'm doing is unfair?"

Literally every hand went up.

I so love it when they make it easy for me...

"Wow, that's pretty impressive," I said, looking around the room. "You're all in agreement. All for one and one for all. Kumbaya!"

Mr. Rugby Shirt in the third row all but pumped his fist in

victory. "Does that mean you've changed your mind, Professor Reinhart? You're postponing the test?"

Silly rabbit.

"No, it means the test has already begun," I said. "Now everyone please take out your cell phones and place them directly in front of you. *It's time to see how united you all really are.*"

CHAPTER 2

I WATCHED and waited a few seconds while everyone took out their phones. *Note to self: buy more Apple stock for Annabelle's college fund.*

Then I went to the blackboard behind me, picked up a piece of chalk, and began writing. It was my cell number. Nothing more.

"Okay," I said, turning back around to the class. "I want you all to pick up your phones and text me the grade you'd like to receive on the final exam. You can choose between an A or a B. Whichever you text me is the grade you'll get."

I wiped my hands free of any chalk, gave a tug on the notched lapel of my navy chambray suit jacket, and started walking blithely toward the exit.

"Wait!" came a chorus of voices. "WAIT! WAIT! WAAAAIT!"

I stopped. "Yes? What's the problem?"

"*That's it?*" they all asked. That and numerous variations on the same theme. "*That's all we have to do?*"

I smacked my forehead. "Gosh darn it, you're right. There is one other thing I forgot to mention. Actually, two other things," I said. "The first is that I'm afraid I can't give you all As. Ten of you will have to choose Bs."

Cue the chorus again. *"That's not fair!"*

"We're back to that again, huh? Fairness?"

"Why would anyone choose a B?"

"That's the other thing I forgot to mention," I said. "Perhaps this will make it easier for you all. If at least ten of you don't choose a B, then you all get Cs, each and every one of you, the entire class. I repeat, a C. All of you. No exceptions."

It was as if I'd just told a roomful of five-year-olds that there isn't a Santa Claus. No, worse. That I had *killed* Santa Claus—and his little furry friend, too, the Easter Bunny. Shock. Anger. Disbelief. *We can't believe you're doing this to us, Professor Reinhart!*

It was beautiful.

Sorry, Sigmund, I now had a new favorite final exam. The setup had gone perfectly. All I had to do was wait for the emotional dust to settle. They would all start to think. First as individuals, then together as a group. It would begin with one simple—

"Question?" I asked, pointing at Mr. Rugby Shirt in the third row. He'd raised his hand again.

"Yeah, I was wondering," he said. "Are we all allowed to talk to one another before we each text you our grade?"

I pretended to think it over for a few seconds, even scratching my chin for added effect. "I suppose I'll allow that," I said. "In return, though, I'll need to put a time limit on any deliberations. Ten minutes should be enough." After a few groans from those who wanted more time, I glanced at my watch. "Make that nine minutes and fifty seconds."

The groans stopped and everyone scrambled like mad to huddle up.

Later, they would learn how they were subjects of an experiment for my next book, and that the tiny cameras and microphones I had installed around the room were recording everything they said and did.

Would they be pissed? Sure. Right up until I announced that they were *all* getting an A on the final for being good sports. In fact, I could already hear the cheering.

But that was then. For now, they were a group of more than a hundred ultra-competitive students at Yale deciding collectively who would sacrifice for the greater good. How would they decide? *Could* they decide?

Would the best of human behavior prevail?

I headed for the exit again so they could all talk freely. I didn't want anything to affect the outcome, especially me. There could be no distractions, nothing to derail the experiment.

And nothing would—I was sure of it.

Silly rabbit.

No sooner had I reached the door than I heard the first *ping*. Then immediately another, followed by a few more. Everyone's phones were lighting up with the breaking news. Including mine.

Something terrible had happened. Just dreadful. The absolute worst of human behavior.

New York City, my home, had been attacked again.

CHAPTER 3

I WAS redlining even before I hit the highway. One hand was maxing out on the throttle of my old '61 Triumph TR6 Trophy; the other was trying for the umpteenth time to reach Tracy. The wind was whipping past me, my cell plastered tight against my ear. To hell with my helmet.

Again the call went straight to voicemail, and again I hit Redial. *Please, please, please! Pick up, Tracy!* We should've never ditched our landline. I couldn't even try him at home.

The news alerts and tweets lighting up everyone's phones in class reported that multiple bombs had gone off in Times Square. A couple hundred were feared dead, if not more.

Like everyone else, I felt the initial shock up and down my spine. Then came an even greater jolt, straight through the heart.

Tracy had told me in the morning that he was planning to take Annabelle to the Disney Store—right in the middle of Times Square. Our adopted daughter from South Africa was only a little over a year old, and yet she was somehow totally smitten with the place. The music, the colors, the characters she didn't even know the names of yet. It all made her smile from ear to ear. She loved that Disney Store more than her binkie, bubble baths, or the monkeys at the Central Park Zoo.

At eighty miles an hour, I started to cry.

Weaving in and out of traffic, riding like a maniac, I could feel the anger in me taking over. My time in London, my years with the CIA. All of it had been dedicated to fighting a war that could never be won, only contained. Terrorism isn't merely a tactic of the enemy; it's the root of their ideology. They *believe* in destruction. They *want* death. And there are no innocent victims. Not to them.

Only to us.

A half hour into the ride, I gave up on trying to call Tracy. A half hour after that, I saw the flashing cherries of patrol cars at the entrance to the Henry Hudson Bridge. Lined up grill to bumper, the cruisers were barricading all three southbound lanes. No one was getting in.

No one was able to make a call either, I was told. At least not on their cells.

"All the carriers were forced to shut down their networks," said the second cop I approached after getting off my bike.

The first cop had all but ignored me. He was too busy directing traffic in what had become a three-point-turn festival with all the southbound cars that had been heading into the city needing to do a one-eighty. Making those turns even tighter were the piles of torn-up pavement from some recent jackhammering. *For once can there be a bridge into Manhattan that isn't under construction?*

"They're saying the terrorists used cell phones to detonate the bombs," the second cop explained. "For all we know there might be more to come."

"I need to get into the city," I said. "How do I do it?"

He looked at me as if I were deaf. Did I not just hear him? "You don't," he said. "No one gets in."

No, you don't understand, officer. I need. To get. Into the city!

I stared at him for a few seconds, hoping he might recognize me. It had been less than a year since I'd had my fifteen minutes of fame by helping to rid Manhattan of a serial killer named the Dealer. In the process, I had gained a couple of nicknames myself, including Dr. Death. For a while I was getting stopped on the street at least once a day. *Hey, aren't you that guy...?* Now it was maybe once a month.

All glory is fleeting, said General George Patton.

So much for staring at the cop. He didn't recognize me. I could've tried to refresh his memory or begun pleading my case, telling him about Tracy and Annabelle, but there was no point. He had his orders. The guy was merely doing his job. Besides, I'd already made up my mind on what I would do.

Time was wasting.

CHAPTER 4

I WALKED quickly back to my bike. Running would've been too obvious. The helmet went on, and the license plate got ripped off and stuffed inside my jacket.

I flipped on the petcock, checked the kill switch, turned the key, squeezed the clutch, and started her up. One quick zig to the left, a sharp zag to the right, and I had the clear path I needed. Now I just needed the speed.

Jamming the throttle, I was redlining again within seconds.

The first cop didn't know what the hell was happening as I blew by him. The second cop, the one I had spoken to, knew exactly what I was about to do but couldn't do anything about it. He looked at me in utter disbelief before turning to the pile of torn up pavement about ten feet in front of the cruisers blocking my way.

One man's rubble is another man's ramp.

I hit the pile hard, pulling up on my handgrips even harder.

There would be no style points. It was ugly. Steve McQueen made it look so easy on the same bike in *The Great Escape*.

My back tire barely cleared the hood of the first cruiser, and I could hear my axle practically snapping as the front tire slammed the pavement. I nearly wiped out—I *should've* wiped out—but somehow I kept my balance.

There was no need to look over my shoulder as I raced onto the deserted lower deck of the bridge heading into Manhattan. Those two cops weren't going anywhere. I was already too far gone. At most, they were radioing ahead to wherever the roadblock was for the northbound traffic, but that would only be to cover their collective ass instead of catching mine.

At the first exit, I peeled off the parkway onto Dyckman Street and into the Upper West Side. Tracy, Annabelle, and I called the neighborhood home. All along, I couldn't stop thinking the unthinkable, that the two most important people in my life—the two I could never imagine living without—were suddenly gone. *Christ, this can't be happening.*

The rest of the ride was a blur as I shot between all the traffic while completely ignoring red lights. In the distance I could hear a slew of ambulances, each one louder than the next, and all of them echoing in my head. It was the soundtrack of a living nightmare.

Finally I reached the front of our apartment building, ditching my bike in the middle of the sidewalk. I sprinted into the lobby and straight for the elevator with no intention of stopping until I saw the doorman, Bobby, sitting on an upholstered bench along the wall. He was completely engrossed in his cell phone. I could tell he was watching news coverage of the bombings.

"Have you seen them?" I asked, half out of breath.

He looked up at me, confused. "Who?"

I would've been confused, too. "Tracy and Annabelle," I said. "Have you seen them this morning?"

Bobby—who everyone called Lobby Bobby, albeit not to his face—acted as if I'd just asked him to explain quantum physics. The fact that I was so panicked only made him more flustered.

"Oh. Um...no, I haven't seen them," he said. "No, wait, *I did see them*. They went out earlier this morning, before the first—"

"Have you seen them since? Did you see them return?" I was talking a million words a minute.

"I don't think so," he said. "Is everything okay?"

But by then he was talking to my back. I was halfway to the elevator. I needed to see for myself. I needed Bobby to be wrong. He was distracted. He usually was, after all. He was often talking to some other tenants or signing for a package. That's what happened.

Tracy and Annabelle had returned home. They were safe. I was going to open the door to our apartment and call out as I always did, *Where's Anna-banana?* Then I'd wait and listen for that glorious sound, the pitter-patter, her little feet shuffling along the floor around the corner of the foyer as she came running into my arms.

But there was no sound when I opened the door. No pitter-patter. The apartment was empty.

Tracy and Annabelle were gone.

CHAPTER 5

"WHAT THE hell are you doing here, Needham?"

Elizabeth stared back at Evan Pritchard, wondering if perhaps she'd misheard her new boss of only two days amid all the chaos. No such luck. The guy was actually pissed off to see her.

"I'm here to help," answered Elizabeth. *What the hell do you think I'm doing here?*

"If you wanted to help me," said Pritchard, "you'd still be up in Boston, where you're supposed to be. Where I sent you."

Is this guy serious?

Elizabeth turned slowly to look at the devastation surrounding the two of them in Times Square as if maybe that might knock some sense into the guy or at least make him ease up. This was the worst attack on US soil since 9/11 and it happened in the same city—their goddamn backyard, for Christ's sake.

Times Square was no longer Times Square. It was a war zone. A coordinated series of C-4 explosions had reduced the stores and theaters to hollowed out shells of twisted metal and shattered glass. It had taken hours to tend to and clear the hundreds of wounded, which meant the dead were still everywhere, covered with bloodstained white sheets. There were too many to count, and yet that's exactly what needed to be done. That and a gazillion other things as part of the investigation. Surely it was all hands on deck for the elite New York–based field unit of the Joint Terrorism Task Force. Including its newest pair of hands, Special Agent Elizabeth Needham.

"Sir, as soon as I heard the news I just assumed that—"

"Of course you did," said Pritchard. "You thought you knew best. That's the rap on you, Needham. You always think you know best."

For a split second, Elizabeth regretted the last three and a half hours of her life, or roughly how long it took her to drive like a maniac from Boston down to Manhattan. But it took only another split second to realize that she'd do it again if given the chance, a hundred times out of a hundred.

This wasn't about her. It was about Pritchard. The guy was bitter. Big time. Six feet plus and roughly 220 pounds of resentment. Worse, he wasn't trying to hide it, not even on the heels of a massive terrorist attack. Her new boss wanted her to know that she wasn't wanted. His elite field unit was handpicked by him, always and without fail. That is, until the mayor got on the phone and told him that the FU, as they loved to call themselves, was being assigned someone new. Detective Needham was now Agent Needham. Pritchard had had no say in the matter. It was a done deal, and Elizabeth knew the guy couldn't stand it. So naturally he couldn't stand her. It was as simple—and effed up—as that.

But Elizabeth held her tongue and the dozen or so jagged-sharp comebacks that were on the tip of it. She knew what she had to do with Pritchard. Go along and get along, or at least get the hell through this miserable, horrible, tragic day. Tell the prick what he wants to hear and then figure out a way to help. Do anything. Do *something*. Search for survivors. Search for bomb fragments.

"I apologize, sir," said Elizabeth. "All I wanted to do was——"

"I get it," said Pritchard. "But look around you, Needham. Look at all the Bureau and Task Force agents who are already here. They're all trying to figure out the same damn thing: *Who did this?* And do you know what they all have in common? Not a single one of them was able to prevent it, including me. So if you really want to help, go back to Boston. Even if there's only a one percent chance your investigation leads to something, it would at least be something we might actually be able to prevent."

Elizabeth hated to admit it, but Pritchard sort of had a point. Still, why couldn't she do both? She could help here today and return to Boston tomorrow. But before she could put that thought into words, Pritchard had already turned his focus to an evidence bag filled with some charred wires that had just been handed to him. He had moved on. His newest agent, courtesy of the mayor, was now supposed to do the same.

Elizabeth walked away. She knew enough to not feel sorry for herself. How could she? She was literally stepping over the dead. As much as she tried not to, she couldn't help gazing at those bloodstained white sheets and the outlines of the bodies they covered.

Suddenly, Elizabeth stopped. One of the sheets was folded back a bit, maybe from a gust of wind. She could see a toddler's hand, a little girl. It was so small. There was a pink Hello Kitty bracelet around her wrist, and all Elizabeth could do was picture the day it was given to her and how much that little girl loved it and how happy it made her. She probably never wanted to take it off, not ever.

Elizabeth froze at the thought of this girl, her legs going numb. The only thing she could do was stare straight up into the heavens. Her years as a detective, the brutal crimes she'd seen, had tested her faith in God to the point where she truly didn't know if he existed. *What god would allow this little girl to die? What god would make all the people who loved her suffer?*

Elizabeth wanted to cry. Instead, she screamed.

In the corner of her eye, she'd seen something. Lots of them. They were in the sky and coming her way. *Everyone's* way.

The attack wasn't over.

CHAPTER 6

"INCOMING!"

Elizabeth yelled at the top of her lungs, her arm rocketing into the air to point north, directly over the building at One Times Square where the ball drops on New Year's Eve.

Everyone around her turned, their necks craning to follow the line of her finger. What they saw coming toward them looked like geese in formation, only these weren't birds. They were drones. Each one was about to drop a bomb, some sort of IED. Hell, you could even see the wiring.

Shoot 'em down! Shoot them all down!

No one screamed it. No one had to.

Elizabeth reached for her gun, as did everyone else who was carrying. She unloaded the clip of her Glock 19, the sky filling with lead. *Pop! Pop-pop-pop-pop!*

BOOM!

The force of the blast knocked Elizabeth hard to the ground. The second blast—*BOOM!*—kept her there as shards of glass from the windows roughly thirty floors above rained down on her. There was no time to take cover. She rolled onto her back, changed out clips, and resumed firing. *How many are left? Three? Four?*

Whoever was controlling the drones could see what was happening. As soon as the first was hit, the others scrambled.

Elizabeth whipped her head left and right, trying to keep track of them. There was now one hovering directly over her.

Single rounds weren't cutting it. There was no way to shoot them all down before—

Shit!

The drone above her released its bomb as Elizabeth fired off the last round in her clip without connecting. She was at ground zero and a sitting duck.

The empty clicks as she continued to pull her trigger sounded like a countdown to her death. All she could do was roll underneath a FedEx truck a few feet away. It wasn't nearly enough protection. She closed her eyes.

BOOM!

Elizabeth felt the blast, the heat singeing her face and hands as the truck buckled and nearly crushed her. It hurt like hell, but it was the best pain in the world because she could feel it. She was still alive. *How the hell?*

Maybe there was a God.

CHAPTER 7

ELIZABETH SLID out from beneath the truck to see what had saved her—but not before hearing it first.

The sound of the gunfire was different, though muffled through her blasted eardrums. The *pop-pop-pop* had been overtaken by the metallic *zip* of submachine guns. The cavalry had arrived in the form of the FBI SWAT team that had been canvassing the perimeter beyond Times Square. One of them had hit the bomb directly over Elizabeth as it dropped, a bull's-eye that had saved her life.

In a double-wedge formation moving up and down Broadway, the team continued to fire. Another drone was obliterated followed by one more, both before they could drop their bombs. Elizabeth's already wobbly knees buckled as she fell to the concrete again from the bombardment, her ears ringing so loudly they were stinging. She couldn't hear. She couldn't do anything.

Finally the SWAT commander yelled out, chopping his hand

through the air. The rest of his team held their fire. Everyone else with any ammo left followed suit.

All eyes remained looking up. Ten seconds became twenty, then thirty. It seemed like forever.

One by one, shoulders began to relax. Guns were holstered. The barrels of the SWAT team's Heckler & Koch UMPs were lowered.

Elizabeth felt a tap on her shoulder and turned. An EMT was talking to her, but it was nothing more than his lips moving. She still couldn't hear. Slowly, she began making out some of the words. The rest she could fill in. He was asking her if she was okay.

"Yeah, I'm fine," Elizabeth lied. She really didn't know for sure. Every part of her hurt.

He pointed to a row of medical tents set up along the nearest cross street. He was saying she needed to be looked at by a doctor.

Elizabeth nodded. It was the most her body could muster. That and hopefully putting one foot in front of the other. At least as far as those tents. She gently pulled up her pant legs, the bloodied fabric of her slacks sticking to her skin. Some of those cuts from the falling glass were well beyond Band-Aids.

She wanted to thank whoever had saved her life, but all the SWAT team members looked alike, as they always did in their combat gear, and now they all were doing the same thing— trying to clear the area. Just because a second-wave attack had been thwarted didn't mean there wouldn't be a third.

They were ushering any nonessentials down the stairs of the subway entrance at 42nd Street and Seventh Avenue. All press and any onlookers were getting the hook, even the uniformed cops who weren't part of the investigation. Elizabeth watched for a moment before spotting Evan Pritchard moving against the flow like a salmon swimming upstream. He was talking on a satellite phone, oblivious to anyone and anything. It figured.

Elizabeth shook her head and began walking toward the medical tents when she stopped on a dime. The sound was faint. A sort of revving. Like a tiny lawn mower that wouldn't start.

Her eyes darted, searching for what was making the noise. She kept looking and looking until—there, in the middle of Broadway—she spotted one of the drones that had been shot down. The bomb it was holding was still intact. *It was live.*

The rush of adrenaline pushed away the pain as Elizabeth started running. Not away from the bomb but toward it.

"Pritchard!" she yelled. He was walking straight for the damn thing and had no idea. "PRITCHARD!"

Others could hear Elizabeth. They could see her waving her arms frantically for everyone still in the street to get back. The SWAT team was now running for cover, corralling the last of the civilians down the stairs to the subway.

For Christ's sake, Pritchard!

Elizabeth ran past the drone, picking up as much speed as she could before barreling into her boss. Never mind that he was built like a brick house. She knocked him clean off his feet, wrapping her arms around him as they rolled toward the curb. He didn't know what the hell was happening, only that he was severely ticked off.

But there was no time for her to explain. Elizabeth scrambled to her feet, pulling Pritchard toward the subway entrance and literally pushing him down the stairs with her.

"What the hell are you doing, Needham?" barked Pritchard as they slammed into the concrete landing ten feet below. He was grabbing Elizabeth with both hands. He was practically shaking her. "Are you insane? You could've killed me. You could've goddamn ki—"

BOOM!

CHAPTER 8

I FRANTICALLY tried again to reach Tracy on his cell. There was still no service.

Pacing back and forth alone in the apartment just made the pain worse. I had to do something, and the worst part was that I knew exactly what I had to do.

Still, I stalled. I turned on the TV to watch the news coverage as if, what? I forgot where Times Square was?

Wait. Hold on. A second-wave attack? When? How? Christ...

The image of Lobby Bobby downstairs came flooding back to me in an instant. I had spoken over him in my haste to get answers. I couldn't help it—I was so desperate to know where Tracy and Annabelle were.

Before the first, he'd said before I cut him off. Before the first *attack,* he'd been trying to tell me.

There was no thinking as I turned away from the TV. One step, then another toward the door. Down the hall. Into the elevator.

If I'd been thinking, I would've known that going to Times Square, or however close I could get to it, wouldn't change anything. I'd be no closer to knowing if Tracy and Annabelle were okay. I'd just be closer to the actual place they might have perished.

The elevator door opened to the lobby. I was looking down, before my head immediately shot up—all because of the most beautiful, wonderful, amazing word I'd ever heard spoken in my entire life.

"Da-da!"

It was Annabelle. She was in her stroller with Tracy behind her. Our little girl was smiling, her baby teeth looking like little white Tic Tacs. I was overcome.

"Anna-banana!"

I took one step out of the elevator and dropped to my knees so I could kiss her and kiss her some more. Then I popped up to hug Tracy. I mean, a real bear hug. God knows the scene I was making, not that anyone could see us around the corner in the elevator bank.

"*Where were you two?*" I asked. But all that really mattered was where they weren't.

I was so relieved to see them alive that I hadn't taken a good look at Tracy. As much as he was happy to see me, there was something not quite right. He seemed to be in a daze. As it turned out, he was still shaken up.

"*We were supposed to be there,*" he said. "We would've been right in Times Square at the moment those bombs went off."

"What happened?" I asked.

Tracy shook his head. He still couldn't believe it himself. "I forgot my wallet."

He said it so softly I wasn't sure I heard him right. "Your wallet?"

"We took an Uber and were almost at the Disney Store when I realized I'd left it in the apartment." He peeked over the hood of the stroller to glance at Annabelle digging into her little baggie of Cheerios. "And you just know you can't escape a Disney Store without buying something. So I told the driver to turn around. A few minutes later, probably right when we would've been walking into the store, we heard the explosions. I'm still in shock."

He looked it, all right. "You went to the Needle, didn't you?"

That's where Tracy always goes to clear his head—the obelisk in Central Park, otherwise known as Cleopatra's Needle. By staring up at the city's oldest outdoor monument, originally built in ancient Egypt, he's able to remind himself that whatever's bothering him, this is just a blip in time. Or, as a Persian Sufi poet once wrote, *this too shall pass.*

"Yeah, only this is the first time the Needle didn't really do the trick," said Tracy. "I'm still numb."

"I don't blame you."

"I tried calling you," he said.

"Me, too," I said.

"All cell service was—"

"Shut down, I know. It still is."

"I used that old pay phone at that Greek diner on 83rd and tried to reach you on campus. Someone in the psych department said you left as soon as you heard the news."

"You'd told me that you and Annabelle were—"

"Going to the Disney Store," he said. "I know."

We both smiled. We used to make fun of couples who finished each other's sentences. Now we were one of them. Again, I hugged him.

"What a day," said Tracy. "What a horrible, scary day."

"Tell me about it," came a nearby voice.

We all knew who it was even before we turned to look. Even Annabelle knew. It was her favorite "aunt" in the world, although Annabelle was still working on her name. Actually, in that moment it sounded absolutely perfect.

"Liz-bet!"

CHAPTER 9

IT WAS the middle of the afternoon, but this was no time for coffee or tea. We never even entertained the thought of beers. Instead, we went straight to whiskey once we all got up to the apartment. Johnnie Black, heavy pours. Elizabeth, Tracy, and me.

As for Annabelle, it was sugar-free apple juice in her favorite sippy cup. Straight up.

"Guys, are you sure it's okay?" asked Elizabeth as we settled in around the kitchen table. "My staying here?"

Gingerly didn't even begin to describe how slowly she was moving. She was bandaged to the hilt on her arms and legs. They were cut up pretty badly, and she had some seriously bruised ribs. In fact, all of her was bruised.

"We're more than sure it's okay," said Tracy. "Stay here as long as you like."

To think, it wasn't too long ago that Tracy questioned my feelings for Elizabeth. Now they're BFFs.

"It should be only one news cycle, two at most," she said. "Then they'll move on and leave me alone."

The terrorist attack—make that multiple attacks—on Times Square would be a story for weeks and months, as well as remembered forever. Elizabeth was referring to the video now making the rounds on the news and YouTube and everywhere else. Somehow a freelance cameraman captured her saving Evan Pritchard's life. She was being branded a hero, and all the news networks suddenly wanted to shove a camera in her face.

"They were literally camped outside my apartment building, at least a half dozen satellite trucks," Elizabeth said. "I told the cabbie to keep driving."

"Why didn't you tell us about the new job?" I asked.

"It literally just happened. Monday morning I was in Deacon's office at City Hall; Monday afternoon I was officially part of the Task Force," she said. "Apparently the mayor has some pull. Go figure."

Elizabeth had been promoted to detective first grade after the Dealer case but Mayor Edward "Edso" Deacon knew he had to do more. For good measure, I'd been sure to remind him.

"He did promise to help you," I said.

"And he kept his promise," she said. "Go figure again."

"Now Deacon's going to exploit you like crazy, isn't he?" asked Tracy. Although it was hardly a question. More like a given.

"Yeah, but at least I won't be a campaign prop," said Elizabeth.

Fortunately, Edso Deacon didn't have another election any time soon. His days of running for mayor were over.

"Thank God for term limits," I said, raising my whiskey.

We all leaned in to clink glasses. Elizabeth let out a moan. Moving only a little had her reaching for her ribs in pain.

"Here," I said, pouring her a refill. "More medicine."

"Do I look as bad as I feel?" she asked.

I was all ready to be the diplomat when Tracy couldn't help himself. He always tells it like it is. Or maybe it was the whiskey kicking in.

"You look like s-h-i-t," he told Elizabeth before glancing at Annabelle in her high chair. He always made sure to spell out curse words around our little girl. I was still forgetting to the point where Tracy was threatening me with a swear jar.

Meanwhile, Annabelle was blissfully still going to town on her apple juice. She looked so happy, and I was relieved that she wasn't old enough to know what had happened today in her newly adopted hometown, so to speak.

The world she's growing up in scares me like crazy. Is she really that much safer here than in the Nyanga township of Cape Town?

Before I could dwell on that too long, my cell started beeping with a flood of incoming texts and phone messages. Within seconds, Tracy's cell was doing the same, followed by Elizabeth's. Service had been restored.

Like teenagers, we all buried our heads in our screens, but it was something Elizabeth muttered that had me stopping to look at her. It was only one word, and barely a word at that. Still, that's all it took.

There wasn't much I didn't know about Elizabeth Eliot Needham by now. The facts as well as the quirks. She was her high school's homecoming queen in Crosspointe, Virginia—a reluctant one at that—and a criminology major at the University of Maryland, where she ran track. She had one sibling, an older sister who lived in Boston. Her mother, Brenda, lived in Seattle, and her father was "somewhere else" ever since he cheated on Brenda when Elizabeth was a teenager. The guy was essentially off-limits as conversation topics went, which actually told me everything I needed to know about Elizabeth's relationship with him. I didn't push.

Then there were those quirks. The meticulousness—everything in front of Elizabeth always had to be neat and tidy and perfectly lined up. She loved pizza but hated tomatoes. She barely made any noise when she sneezed. Oh, and she could sing the alphabet backward as if singing it forward. I've tried and tried and I still can't do it.

But above and beyond all that was the one fact that doubled as a quirk. Elizabeth absolutely, positively lived for working cases.

So nothing piqued her interest more than something that might help her solve one. On her phone right then had come something—I could tell—and all it took was that single little word.

"Huh," she'd said.

CHAPTER 10

"WHAT IS it?" I asked.

I could practically read her mind as she was quickly deciding how to answer. On the one hand, the Joint Terrorism Task Force was like Las Vegas—what happens there, stays there. She couldn't discuss anything specific involving her unit. Those were the rules.

On the other hand, it was me who was doing the asking. I'd trusted her with my CIA past. The CIA was like Vegas even before Vegas was like Vegas. I'd even introduced her to the Byrdman—Julian Byrd—the J. D. Salinger of hackers in terms of reclusiveness. Vladimir Putin would kill to know how to find him. Literally. After all, Putin's foreign bank accounts and cryptocurrency holdings didn't magically disappear by themselves after the Russians meddled with our elections. *Payback is a bitch. Huh, Vladdy?*

Of course, even if Elizabeth was fine telling me, there was still the issue of Tracy being at the table. Then again, Tracy had been the first to insist she stay with us while waiting out the news vans surrounding her apartment building. She was our guest. Plus, who was he really going to tell?

"Ah, screw it," said Elizabeth.

After another swig of Johnnie Black, she told us about her trip up to Boston and the first case she'd been assigned to on the Task Force. Or rather, "this *so-called* case." She clearly wasn't happy about it.

An Iranian-born professor at MIT, a nuclear physicist, had died accidentally during an act of self-love gone awry. That's a very polite way of saying that he suffered a heart attack with a tiny liquor bottle inside him where the sun doesn't shine.

"So, what exactly are you investigating?" asked Tracy.

"I'm not sure," said Elizabeth. "My new boss—who hates me, by the way—said that no two words make him twitch more than *Iranian* and *nuclear*. So when an Iranian nuclear physicist suddenly turns up dead, he wants to look into it no matter how certain the police are that it was an accident."

"And you?" I asked. "How certain are you?"

"This professor had been watching a porno in the hotel room and there was excessive Viagra in his system. He also was on prescription meds—OxyContin and an anti-inflammatory. It's all embarrassing as hell, especially with his turning that liquor bottle into a sex toy, but it's not exactly suspicious," she said. "As for his colleagues and neighbors I interviewed up in Boston, they all said the same thing. Iran was his homeland, but this was his home. The guy loved America. Everything points to him being alone in that hotel room when he died, and given what he was doing, it makes complete sense."

"So, what's changed?" I asked, motioning to her phone. "Why the *huh*?"

"It's the hotel where the professor was staying. Their surveillance cameras showed him leaving to meet some colleagues for dinner, but they didn't have any footage of him returning that night. At least they didn't until now," she said. "Can I borrow your computer?"

"Here, use mine," said Tracy, getting up to grab his laptop from the living room. In the meantime, Elizabeth handed me her phone so I could see the text she got.

"It's from one of the detectives on the case," she said.

1 mystery solved. Another created.

That was followed by a file number on what was the NYPD's version of an encrypted Dropbox, a way for cops and detectives to share files securely. Sure, Julian could probably hack into the server with both eyes closed, but that was Julian. The Byrdman was one of a kind.

Elizabeth logged into the site on Tracy's laptop, glancing up at us before entering her JTTF password. Tracy and I jokingly made a show of covering our eyes to prove we weren't looking, only to see that Annabelle thought we were playing peekaboo. She covered her eyes, too.

"Here it is," said Elizabeth, turning the screen so Tracy and I could see. She double-clicked the file. The footage flickered before smoothing out.

"Is that the guy?" asked Tracy, pointing.

"Yeah, that's him," said Elizabeth. "Dr. Jahan Darvish."

The recording was in color, albeit not very crisp. No surprise, as it came from a surveillance camera. Still, we could all clearly see the professor walking through the door of what looked to be a back entrance of the hotel.

He wasn't alone.

There was a woman clutching his arm. She was wearing a white blouse with a scoop neck, a black skirt, and black high heels. That much we could see.

But the mystery was what we couldn't see.

"Huh," I said.

CHAPTER 11

I WAS sure of two things before going to bed. One, the sun would rise in the morning. Two, life would go on.

We had watched the news coverage of the attacks into the night, and there wasn't enough whiskey in the world to dull the pain and heartache as some of the victims became known.

There was the story of a mother and her twin nine-year-old sons visiting from Lincoln, Nebraska. The father had stayed behind at their midtown hotel for a work call while they toured the wax statues at Madame Tussauds New York, a Times Square favorite. In the blink of an eye, the man was now a widower and childless.

There was the drama club from a high school in Flushing that was on a field trip to see a musical at the Lyric Theatre. Every student except two was killed by the explosions. One of the four chaperones, the vice principal of the school, survived only because she went back to the bus to get her sweater. She's the one who spoke to the media, or at least tried to. The poor woman couldn't stop crying.

It was too soon for any official list of the dead to be released. The police were neither confirming nor denying any particular name. Eventually they would all be known, and all I could do was breathe in deeply and exhale at the thought of how close Tracy and Annabelle had come to being among them.

"Are you okay?" asked Elizabeth.

I was staring out the living room window early the next morning. I'd just changed Annabelle's diaper, and Tracy was now dressing her.

The sun had come up and life—no matter how cruel at times—would indeed go on.

"I'm okay," I said. "More importantly, how are you?"

"I still feel like s-h-i-t, but I'll be fine," she said. She couldn't shower because of all her bandages, but she was dressed and ready to go. "Thanks again for the change of clothes."

She had on one of my old gray hoodies and a pair of "mom" jeans left behind by Tracy's sister when she last visited from Providence. While it ranked among the top ten of unflattering ensembles, leave it to Elizabeth to somehow look good in it.

"Are you heading straight to work?" I asked.

She nodded. "I'll let you know what I find out."

I knew how anxious she was to get to her office and see what she could learn about that mysterious white glow obscuring the face of the woman in the hotel with the nuclear physicist. Elizabeth assumed either there was a technical glitch with the footage or someone had tampered with it. She had asked me what I thought, and I had told her I didn't know.

I hated lying to her.

The glow was neither a glitch nor the result of tampering. Something else had caused it, but I couldn't tell her what it was. Not yet.

Or maybe not ever.

What's done is done, wrote Shakespeare in *Macbeth.* Were that only true for me.

My past won't leave me alone.

In fact, it was about to come after me in more ways than I could've ever imagined.

CHAPTER 12

"YOU'RE GOING to be late," I told Tracy after Elizabeth left.

"So I'm a little late," he said, continuing to shower kisses on Annabelle, who was playing with her Baby Stella doll in his lap on the living room couch. "I'm jealous. You get to be with our beautiful girl all day. And I have to..." His voice trailed off into a sigh.

Sometimes the only thing worse than not booking an acting gig for a while is booking one that you dread. In Tracy's case, it was a 3-D motion capture shoot. He was half doing a favor for a friend, Doug Chadwick, a programming engineer with a gaming company based in Hell's Kitchen. It wasn't a full favor for one simple reason. The gig paid pretty well. At least as well as one can imagine for jumping around all day wearing a green leotard covered with ping-pong balls.

Doug had already called to apologize. He wanted to cancel the session in light of the attacks, but the studio was already paid for. He couldn't postpone or get a refund.

Tracy finally handed Annabelle to me and headed for the door. "Okay," he said with a wave, "I'm off to win an Oscar."

Two minutes later, he was back. Or so I assumed when I heard the knock on the door. Tracy had a habit of forgetting his keys.

I lifted Annabelle and carried her to the door with me. The previous owners of our apartment had been a little fanatical about security. In addition to motion-activated sensors in every room, they had installed a self-locking front door. It wasn't the worst feature to have in a big Manhattan apartment building, so we didn't change it.

"Let me guess," I said as I opened the door.

Guess again, Dylan...

The man standing in front of me seemed as startled as I was. "I'm sorry—"

"No, I'm sorry," I said. "I thought you were someone else."

"Are you Dylan Reinhart?" he asked.

The average adult brain has anywhere from 100 to 500 trillion synapses. All of mine, no matter what the count, were firing at once. Something wasn't right.

A well-dressed Arab with a British accent had just shown up out of the blue on my doorstep. I didn't know him from Adam, but I was fairly certain his question was a formality. He knew damn well that I was Dylan Reinhart.

No point in my being coy. "That's me," I said. "I'm Dylan. And this here is Annabelle."

"She's beautiful," he said. His somewhat stoic demeanor softened. *"Hello, Annabelle."*

Annabelle buried her face in my shoulder. "As you can see she's not terribly good with strangers," I said. I didn't actually punch the word *strangers,* nor did I have to. The word itself did the trick.

"Oh, yes, of course. My apologies," he said, reaching inside his suit jacket, which was clearly custom-tailored. He handed me his card. "I'm Benjamin Al-Kazaz."

Different cultures have different etiquette when it comes to giving someone a business card. The Chinese always use two hands. In India, you use the right hand and *only* the right hand to extend a card.

But what we all do once we get the card is universal. It's human nature. We all look at the card.

BENJAMIN AL-KAZAZ, ATTORNEY AT LAW. No address, just a phone number.

I looked back up at him, catching his stare. He was around my age, maybe a few years older. Clean-cut, no beard.

What I noticed most, though, was the furrowed brow above his very dark eyes. It spoke volumes. He was not the bearer of good news.

"I'm afraid to ask," I said.

"I'm here regarding an old friend of yours. Ahmed Al-Hamdah?"

He could've stopped right there. I knew what was coming. The only question in my mind was *When did it happen?* But I couldn't ask that because that would be revealing too much. About me. About my past.

So instead I said what I was supposed to say. I said what Ahmed would say if a stranger had asked him about me.

"I'm sorry, who?" I asked.

Al-Kazaz nodded with a hint of a smile. "He told me that's what you'd say." The smile then disappeared. "I'm afraid your friend, Mr. Al-Hamdah, is dead."

CHAPTER 13

"COME IN," I said, stepping back from the doorway.

"Thank you," said Al-Kazaz.

I led him into the living room, offering him a seat in one of the armchairs opposite the sofa. Annabelle was still playing shy, so I put her down beside her pink pop-up tent, which she absolutely adores, and then grabbed her Baby Stella doll. She smiled wide as I handed it to her. All was good in her world.

My world was less so. A lot less.

I'd first met Ahmed Al-Hamdah as a field operative in London. My cover was a research fellowship at Cambridge. His was as a ThM candidate at Oxford—a master of theology. He'd been recruited by MI6 to be their eyes and ears in the Baitul Futuh Mosque in South London, the largest mosque in Great Britain. Our paths crossed during a joint CIA and MI6 operation to foil a bombing at Westminster Abbey. We foiled it, all right, but it nearly got me killed. One chilly night in November, when my cover was blown, Ahmed saved my life.

"Can I get you something to drink?" I asked Al-Kazaz. "Coffee?"

"No, thank you," he said.

I sat down on the sofa, grabbed a knee with each hand, and stared for a moment at the stranger I'd just invited into my home. The only things I knew about him were what he'd told me. In other words, I knew nothing about him.

He, however, knew my name and where I lived. He also knew that Ahmed was at the very least a friend of mine. I couldn't help but wonder: did this stranger know my past?

"It's been years since I've seen or talked to Ahmed," I said. "Was there an accident? Had he been sick?"

Fat chance. Ahmed had still been an operative, although now with the CIA. The Agency doesn't exactly promote this fact in their recruiting pamphlets, but the probability of an operative dying in the line of duty is 28 percent. If you happen to be a Muslim operative, it jumps to 44 percent.

Al-Kazaz shook his head. "Ahmed was killed in the Times Square bombings yesterday."

I didn't have to fake my surprise. "How do you know?" I asked.

"I know."

"*How* do you know?"

"I have to be honest with you, Dr. Reinhart. I'm not privy to what Ahmed really did for a living. I have my suspicions, but it wasn't my place to ask," said Al-Kazaz. "Ahmed told me he was an insurance executive when he hired me years ago, although I haven't known many insurance executives who wanted to exchange a text every day in order to confirm they're still alive."

"Excuse me?" I asked.

"It was an unusual arrangement, and it's what ultimately led me to you," said Al-Kazaz. "Every day, precisely at noon, I sent

Ahmed a one-word text. If he responded in a certain way, I knew it was him and that he was alive."

"May I ask what the one word was?"

"It was actually a name. Gary."

"Gary?"

"Yes. And every day for the last three years, without fail, Ahmed texted back the same response within sixty seconds."

"Cooper," I said. It was pure reflex. Ahmed loved westerns. His favorite movie was *High Noon*. He used to talk my ear off over pints of Guinness about how cool Gary Cooper was.

Al-Kazaz nodded. "Only yesterday, there was no Cooper," he said. "I immediately had a bad feeling given what happened in Times Square. I called a friend of mine with the police. Ahmed's wallet had been found on one of the bodies."

"I'm confused," I said, which wasn't entirely a lie. "Was my name in his wallet or something?"

I knew that wasn't a possibility, but the dots still weren't connected. How did this attorney get to me via Ahmed?

"I had one other responsibility besides texting Ahmed every day at noon," said Al-Kazaz. "He gave me your name and your address. If he were to die, I was immediately supposed to come see you."

"Why?" I asked.

He reached into his pocket. "To give you this," he said.

CHAPTER 14

"WHAT IS that?" I asked.

"I don't know," said Al-Kazaz, holding up the envelope. "I don't think I'm ever supposed to know. But you are."

He leaned over the coffee table, handing it to me. It was your typical number 10 white envelope. No writing on either side. Sealed.

"How long did you say you've been holding on to this?" I asked.

"A total of three years, although Ahmed asked for it back a few times. I figured it was to make some changes. Updates, perhaps. He'd always return a new envelope to me within a day or two."

"Do you remember the last time Ahmed asked for it back?"

Al-Kazaz thought for a second. "Maybe six weeks ago?"

"And he never told you what was inside?" I asked. "Not even a hint?"

"No, nothing," he said. "I was curious, of course, but there was also a part of me that wasn't sure I wanted to know. Do you know what I mean?"

"Sure, I understand," I said. "You're an attorney. What you don't know can't be used against you, right?"

"Something like that."

"Ahmed obviously trusted you, though. You were good friends?"

"Actually, no," said Al-Kazaz. "We weren't friends at all."

"I suppose that makes sense. A friend might ask too many questions. Besides, sometimes it's easier to trust a stranger."

"You might be right."

"Still, it's not like you two didn't have anything in common," I said. "Saudis with British accents? I can't imagine that's a coincidence."

"How did you know I was Saudi?"

"I'm assuming based on your last name."

"Huh," said Al-Kazaz. He looked impressed. "Most Americans wouldn't have a clue."

"Most Americans have never traveled outside the United States," I said. Something like half, in fact. Accordingly, most don't know the definition of *xenophobia*.

"Is that where you first met Ahmed?" he asked. "Overseas?"

"Yes, we were both students in England. Some years ago we made plans to meet up in Saudi Arabia, but they fell through. I think Ahmed had to attend some insurance conference in Geneva," I said. "What about you? Have you been back there recently?"

"To Saudi Arabia? No, it's been many years."

"Of course, who could blame you, right? Your country hasn't exactly put out the welcome mat for Benjamins, have they?"

He gave me a blank stare.

"Oh, my goodness, do you smell that? Actually, I hope you

don't," I said suddenly, turning to Annabelle. "I'm sorry, it seems someone is in desperate need of a diaper change."

Al-Kazaz took his cue. "I've already claimed too much of your time as it is," he said, standing.

I scooped up Annabelle and shook his hand. "It's horrible we had to meet under these circumstances, but I appreciate your honoring Ahmed's wishes," I said. "Thank you for bringing the envelope."

"You're welcome."

I walked him out, watching as he made his way down the hallway to the elevator. Annabelle was watching him, too. I gave her a squeeze and whispered in her ear, "Thanks for taking one for the team, Anna-banana."

I'd smelled something, all right. But it wasn't her diaper. It was Al-Kazaz, who was full of crap. If that was even his real name.

Whoever he was, he had delivered a near perfect performance. In fact, he probably would've had me were it not for one little mistake.

CHAPTER 15

"NICELY DONE, Needham," said a fellow agent walking by as Elizabeth stepped off the elevator. Elizabeth didn't even know his name.

"Thanks," she said.

She delivered about a dozen more thank-yous en route to Evan Pritchard's office in the back corner of the JTTF field unit. It was the proverbial morning after and everyone was up to their necks in chasing leads and poring over past intelligence reports, but at some point they had all managed to see the video of Elizabeth saving their boss's life. They'd also heard she was the first to spot the drones in the second-wave attack.

"Oh, great. There she is, the bane of my existence," said Pritchard's assistant, Gwen, sitting behind her desk outside Pritchard's office. Gwen, pushing sixty, was five foot nothing and ninety-eight pounds of chutzpah and sarcasm. "You had to do it, huh, rookie? You had to save his life so he could continue to make mine miserable?"

There was absolutely nothing to laugh about in the wake of the attacks, but Gwen didn't give a damn. Her brother had worked for Cantor Fitzgerald and was on the 105th floor of One World Trade Center the morning of 9/11. If poking a little fun helped her fend off having to relive the memory of that day all over again, so be it.

"Any chance I can get in there for a few minutes this morning?" asked Elizabeth, nodding at Pritchard's door. It was cracked open about an inch.

"Send her in!" came Pritchard's booming voice. He sounded like James Earl Jones talking through a megaphone. "And if you want me dead, Gwen, you're going to have to do it yourself."

Gwen winked at Elizabeth. "Finally, something to live for," she said. "He's all yours."

Elizabeth stepped inside Pritchard's office. It was only the second time she'd been in there, the other being on her first day when he told her she needed to go to Boston. She hadn't even been assigned her own desk yet.

"Is it good?" Pritchard asked immediately.

"Is what good?"

"Whatever it is you have for me, Needham, because you're sure as hell not here just so I can thank you again for saving my life," he said.

"No, once was enough," said Elizabeth.

"All the same, thanks again," he said. "You were heads-up out there, good under pressure. That's the kind of people I need, that this unit needs. Now, what do you have for me?"

Elizabeth blinked a few times, trying to digest Pritchard's flash of humanity. She wondered how much of his act was just that, an act. The guy was far from loved in law enforcement circles, but he was universally respected. Revered, even. Gwen's kidding around about wanting him dead was exhibit A. She clearly thought the world of her boss.

"Earth to Needham," said Pritchard.

"Yeah, sorry," said Elizabeth, snapping out of it. She quickly got down to business, directing him to the file of Professor Darvish and the mystery woman returning with him to his hotel.

Pritchard paused the footage on his computer to stare at the white glow around the woman's face. "Hmmm."

"My first thought is that it's either a glitch or someone tampered with it," said Elizabeth.

"Yeah, we'll have the geeks in the lab look at it," he said.

"Who do I call for that?" she asked.

"No one."

"Excuse me?"

"I'm taking you off the case, Needham," he said.

CHAPTER 16

"WHY?"

"Think about it," said Pritchard.

"I am," said Elizabeth. "I'm thinking about what you told me yesterday about trying to stop the *next* attack, that your agents are needed on all fronts."

"They still are," he said. "But you specifically are needed now on the attacks that happened yesterday."

It was the way he said *specifically*.

"This wasn't your decision, was it?" she asked.

"As I said, think about it."

Elizabeth winced, realizing. "The mayor?"

"I suppose I couldn't really blame him," said Pritchard. "As much as I hate politics, the optics for him are too good to ignore. He'll let it leak that he got you assigned here. In other words, *he's* the one who saved my life yesterday."

"When did Deacon call you? If you want, I could—"

"Needham, I didn't get where I am by waiting for the mayor to call me. As far as he knows, you were always on the case."

Elizabeth nodded. She knew what he meant. Mainly, because she knew Mayor Deacon. All too well. His pretty protégée was now the poster girl of bravery for what the press was calling the Times Square Massacre. If Deacon found out that she wasn't actually working to catch the masterminds behind it, he sure as hell was going to pick up the phone and call Pritchard.

As much as Pritchard hated politics, he was keenly aware of one of its first rules: always get out in front of any potential problem. In other words, *anticipate*. Just the sort of thing you want to be good at when your job is preventing terrorism.

It all made sense to Elizabeth.

Still, there was this little something kicking around inside her head. An image. It took all of a split second, quicker than quick. It was the look that flashed across Pritchard's face while he was staring at the footage of Darvish and the woman. That glow obstructing her face wasn't necessarily a mystery to him.

Or maybe Elizabeth was just imagining the whole thing.

Sure, that had to be it, she told herself. There was a 99 percent chance it was nothing, a figment of her imagination. Besides, it wasn't as if she were in a position to ask him about it. If there was something Pritchard wanted to share with her about that glow, he would've shared it. *Right?*

"Okay, I'm off the Darvish case," said Elizabeth, playing the good soldier. "Times Square. What would you like me to focus on?"

She'd barely finished the question when the answer came barging into Pritchard's office. He was clearly an agent, but she hadn't seen him before.

"We have an address," the guy said.

"Where?" asked Pritchard.

"Jersey City."

Pritchard nodded, rubbed his chin, and turned to Elizabeth. "Want to go for a ride, Needham?"

CHAPTER 17

MEN AND *their toys* . . .

Elizabeth stared wide-eyed at all the equipment, the endless gadgets being prepped and primed, during the half hour drive from lower Manhattan out to Jersey City in what was the back of a moving truck, or so it appeared to anyone seeing it from the outside. A1 SHLEPPERS, read the signage.

Inside the truck was a command central that looked to Elizabeth like some Hollywood take on what the future of law enforcement might one day be. Some of the things she could take a stab at based on her training—like what appeared to be an electromagnetic-pulse gun for tripping IEDs from a safe distance. With some of the other items, she had no clue. *What the hell is that neon-green goo that guy is mixing?*

Screw Hollywood. The future is now.

Elizabeth was one of only two women among the two dozen or so agents, a mixture of the JTTF's federal, state, and local law enforcement officers, the FBI SWAT team, and the additional

FBI agents who had just arrived from the Operational Technology Division at Quantico. A few times she was tempted to lean forward and ask Pritchard what the plan was, and each time she held back. He was sitting in the row of seats on the opposite side of the truck, heavily engaged in conversation with a square-jawed agent in full tactical armor named Munez, presumably the SWAT team leader.

Pritchard's body language could be summed up in three words: do not disturb.

All Elizabeth knew so far was what the agent in Pritchard's office had explained. Whoever placed those bombs in the first-wave attack on Times Square didn't do so randomly. They did their homework to ensure that none of the street-level surveillance cameras would spot anything suspicious beforehand. There were no knapsacks left unattended. No sudden appearance of workmen who couldn't be accounted for by either the city or any business. Ironically, the one thing the terrorists didn't account for, especially in light of their second-wave attack, was the mother of all drones: a satellite.

Then again, you can't really plan for something you don't even know exists.

"One of the keyholes from NROL-71 picked up a guy wearing a coat into the Lyric Theatre and leaving minutes later without it," the agent had told Pritchard. "We tagged him returning to a house in Jersey City. Unless he left without his phone, he's still there."

"NROL?" Elizabeth had asked, not waiting for an introduction.

"National Reconnaissance Office Launch," said the agent. Otherwise known as a secret satellite.

Elizabeth could tell the agent had been up working all night. Beneath the stubble and wrinkled mess of a suit, though, was a good-looking guy. If Ryan Gosling had a brother, perhaps.

"Needham, meet Sullivan. Sullivan, meet Needham," said Pritchard, doing the honors. "Needham just joined the unit."

"And not a minute too soon," said Sullivan. "Nice tackle yesterday."

He had clearly seen the video, too.

What he wasn't getting to see, however, were the fruits of his labor. Sullivan wasn't in the truck, probably because he was running on fumes. Dead tired is no way to be when raiding the home of a terrorist. Especially since terrorists tend to have a very strong aversion to being taken alive.

Hence, all the toys in the truck.

"Two minutes!" barked the agent sitting by a GPS display mounted on the wall behind the driver. He smiled wide. He lived for this shit; they all did. And thanks to her new boss, Elizabeth was along for the ride.

For the first time, Pritchard looked over at her and caught her eye.

How's your first week on the Task Force going, Needham? Having fun yet?

CHAPTER 18

WHEN THE truck stopped, things really got moving. One after another, all the toys were put into play.

Elizabeth tried her best to watch and learn. If there had been a ticket for her seat, it would've read *obstructed view*, but she could see just enough of one of the myriad surveillance screens toward the front of the truck to get a sense of what was happening, and what she couldn't see was filled in by what she could hear.

"Jesus, we might as well be back in Baghdad," muttered one of the agents at the console while shaking his head. He was looking at an external camera feed of the neighborhood.

Jersey City was never going to land on anyone's top ten list of places to live, and the house that matched the address was a sorry reminder of that. It was a run-down 1950s split-ranch with aluminum siding that had turned a shade of puke green. Four windows in the front, two on either side of the front door. All curtains drawn closed.

"Give me thermal…"

The screen changed to an overhead shot of the house using an infrared camera, which was too detailed to be from a satellite. No one commented on the irony, but it certainly wasn't lost on Elizabeth. *Drones.*

That explained the *launch van* remark she'd overheard Pritchard make to someone before they boarded the truck. Apparently there was a sister vehicle in the vicinity that had released the drone. Make that drones, plural, after the thermal imaging revealed no movement inside the house.

"Send in Santa Claus…"

Down the chimney went another drone as the monitor switched to a split screen. The infrared feed showed this second drone to be no bigger than a bumblebee.

What had to be one of the world's tiniest lenses was providing crystal-clear images, room by room. At least the rooms the drone could get into. Some of the doors were closed.

"Switch to Doppler, twenty kilohertz…"

What the drone couldn't see, the drone could feel. Sound waves. And when there was still no motion detected, the drone could smell. A built-in filter could test the air for trace explosives, the readings streaming straight back to the truck.

This was truly the Swiss Army knife of drones.

"Well?" asked Pritchard, arms crossed, standing behind the men at the console.

One of them turned to him, a baby face with a perfect left part in his hair. He reminded Elizabeth of a guy in her high school chemistry class who always had raised his hand when the teacher asked a question.

"Double-checking p and z," he said, tapping away feverishly on a keyboard. He was accessing the planning and zoning files for the city. "Yeah, no basement and no attic. There's a boiler room with heating and cooling off the kitchen." He looked up at Pritchard, nodding confidently. "Looks like no one's home, sir."

Pritchard turned to Munez, standing next to him, who immediately took his cue. "Okay, we pulse the house first for IEDs. Four men on the perimeter, one to a side. Williamson, Foltz, Hernandez, and Meyer, that's you."

The four guys stood in unison. They sounded like a law firm but looked like linebackers. Each got handed an electromagnetic-pulse gun—not exactly standard-issue equipment—and out the side door they went.

Within minutes they were back. All clear, they reported.

It was Pritchard's call now. Munez turned to him, followed by everyone else. Elizabeth included.

Pritchard shrugged. "Let's go stretch our legs," he said.

CHAPTER 19

SAY NO more. Everyone on the truck knew exactly what that meant. *Roll out!*

Endless training, tactical drills, event scenarios, simulation exercises, and actual combat experience all kicked in at once as the truck emptied with perfect choreographed precision. It didn't matter how many drones or how much technology was telling them that no one was inside that house. Being human would forever have one major advantage over any machine.

The ability to doubt.

"What the hell are you doing, Needham?"

"What do you mean?" Elizabeth asked.

Pritchard was eyeing her like he would a dog chasing its tail. The look was worse than that, really. At least the dog would've been moving. Elizabeth was just sitting there, unsure of her role.

"Are you waiting for a personal invitation? Grab a vest, and let's go," he said.

Elizabeth quickly strapped on some body armor and followed Pritchard out of the truck and past the outer circle of

SWAT officers with their backs to the house, guarding the perimeter. She practically had to jog to keep up as Pritchard then marched through the inner circle, who were covering every angle of the house itself, front and back, while providing cover for the two-by-two configuration led by the team leader. Munez's group was gathered by the front door.

Surely it would be somebody—*anybody*—else besides Pritchard who would be first in, thought Elizabeth as she drew her gun. Her fingers tingled a bit as they always did when holding her Glock.

She stared at Pritchard. She was wrong. He continued straight past the team leader and started knocking, no hesitation. It was badass. He didn't even position himself along the side of the door to shield his body.

"Who's got the Push Pop?" he asked, after knocking a second time with no answer.

From behind Elizabeth stepped another officer holding what, sure enough, looked like a Push Pop straight from a candy store. The flavor? Green goo.

The officer lined up the device directly over the lock on the door, pushing the goo from a tube into the keyhole. Within seconds, the goo had hardened enough to mimic the key without sticking to the cylinder. Voilà. The door was unlocked. No muss, no fuss.

No trace.

The world's fastest issued FISA warrant was now in play.

The outer and inner circles around the house held their marks as Pritchard drew his old-school SIG Sauer P228 and pushed open the door.

Waiting a few Mississippis before entering was Pritchard's last nod to the outside chance that anyone was inside. On the count of three, he strolled in as if he owned the place.

"Your turn, Munez," he said.

Right behind him, the SWAT team leader instructed his four officers to go room by room—one pair starting upstairs, the other on the first floor. They were all back in the living room within a minute. Small house.

Dirty as hell, too. Leftover takeout food was littered everywhere. Elizabeth didn't know which putrid odor to gag on first when she'd walked in. A half-eaten falafel by the fireplace was swarming with ants.

What was nowhere to be seen, though—in addition to the suspect—was any suggestion that the house had been used to make bombs. In that sense, it was as clean as a whistle.

"Well?" asked Munez, flanked by four team members.

"Get me a twenty-yard radius on the guy's phone," said Pritchard.

Munez reached for his radio, making the request. Within seconds came a *ping* from the one and only place to sit down in the living room, a faded brown couch with large tears in two of its cushions. Lodged between them and barely visible was the cell phone that had led them to the house.

"That explains his not being here," said Pritchard, pulling a sleeve over his hand to pick up the phone without adding his fingerprints. He sat down on the couch.

"What now?" asked Munez.

"We wait back in the truck," said Pritchard. "At least for an hour or so. If he doesn't show, we'll set up surveillance and call it a—"

Pritchard's voice trailed off as he slowly tilted his head. He was looking sideways at the floor, his eyes fixated on the stained and tattered Persian rug directly underneath Elizabeth's feet.

Pritchard raised his forefinger to his lips. *Shhhh.*

CHAPTER 20

PRITCHARD QUICKLY resumed talking, rambling on about setting up around-the-clock surveillance of the house and how the teams should be manned.

But no one was listening. They weren't supposed to. It was Pritchard's hands that were doing the real talking.

He was pointing at the slight curve of the wood floor beneath the rug. His other hand was motioning for two of the officers to move the coffee table sitting on top of it. As for how the table should be moved, that was a given.

As quietly as humanly possible.

Elizabeth stepped back off the rug, eyeing the slight curve of the floor. The wood was warped. It was an old house. The warping could've been caused by years of winters and summers, heat and cold. Over and over.

Or it could've been something else. Like a section of the floor had been removed and put back, on and off. Over and over.

Pritchard clearly had a gut feeling it was the latter.

The second the coffee table was moved, he pointed down and spun his finger. Still, he kept talking, the sound of his booming voice masking the footsteps of the officers as they rolled up the rug.

Everyone stopped and stared at what was underneath. It sure looked like a hatch.

The circle was no bigger than a manhole cover, the deep cut along the perimeter the product of a reciprocating saw and a pretty steady hand. The cut itself was also wide enough to get your fingers in and lift.

Why a circle and not a square? Elizabeth knew why. She figured everyone else in the room did, too. It was a common question in law enforcement interviews. *Why are manhole covers round?*

So they can't fall in.

"You guys see that Yankees game last night against the Angels? Man, that Mike Trout has got some serious range in center field. I've got to hand it to him," said Pritchard, holding out his hand.

Everyone nodded, including Elizabeth. Never mind that she knew—or cared—as much about baseball as she did seventeenth-century Russian poetry. Pritchard was asking for one more toy.

The house that didn't have a basement according to planning and zoning apparently now had a basement. Or at least something underground—something deep and dank enough to shield body heat from thermal imaging. It was time for plan B.

Make that plan R.

CHAPTER 21

THE SWAT commander, Munez, reached for the Range-R radar device strapped to his left hip, handing it over to Pritchard. No bigger than a stud finder but definitely its far more advanced cousin, the device used stepped-frequency continuous-wave radar to detect motion behind walls. Or, if need be, below hatches.

Pritchard continued talking baseball as he pressed the device flush against the floor. The Yankees needed better starting pitching. The bullpen was overused. What else was new?

All the while, he kept his eyes trained on the device's readout. Finally he shook his head. There was no movement happening underneath them.

Munez quickly bit off the cap of a pen and wrote something on the palm of his hand. He held it up. One word: *Rover?*

Pritchard shook his head again. It was either a calculated risk or an insane amount of impatience. The hatch could've been booby-trapped, but bomb-squad rovers had only one gear: slow. Pritchard didn't want to wait.

No one else wanted to wait either. Without prompting, the two officers who had rolled up the carpet positioned themselves on either side of the hatch, ready to lift. Everyone else formed a wide circle, their guns all aimed at the hole that was about to be.

"Get out of here," Pritchard whispered to Elizabeth.

She wasn't sure if she heard him right. "What?" she whispered back.

"I said, go wait by the truck."

Elizabeth was never so sure of a decision in her life. *Wait outside?* "Fuck the truck," she said.

Pritchard smiled. Then he held up three fingers. *On the count of three...*

Up came the hatch, immediately tossed to the side like a Frisbee. Every hand on every gun tightened, all eyes waiting for some kind of movement or sound. There was neither.

"Stick," said Pritchard.

The officer to his right quickly handed him his search mirror. It didn't exactly qualify as another toy, but it was the only tool for the moment.

Pritchard extended what amounted to a glorified selfie stick, angling the mirror while Munez shone a light into the hole. From her angle, Elizabeth could make out part of a ladder.

"Anything?" asked Munez.

Pritchard didn't answer. Instead, he handed over the mirror to Elizabeth and climbed down the ladder. "That explains the no movement," he announced moments later, his voice slightly echoing.

Elizabeth thought he meant the space was empty. It seemed like the only explanation.

Then she caught a glimpse in the mirror of what was lying next to Pritchard's feet. There was another explanation.

The dead don't move.

CHAPTER 22

LANDON FOXX shook my hand and promptly told me how he really felt. "You shouldn't be here, Reinhart," he said.

"That's odd," I replied. "I could've sworn you were the one who gave me the address."

"Yeah, I know," he said. "But you still shouldn't be here."

And there in a nutshell, ladies and gentlemen, is what it's like working for the CIA. A constant diet of contradictions that still somehow manage to make sense.

Some things never change.

The *here* where I wasn't supposed to be was a dimly lit hallway outside an operating room in the basement of a safe house in Brooklyn that was currently doubling as a mortuary. Foxx, the CIA's New York section chief, had acquiesced and allowed me to be here—against all rules and protocol, not to mention the fact that he never much liked me—because he knew what good friends Ahmed Al-Hamdah and I had been.

He also knew that Ahmed once had saved my life back in

London. It was only right that I be able to pay my last respects. No matter how wrong.

The "official" count of the dead from the Times Square bombings stood at 216. That's what was being reported all over the news. The actual count was 217.

Ahmed would forever be unaccounted for in every sense of the word. His parents were killed in a car accident when he was a toddler. He was an only child. The aunt who then raised him in London died from cancer while he was at Oxford. She never knew he'd been recruited by MI6. No one did.

Ahmed was required to lose touch with the friends he'd made at school. He was also forbidden to make any new ones outside work. The same rules applied when he later joined the CIA. The reason he and I first bonded was shared grief. I'd also lost someone I loved to cancer. Moreover, the same cancer as his aunt: pancreatic. My mother had died four months after she was diagnosed, when I was thirteen.

By the time Ahmed moved to the US, he was a true nowhere man. Those who crossed paths with him "off duty" knew him by a fake name. Even then, they rarely saw him. So rarely, in fact, that he once joked, *It will be years before everyone realizes that they haven't seen me in years.*

Now, for sure, they were never going to see him again. They'd never know why either. Only a handful of people on the planet would ever know he had perished in the initial Times Square attack—after sacrificing his life trying to stop it.

Oh, the glamorous life of a CIA operative.

"He was embedded with a cell here that was connected to another cell that carried out the bombings," said Foxx.

"Multiple cells?" I asked. The mere thought of there being one active in the area was bad enough. But two?

Foxx straightened his broad shoulders and nodded. In his

mid-fifties without an ounce of body fat, the guy was a total gym rat and addicted to running marathons. That was how he managed the stress of the job. It was far healthier than wearing out a barstool.

"We get smarter, they get smarter," he said. "Picture a bunch of capos working for a single mob boss, only the capos don't actually know one another or even the identity of the boss himself. That's what we're dealing with."

Yeah, that was smarter. "In other words, no single member can ever bring down the entire operation."

"Exactly. Only Ahmed was on the verge of doing just that. He'd infiltrated one of the mini cells and had just cracked another. That was the one that carried out the bombings," said Foxx. "Ahmed was literally running toward Times Square in hopes of defusing at least one of the bombs when he was shot. By then he'd been exposed."

Foxx watched me flinch. He knew the details of what had happened to me in London. I'd been exposed during the Westminster Abbey sting. Ahmed killed my would-be assassin a mere second before the son-of-a-bitch would've been my assassin.

"Tell me more about this cell," I said.

"You know I can't do that. I've already told you too much."

That's what you think, Foxx. But we're only getting started. You just don't know it yet.

I slid my heel along the concrete floor, the scraping sound echoing up and down the hallway. Timing is everything.

"Oh, I almost forgot," I said. "Did I mention the guy who came to visit me yesterday?"

"What guy?" asked Foxx.

"The one who's part of the cell," I said.

CHAPTER 23

FOXX FOLDED his arms, rolled his eyes, and let out a deep and pissed-off sigh all at once. "Way to bury the lede, Reinhart. And you wonder why I never liked you."

"I never wonder at all," I replied. "I know *exactly* why you never liked me."

"You were reckless."

"I took risks."

"You withheld information from the Agency."

"I was careful whom I told things to."

"You were a wiseass."

"Yeah, okay, you got me there," I said. "Guilty as charged. Now, do you want to hear about this guy or what?"

I told Foxx everything about my visit from Benjamin Al-Kazaz, or rather, the guy posing as a lawyer by that name. He'd somehow connected me to Ahmed but clearly didn't know if I was CIA or merely an old chum from our London school days. Hence the charade.

"How did you know the guy was lying?" asked Foxx.

"He picked the wrong fake name."

"Al-Kazaz?"

"No, his first name," I said. "I made a joke about his returning to Saudi Arabia and how they're not exactly welcoming Benjamins these days. He had no idea what I was talking about."

"That makes two of us," said Foxx.

"A few years back," I explained, "the Saudi government banned a bunch of baby names. There were about fifty in total, and if you were a Saudi, there's no way you wouldn't know about it. One of the names, if not number one with a bullet, was Benjamin."

Foxx didn't need any further explanation. It was all the more obvious to him given that he'd been stationed in Israel during Obama's first term. "Really?" he asked. "Because of Bibi?"

"Yep." Saudi parents were now forbidden from naming a boy Benjamin because of Benjamin Netanyahu, the Israeli prime minister. Talk about holding a grudge.

"So this guy, Al-Kazaz, or whatever his real name is, isn't a Saudi, and he knew Ahmed was dead. Why did he want you to think he was Ahmed's lawyer?"

"Because of this," I said, opening my hand.

Foxx stared at the tiny flash drive in my palm. "He gave that to you?"

"In a sealed envelope, yes. He claimed it was from Ahmed and he'd been holding it for him. If Ahmed died, he was supposed to get the envelope to me."

Foxx eyed the flash drive. "It's probably a virus—a way for him to hack your files and learn more about you."

"Not probably," I said. "That's exactly what it is."

"Wait. You actually—"

"Of course I plugged it in," I said. "That's what someone

who's never been in the CIA would do, right? I just made sure to use an old laptop. Lecture notes, research for my next book—the guy saw the life of an ordinary college professor, that's all."

"Did he actually fake a letter from Ahmed?"

"No, this guy was cleverer than that. He put a file on there that wouldn't open. Meanwhile, the virus gets embedded and he becomes a ghost. The phone number on his fake business card? It's out of service."

"What about fingerprints?" asked Foxx. "The envelope he handed you? Or the business card?"

"Both clean," I said. "I figure he was using tips on his fingers." Tips are ultrathin silicone patches used to cover one's fingerprints. Bomb-making terrorists are big fans of them.

Foxx continued to grill me like a prosecutor. That was his style. "Any cameras in your building?"

"Plenty," I said. "But he wore a baseball cap in the lobby and in the elevator."

"So we've got nothing to go on, huh?"

"I'm just thankful he doesn't either," I said. "I've got a family, and he knows where I live."

The sound of the door opening next to us brought our conversation to a halt. A head peeked out. There are only a handful of imams in the world working secretly for the CIA. This was one of them.

"Okay," was all the imam said. It was all that was needed.

Foxx turned to me. "Go ahead, take a few minutes."

"Thanks," I said.

I knew what I would see when I entered the room. Ahmed had long ago educated me on the death rituals of Muslims, beginning with the body being bathed and shrouded in three sheets. The imam was slightly breaking with tradition by leaving Ahmed's head uncovered until after I could say my final good-bye.

Still, knowing what to expect isn't always the same as when it actually happens.

I stood there and stared at Ahmed's face, the sadness running through me. I felt numb.

Then came the guilt. I knew it wasn't rational, but I felt it just the same. He had once saved my life. I wasn't able to save his.

Suddenly all I could think about was Ahmed's love of westerns. It now made more sense than ever. The best ones always feature a loner on the wild frontier, someone who never looks for the spotlight or needs to take credit for doing the right thing.

I'd left the Agency for all the right reasons. No regret. But standing there next to my old friend, that's all I could feel. I somehow owed him justice.

What would Gary Cooper do? Right, Ahmed?

Of course, I had no way of knowing that I was about to find out.

My high noon was coming.

BOOK TWO

MASQUERADE

CHAPTER 24

THE ROOM was as hot as hell. It reeked of sweat and mold and something even worse.

Fear.

That's him. He's arrived.

The impeccably dressed man they all called the Mudir, the Governor, came walking into the room with a black duffel bag casually draped over his shoulder as if it were filled with laundry or whatever else someone might carry around who wasn't actually a mass murderer.

Without a word of greeting to the thirteen men seated on the folding chairs in the basement of the mosque, he placed the duffel on a metal table with rusted hinges and slowly unzipped it. One by one, he removed the guns—all Russian made and all of them chosen for a specific reason, a feature or attribute that would help ensure the greatest amount of casualties.

Finally the Mudir spoke.

"Six of you will use the AS Val," he said, holding up the assault rifle often used by Spetsnaz, the Russian Special Forces. "Its integrated suppressor will silence your rounds and delay the initial panic. The fewer people who are running, the more of them you can kill."

The Mudir then lifted the AK-47, explaining that another six men would be stationed at the three main staircases connecting the lower level to the main concourse. There would be two men per staircase, both positioned halfway down the steps so as to ambush all those trying to escape from either level. "The two shooters will stand side by side. One aiming up, one aiming down. Fish in a barrel."

All the men in the room had been embedded in the US for close to five years. They were well versed in American slang and idioms. They all spoke English fluently. None of them were married. All of them had jobs. These were the requirements.

Lastly, the Mudir raised the MP-443 Grach, the standard-issue semiautomatic pistol of the Russian military. He explained that all twelve men would be armed with the pistol in addition to their assault rifle. "It will function as backup should your rifle jam."

That took care of the weapons portion of the presentation. The Mudir next discussed timing and transportation. As he spoke he began seeing what he expected. A few of the men were stealing glances around the room, doing a head count to themselves. They were confused by the math.

The Mudir kept referring to the dozen men who would take part in the attack, but there were thirteen of them in the room. Was someone going to play a special role not yet discussed?

Yes.

"Are there any questions?" asked the Mudir.

One of the men raised his hand. The Mudir nodded at him. Permission to speak.

"Why are there thirteen of us here if only twelve are needed?" the man asked.

The Mudir smiled. The trick to turning men into murderers was to show them how little control they had over their own fate. Life was not precious. It was not special. It wasn't anything.

And if you truly believed in what you were doing—your god and your cause—then life was yours to take from others at any time.

It required radical thinking to radicalize people.

"I didn't hear you," said the Mudir, walking toward the man who had raised his hand. "Can you repeat what you said?"

No, he couldn't. All the man could do was stare at the MP-443 Grach in the Mudir's hand before literally pissing himself in his folding chair. "I'm sorry," he said finally.

"I'm not," said the Mudir.

Raising his arm, he pumped a single round from the semi-automatic pistol right between the man's eyes. The shot was so clean the man barely moved as blood poured out the back of his head like water from a spigot.

The Mudir returned to his large duffel on the table, looking around at the twelve remaining men who would carry out the attack on the train station on July 4th.

"Does anyone else have a question?" he asked.

CHAPTER 25

TRACY SHOOK his head with a chuckle as he dipped a spring roll into some hot mustard. "You've gotta admit, this is pretty funny," he said.

"What is?" I asked.

"This," he said, looking around our living room. "*Us.*"

"What about us?" asked Elizabeth.

"A straight girl shacking up with two gay white guys who have a black South African baby," he said. "And we're all eating Chinese food. This is either a Benetton ad or the pilot for a sit-com that's trying way too hard."

Tracy had no idea where I'd been that afternoon, but after paying my last respects to Ahmed, I was in desperate need of a laugh.

Elizabeth laughed, too. She was in the middle of slurping a lo mein noodle, and that only made her laugh harder. She was still banged up, still in some pain, but it was good to see. By the looks of her when she first walked in, her day had been as much of a bummer as mine. It certainly didn't help that reporters were continuing to stake out her apartment building.

We'd just put Annabelle down for the night and were sitting around on the floor of the den eating takeout from Han Dynasty and watching the news. It was twenty-four seven about the bombings—the victims, the survivors, and now the search for the terrorists responsible. Naturally, the blame game had begun. The police? The FBI? The CIA? The NSA? Homeland Security? Who dropped the ball?

"Do you want me to change the channel?" I asked Elizabeth.

"I would love you to," she said, "but don't. I need to watch, like it or not."

She was right. It was part of her job now.

The only thing she'd shared with us—the only thing she was *permitted* to share with us—was that she'd been assigned to the Times Square investigation. Tracy and I didn't ask her for any inside scoop, and she knew enough not to offer one. I was wondering, though. Had she been briefed about Ahmed and his being embedded with the terrorist cell? Would she ever be?

There was something else, too. Elizabeth had gotten what she wanted. She'd been taken off the Professor Darvish case. But somehow she hadn't seemed all that pleased about it when she told us. What was bothering her?

Hold that thought.

The sound of Annabelle crying suddenly filtered to us from down the hall. "I've got her," I said, starting to get up.

"No, let me," said Tracy, beating me to it. "It's my turn."

Parenting is life's biggest learning curve, but Tracy and I at least had the balancing act part of it down pat. We didn't actually take turns tending to Annabelle. It's not like either of us kept count of who did what for her. It was more instinctual. We both just had a sense of when one of us should step in for the other. *Can you really be good parents without that?*

"I'm calling that last dumpling, though," said Tracy, pointing at the box in front of me as he headed for Annabelle's room.

No sooner had he gotten there than Elizabeth turned to me. "I need to ask you something," she said.

"Anything," I answered, although I immediately regretted it.

"Before Pritchard reassigned me this morning I showed him the video of Darvish and his mystery woman," she said.

"And?"

"And Pritchard pretended to have no idea about the white glow obscuring her face."

"How did you know he was pretending?"

"It was a look he had," she said. "It was super quick, came and went in an instant, but I saw it. I know I did."

"What kind of look?"

"The same kind you gave me last night when I showed you the video," she said. "You already know what's causing that glow."

"You're that sure, huh? All based on a look?"

"Actually, I wasn't sure until after I walked into your apartment tonight. *That* was the clincher."

The second she said that, I knew she had me. I hated it when Elizabeth reminded me of how smart she was. But I loved it even more.

"Go ahead," I said.

"You haven't once tonight mentioned the video. You haven't asked about my meeting with Pritchard, what he thought about the glow, anything..."

"You're right, I haven't," I said.

"Because you don't want to talk about it."

"Or maybe I *can't* talk about it."

"Too late," she said. "What are you not telling me, Dylan Reinhart?"

CHAPTER 26

I GLANCED down the hall, listening to the faint sound of Tracy singing softly to Annabelle.

When we first brought her home, we discovered she was basically lullaby-proof. None of the staples like "Hush, Little Baby" seemed to calm her down. Desperate one night, Tracy and I riffled through his iTunes playlist like a couple of possessed Casey Kasems. Much to our relief—and delight—we discovered that our baby girl was a Beatles fan. Tracy was now in the middle of one of her favorites, "Penny Lane."

"Tracy really has a nice voice," I said. "Don't you think?"

"You're stalling," said Elizabeth. "That's what I think."

She'd intentionally waited until we were alone before asking me about the glow, and that only made me feel worse. She knew my darkest secret and Tracy didn't.

I'd become all too adept at concealing from Tracy anything having to do with my CIA days. But my decision not to tell him—made so many years ago and done, I was convinced, for his protection—had always hung over me. At that moment it felt as if there were a giant boulder perched on a ledge in the middle of an earthquake, and I was standing directly below it wearing a pair of lead shoes.

Still, Elizabeth wasn't about to take *No comment* for an answer.

"It's called Halo," I said. "That's what's causing the glow."

"*Halo?* I don't know what to ask first," she said. "How does it work or who created it?"

"It was developed by a CIA lab back when I was stationed in London," I said. "As for how it works, I'll be damned if I understand all the science behind it."

Elizabeth blinked in disbelief. "Did you just admit to ignorance?"

"Bite your tongue. I said I didn't know *all* the science. The device, sometimes disguised as a necklace, reflects infrared waves, along with some visible light, and distorts any CCTV image. The effect is that blur of white you saw."

"With a simple necklace?" she said.

"That's the gee-whiz part. They've been able to produce the effect with what look like ordinary beads."

Wait for it, Dylan. In five seconds, she'll forget all about the science and realize the implications. Five, four, three, two...

"Jesus," said Elizabeth. "So this woman with Darvish is CIA?"

"It's possible."

"Could she have killed the professor and made it look like an accident?"

"Also possible," I said.

"Would Pritchard know something like that?"

"It's highly unlikely anyone in your unit would know, including your boss."

"But he could know about Halo, right?" she asked.

"We're back to it's possible," I said. "But you can't ask Pritchard because—"

"You and I never had this conversation. I get it. Besides, I'm not even assigned to the case anymore."

"You could've fooled me," I said.

"Can you blame me? We need to find out who this woman is."

"*We?*"

"You want to know, too, don't you?"

"Not necessarily. If she's an operative, I'll take it on faith that she was acting on good intelligence—information that no one inside the Agency is about to share with me."

"What if she's not, though?"

"Acting on good intel?"

"No," said Elizabeth. "What if she's not CIA?"

It was a fair point. Halo's technology had been around nearly a decade, albeit in the hands of a very select group. That didn't mean, though, that someone else hadn't gotten hold of it. The wrong hands.

"What time does Bergdorf's close?" I asked.

There wasn't a more out-of-left-field question I could've thrown at Elizabeth in that moment. Her face confirmed it. *"Bergdorf's?"* she asked. *"Why?"*

I reached for my phone, quickly googling the store's hours. It was already past seven. "We need to do some shopping," I said. "Then we need a huge favor."

CHAPTER 27

"I'M REALLY going to hate returning these," said Elizabeth, gazing down at the shoebox in her lap as we pulled away in the cab from Bergdorf's. We caught a break. The store stays open until eight during the week.

I turned to her. "Who said anything about returning them?"

"Yeah, right," she said with a laugh. Then she realized I was serious. "Dylan, that's crazy. I can't keep these."

"Why not?"

"For starters, they cost over nine hundred dollars."

"Yeah, what is it with women's shoes? You girls know you're getting scammed, and yet you still buy them like drugs," I said. "Anyway, that's not a good enough reason not to keep them."

Elizabeth opened the box, taking out one of the Christian Louboutins and staring at it, transfixed. She was clearly in love. Still, as if snapping out of it, she shook her head.

"I'll give you a better reason why to return them," she said. "They're just going to sit in my closet."

"I've been meaning to talk to you about that," I said.

Elizabeth rolled her eyes. "Please don't. My sister already gives me the you-need-to-get-a-boyfriend speech about once a month."

"She isn't very persuasive, is she?"

"No, I'm just that pathetic."

I didn't say anything. Apparently I was supposed to.

"For the record," said Elizabeth, shooting an elbow into my ribs, "this is the part where you tell me that I'm not actually pathetic and I simply work too hard."

"Oh, you mean the old married-to-your-job cliché?"

"If the shoe fits."

"Okay, here you go," I said, clearing my throat. "You're not actually pathetic. You simply work too hard."

"That wasn't very persuasive."

"You don't believe it so why should I?"

"Do you really think I use my career as an excuse to avoid dating?" she asked.

"Actually, no. I think the excuse you use is your father cheating on your mother."

"Wow, you went there, didn't you?"

"Hey, you asked."

"I'll make a deal with you," she said. "You don't try to psychoanalyze me, and I won't make the joke about gay men knowing more about women's shoes than most women."

"That's an even bigger cliché than being married to your job."

Elizabeth chuckled. "It is, isn't it?" She turned the shoe upside down, staring at the signature red sole of all Christian Louboutins. "So is this idea of yours going to work?" she asked.

"It's worth a try," I said.

A few blocks later, we pulled up in front of a converted warehouse in Hell's Kitchen near the corner of West 44th Street and

Tenth Avenue. SILVER KEY STUDIOS read the sign over the entrance.

Tracy's friend, Doug Chadwick, was waiting for us in the lobby. I shook his hand and introduced him to Elizabeth.

"Thanks again for doing this," I said.

"I haven't done anything yet," he answered, "but Tracy said the magic word."

"What's that?" I asked, trying to remember what I'd heard Tracy tell Doug over the phone back at our apartment. I assumed he didn't mean *please.*

"Tracy said what you were hoping to do was practically impossible." Doug smiled wide. "I live for impossible."

CHAPTER 28

TAKE AWAY Doug's thick lumberjack beard, pierced eyebrow, rimless glasses, and Woodstock revival wardrobe and replace them with a permanent glass of single-barrel whiskey, a British accent, and the "screw you with a capital *F*" attitude of a devilishly unparalleled hacker, and you'd basically be looking at Julian Byrd's separated-at-birth brother.

Or, in other words, he was nothing like Julian.

Except for one thing.

Like Julian, Doug Chadwick clearly didn't appreciate being on the surrender side of a challenge. Especially one involving a computer.

"Follow me," he said.

Once again, life was just as much about who you know as what you know. Tracy had been introduced to Doug through an actress he'd met on the set of a shampoo commercial. Almost a year later to the day, Doug hired Tracy for his 3-D motion-capture shoot.

And tonight, Doug was about to help us identify a woman based solely on the way she walked in a very particular pair of high heels. At least that was the plan.

Elizabeth and I had Tracy to thank for setting this all up. He was also being a mensch for staying home with Annabelle. It was a double favor. But it was Doug who was doing us the huge favor.

"Just let me know what the hourly rate is," I said as we entered one of the studios at the end of a long hallway.

"Zilch," he said. "The booking agent felt bad for holding me to my session the day after the bombings, so this one's a freebie."

"What about your time, though?" I asked. "I need to pay you something."

"Nah, don't worry about it. To be honest, making Tracy jump around for hours in that ridiculous green leotard makes me feel a bit guilty for not paying him more," he said. He turned to Elizabeth. "Speaking of that leotard, I assume you have the honors?"

"I'm afraid so," said Elizabeth. "And green is so not my color."

Doug's involvement required a delicate dance for us in terms of what we could and couldn't tell him. We'd already emailed him the hotel surveillance footage of Darvish the night of his death. As far as Doug knew, he was helping the police identify the woman on the professor's arm. We obviously couldn't share why we wanted to know who she was or the real reason her face was obscured. If he asked about the glow, I was going to tell him it was the result of the footage being tampered with, but I had the feeling he wasn't going to ask.

"Okay, walk me through what you're thinking," he said, eyeing the shoebox in Elizabeth's hands. "So to speak."

"It's simple," I said. "While we can't see the woman's face, we can see her walk, and everyone has their own unique way of walking. Almost like a fingerprint."

"Almost, but not exactly," said Doug.

"Right, but close enough that we might be able to model this woman's precise gait. Of course, to do that—"

"You'd have to have her precise shoes. Lucky for you, she was wearing Christian Louboutins," he said.

I nudged Elizabeth. "*See?* He knows women's shoes and there's no way he's gay."

Elizabeth rolled her eyes. "Just ignore him, Doug. That's what I do." She took the shoes out of their box and handed them over.

"Yeah, I once dated a girl who was addicted to Louboutins," said Doug, giving them a look. "She couldn't afford them and I couldn't afford her. Are you sure these are the right ones, though? The difference of even a few millimeters in the heel height would throw off every calculation."

"They're the right ones," said Elizabeth, "and the heel is exactly a hundred millimeters. It's the only way they come."

Scam or no scam, you don't get to sell shoes for close to a thousand bucks a pop by making a gazillion different styles. The cross straps and open-toe design with a vamp heel narrowed the field down to just one, and there was no escaping the irony.

Louboutin made shoes with names like Fifi, Bibibop, and Doracandy.

This particular shoe, however, was called the Malefissima.

Latin root word *mal,* meaning bad.

Or evil.

CHAPTER 29

ELIZABETH RETURNED from the bathroom after changing into the skintight green leotard that gave new meaning to the word *unflattering,* even on her.

"You're right, Doug," she said, cringing, and not just from her cuts and bruises. "You're probably not paying Tracy enough."

Doug quickly lined her legs with the reflective markers otherwise known as "those tiny ping-pong balls." Her job now was to walk the world's shortest catwalk, back and forth in front of an elaborate station of cameras, behind which was an even more elaborate console of screens.

"Work it, girl!" I said.

Doug was multitasking at the keyboard, modeling the movement of the woman with Darvish in addition to the measurements he was getting from Elizabeth. The only fixed element was the shoes, so everything else—stride differential, for instance—had to be accounted for and adjusted using multiple algorithms that also took into account things like skin tone and body mass. And that was only for starters. The real math hadn't even begun.

So much for my having a statistics PhD from MIT. My head was spinning just thinking about it.

"Doug, any sign of the file?" asked Elizabeth.

All the computing in the world couldn't help us unless we had something to apply it to. That was the file we were waiting on—additional surveillance footage from the hotel covering the days leading up to Darvish's death. The detectives assigned to the case had acquired it, as per protocol for their investigation, and had even checked to see if there was any sign of Darvish's mystery woman. But they were searching for someone with the same glow. We weren't.

An operative or anyone else doing reconnaissance before taking out a mark wouldn't bother using Halo. She would assume she didn't need to.

"How the hell can anyone go back and identify her without having seen her face?" asked the detective Elizabeth had called on our way to Bergdorf's. She'd had him on speaker. He was peeved that she'd interrupted his dinner, especially because the file was only supposed to be viewed on the department's encrypted server.

"You're a detective, *figure it out,*" snapped Elizabeth. She wasn't digging the guy's attitude. "In the meantime, just send the damn file to the following address."

Doug checked his email again. It hadn't arrived the first time he looked. Two's a charm. "There it is," he said. "Got it."

But there was still more to do before using it. After filming Elizabeth in the Louboutins, he also had to film her barefoot to create a baseline. After all, it's not like our mystery woman would've worn her Malefissimas while doing her reconnaissance.

She did scout the hotel, right? She had to have done a walk-through before the night she returned with Darvish. Otherwise, we were wasting our time.

A lot of time.

"Are you sure you don't want to go home and get some sleep?" asked Doug as he began the task of singling out every woman who could be seen in the surveillance footage from the hotel, over a hundred hours' worth.

We were hardly about to bail on him, though.

"We'll sleep when you sleep," I said. It was the least we could do. Or, at least, try to do. By about 3:00 a.m., Elizabeth and I had both dozed off on a couch behind Doug's console. Had he actually known we were asleep he probably wouldn't have yelled. But I'd never been so happy in my life to be jolted awake.

Doug had been at his keyboard for six hours straight and looked every minute of it. His eyes were bloodshot, his hair the full-on Johnny Depp from *Edward Scissorhands*. Yet all I could really see was his smile. It was the same one he'd flashed when we first met him. Only wider. Much wider.

"Well?" I asked.

"Impossible, my ass," he said.

CHAPTER 30

IT TRULY was a thing of beauty.

In nerd terms, Doug had overlaid an algorithm onto every single frame of the footage, identifying and measuring all movement against an extrapolation of how the mystery woman would walk in every heel size using the baselines of Elizabeth both in the Louboutins and barefoot.

In non-nerd terms? *He crushed it.*

From over a thousand possible women, Doug had narrowed the field down to five.

The first two were white, albeit with either slightly darker complexions or tans—most likely the spray-booth variety.

"Is that one Hispanic?" asked Elizabeth, pointing at the third.

"Could be," I said. "She could also be a Filipina."

"What about the last two?" Elizabeth leaned toward Doug's main monitor. "Can we zoom in on them?"

Doug punched some keys. The more he zoomed in, though, the more pixelated the image got.

"Hard to tell," I said. "She could be South American, Indian, Middle Eastern, none of the above? Take your pick."

"Not that it makes a difference," said Elizabeth.

We all could agree on that. Knowing the woman's ethnicity was a long way from knowing her name and address.

"What now?" asked Doug.

"That depends," I said. "Porterhouse or bone-in rib eye?"

"Huh?"

"The steak dinner that I'm going to buy you."

"Thanks, except you still don't know who your woman is."

"No, not yet," I said. "If only she could've been your ex-girlfriend with the Louboutin obsession, right?"

He smiled, but it was half-hearted. To say he was now fully vested in the outcome was an understatement. Who could blame him? He'd gotten us so close. Even if he'd narrowed the choice down to one, though, it wasn't as if we could immediately identify her.

I was pretty sure that realization was settling over him when he suddenly snapped his fingers. He'd answered his own question.

"Facial recognition software," he said. *That's what's next.*

I nodded. "Yep."

The next step was seeing how many of these women we could identify through either mug shots or driver's license photos. Both the NYPD and the FBI had the facial recognition software sophisticated enough to accomplish that.

But there's a difference between taking the next step and being a step ahead. Already this was feeling like a chess match.

What were the chances that our mystery woman was really going to show up in either DMV records or a criminal database?

Sometimes the best covert agents and operatives are the ones who hide in plain sight. No one knows who they are because no one ever suspects that they're anything different from what they want you to believe.

Other times it's the exact opposite. The best are the ones who are so far off the grid it's as if they'd never existed.

All I knew was that we had to allow for both possibilities.

Or maybe worse. *Neither* of the two.

What if this woman was a category all to herself?

CHAPTER 31

I HATED doing what I did next. But it had to be done.

Elizabeth and I cabbed it back to Tracy's and my apartment. She was due at work in less than four hours and needed every minute of sleep she could get until then. "Is it weird if I wear the Louboutins to bed?" she joked before saying good night.

As far as she knew I was crawling into bed, too, equally as exhausted. I'd even said something on the way up in the elevator about needing to be quiet so as not to wake up Tracy.

But I never went into our bedroom.

After taking a peek at Annabelle—she looked so adorable snuggled up in her crib—I was back in the elevator and heading to the garage down the block for my motorcycle. I reattached my license plate with some tape. *I hope it holds because it's time to break some speed laws...*

I'd already sent the text, asking if he was still awake. It was a formality. Julian and Dracula kept the same hours. I didn't want to show up unannounced, though. The secret to a lasting friendship? Don't abuse it.

"What have we gotten ourselves mixed up in now?" asked Julian in his thoroughly British accent, greeting me at his steel door that was ten feet behind another steel door that was past the security gate to a warehouse for a medical supply company in Fort Lee, New Jersey, that nobody had ever heard of, primarily because it didn't actually exist.

"*Mixed up?* Do I look like I'm mixed up in something?" I asked.

"It's past four in the morning," he said. "You bloody well better be."

I followed Julian back to his office, smiling at the familiar sight of his giant desk made from the wing of an old Fokker Eindecker, the first German fighter plane.

"Is that Vegas?" I asked.

All the walls still doubled as seamless projection screens carrying a live feed from Julian's latest hacking conquest. I was looking at a busy casino poker room through its own security cameras.

"No, it's Macau," said Julian. "I'm trying to pick up some tells on a couple of regulars. I'll be there next month."

"I didn't think you took vacations."

"You're right, I don't," he said. "But enough about me, right?"

That was Julian's version of *Don't ask, don't tell*. I shouldn't bother asking why he was going to Macau because there was no way he was telling.

"Here," I said instead, handing him my phone. "There are five women in total. You're looking at the first. Swipe left to see the other four."

"You came here in the middle of the night to show me how Tinder works?"

"Yeah, like I would actually know."

Julian looked at all five screenshots from the hotel's surveillance footage. Once, then twice over. "Okay, now what?"

"Does one of them look familiar to you?" I asked.

"Before I answer that, answer this," he said. "How did you get involved in whatever this is?"

"You remember Elizabeth, right?"

Julian rubbed his chin sarcastically. "You mean, the pretty detective and only unauthorized person—other than yourself, of course—to ever set foot in this office? Oh, and the woman who was just all over the news for saving her boss's life? Nope, can't say I recall her."

"Yeah, well, Elizabeth is why I'm here."

"Interestingly enough, though, she's not. I'm guessing that's because of the possible identity of one of these five women. You're thinking she might be CIA. Elizabeth might even be thinking that, too. But if one of them actually is an operative, Elizabeth can't know her identity."

I once saw Julian solve a Rubik's Cube in less than fifteen seconds. With one hand, no less.

"Okay," I said. "Go ahead and say it. If you recognized one of these women as being an operative, you sure as hell couldn't tell me, right?"

Julian smiled. "Still, here you are asking..."

"I don't have to anymore," I said. "You don't recognize any of them."

"How do you know?"

"Your shoulders are relaxed. They tense up whenever you lie." I motioned to the wall and the casino in Macau. "Like a player who's bluffing."

"Remind me never to play poker with you, Reinhart." Julian glanced at my phone again. "No, I've never seen any of those women before. Then again, it's not like the Agency puts out a yearbook. And if you're about to ask me to hack—"

"Into the Agency's files? No, of course not," I said. "But I do need to identify all five of them."

"I'm guessing that would require something beyond DMV and criminal databases. In other words, the kind of facial recognition software that doesn't officially exist."

"You tell me," I said. But he already had.

As only Julian could.

CHAPTER 32

I TURNED to look at one of the walls again. Gone was the poker room in Macau. In its place was me. Everywhere.

I was so busy watching Julian's shoulders I hadn't seen his hands. He'd opened all the photos on my phone, transferring some of them to his computer. His entire office was now covered with different shots of me. Me with Tracy. Me with Annabelle. All three of us together.

"That's a nice one, all of you there in Central Park," said Julian, pointing.

Yes, it was a nice shot. Some woman had offered to take it after telling us in true Upper West Side fashion that she supported gay adoption 110 percent.

Only looking at the picture now I was barely recognizable. My face was contorted, and that was just for starters.

"What's with all the red explosions?" I asked.

"I know," said Julian. "It sort of looks like a pimple commercial."

"Yeah, if it was directed by Michael Bay," I said. Red spots were blowing up all over my face, one after another in rapid-fire succession. "That looks like more than measuring going on."

"It's called animatronic echo mapping. The next step in biometrics. It can predict muscle movement based on fixed intervals."

Facial recognition software generally relies on measurements between key features: the eyes, ears, mouth, and nose. Its limitations derive from the inability to account for different facial expressions. But what four-star general smiles when he gets his face scanned before entering the launch room at NORAD? In other words, the limitations haven't been too limiting. Until now, apparently.

"The times, they are a-changing, Dylan," said Julian. "It used to be I could hack into any facial recognition system by simulating a single expression. A freeze-frame. Now it's all about movement. Instead of passwords, most Swiss banks have recently switched to using sentences, and not just for a voice match. Every move of the mouth for each vowel sound has to match as well."

"So this echo mapping is your way around that?"

"An eleven-foot ladder for a ten-foot wall," said Julian. "From a series of still photos I can essentially animate you. If I can do that, I can *be* you."

"And empty my Swiss bank account?"

He grinned. "If need be."

"Good to know if I actually had one," I said. "Even better would be knowing how this is going to help me identify the five women."

Julian looked down at my phone. "These are still frames from surveillance footage, right? So, what I need is the footage."

I felt like a Boy Scout handing him the flash drive I'd made with all the recordings. I'd come prepared.

Julian began downloading the files, and I was starting to get the picture, so to speak. Julian was a hacker, not a programmer. This wasn't his program, but he was well equipped to reverse engineer it and tinker with its application. In doing so, the possibilities were literally endless. Forget about only being able to search mug shots and driver's license photos. Now you could identify almost anyone using the internet, and not only by their photos. That was the true innovation. All videos were now in play. Snapchat. YouTube. You name it.

The times, they were indeed a-changing.

As fast as I'd appeared, I was now gone from Julian's walls. In my place were the five women, one shot after another, amid the barrage of red bursts. It felt like the room was exploding.

Then, it all suddenly stopped.

"Winner, winner, chicken dinner!" said Julian with a clap of his hands.

I spun around on my heel, my head craning to look at every wall. "Which one?"

"Right shoulder, three o'clock," he said.

I turned. Fittingly, I was staring at a still frame taken from a video. She was standing at a podium. It was as if she were staring right back at me. "How do you know it's her?" I asked. "How do you know she's the one?"

He made a few taps on his keyboard. "Because of this," he said.

CHAPTER 33

SHE DIDN'T have a mug shot, and according to the motor vehicle departments in all fifty states, she didn't have a driver's
license either. But she did have a job.

Julian enlarged the description underneath the video he'd
found. It was from the website of New York University. *Professor
of Philosophy Sadira Yavari speaking at the Great Thinkers Summit,*
it read.

Before I could even ask for it, Julian pulled up her bio from
another page on the website that listed all the NYU faculty.

Sadira Yavari was an Iranian-born professor who had
taught philosophy at the university for seven years. Her focus
was epistemology, the study of knowledge and justified belief.

"It can't be a coincidence," said Julian.

"Which part?" I asked. "That she and Darvish are both Iranian or both professors?"

"*Both,*" he said.

On the one hand, he was right. The fact she was Iranian was proof enough for me that she had been the one with Darvish at the hotel. That she could also claim to be a professor only further explained how she was able to get close enough to him to end up in his room.

On the other hand, "Do you notice something odd about her bio?" I asked.

Julian read it again. He nodded. "Seven years."

That's how long Yavari had been teaching at NYU. An operative would never be in one place for that many years. Two was the norm. Three, max. Never as long as seven. My stint at Cambridge lasted thirty months. Coincidentally or not, I got made after twenty-nine.

"Of course, there is a simple explanation," I said.

"A civilian recruit? It rarely happens," said Julian, "and even less so with a woman."

"Rarely, but not never."

Sadira Yavari could've been recruited by the Agency for a specific assignment because she matched a unique profile that was needed—in this case an Iranian-born professor, and a very attractive one at that. But recruiting civilians fully entrenched in their civilian lives is a hard sell. Like ice-to-Eskimos hard.

And Julian was right—it's even harder with women. As opposed to men, women don't secretly harbor thoughts of being James Bond.

"Is it possible? Sure," said Julian. "Think limited scope. Maybe all she had to do was cozy up to Darvish and set the table for someone else to kill him."

"With a heart attack? And a bottle lodged up his—"

"Yeah, I read the report. You can spare me the details."

Regardless, it prompted a question: had the two professors

previously known each other? "What do we have for phone records?" I asked.

I watched Julian work his keyboard, his fingers a blur. He had both cell and landline numbers for Darvish and Yavari within seconds. Just as quick, he cross-checked all their billing statements for the past couple of years.

"No calls or texts between them," he said.

"It makes sense. A one-night stand."

Julian eyed Yavari again on the wall. Actually, it was more like ogling. She truly was gorgeous. Long dark-brown hair and high cheekbones. She looked a bit like Amal Clooney. "A one-night stand would've certainly worked for me," he said.

Julian clicked on the video of her from the NYU website so we could hear her voice. Sure enough, she sounded as good as she looked. Poised. Intelligent. In complete control.

She was telling a funny anecdote about taking the wrong subway all the way out to Queens when she first moved to Manhattan. The point being, as much as she believed she knew where she was going, the truth was that she had no idea. It was a parable for epistemology.

"But what if I had guessed right?" she asked the audience. "Does taking the right subway unto itself prove that I knew where I was going?"

On cue, the person filming her lecture turned the camera on the audience. Some heads were nodding; others were bobbing as if pondering the question. Everyone was fully engaged. Sadira Yavari had the room, as they say. They were hanging on her every—

"*Wait!* Hold it," I said.

Julian paused the video. "What is it?"

I couldn't believe what I was seeing. "Third row, second from the right. Do you know him?"

"No, but you obviously do," said Julian. "Who is he?"

"I'm not exactly sure, but I've met him. He's even been inside my apartment."

"And you don't know his name?"

"No," I said. "But I know what his name definitely isn't. *Benjamin Al-Kazaz.*"

CHAPTER 34

ELIZABETH'S SUNGLASSES were pulling double duty as she opened the door to the Starbucks around the corner from Dylan and Tracy's apartment. In addition to shielding her from the press in the wake of the Evan Pritchard video, the dark-tinted lenses were concealing the Samsonite-sized bags under her eyes on the heels of less than four hours of sleep.

She was exhausted. She was also running late. Pritchard had scheduled an early briefing with all agents assigned to the Times Square bombings. It started in twenty minutes. Her Uber was due out in front of the Starbucks within moments.

"I'll take a large coffee, please."

"We don't have large," said the girl with the purple-dyed hair behind the counter. "Did you mean a *venti*?"

Elizabeth could count on two fingers how many times she'd ever set foot in a Starbucks. She always preferred her coffee from diners. So did her wallet. But there was no time this morning. "Sure, I'll take a venti—whatever your largest size is," she said.

"Well, our largest size is actually a *trenta*. It means thirty in Italian. As in, ounces. Venti means—"

"Yeah, venti means twenty. As in, ounces. I get it," said Elizabeth.

"So which one do you want, a venti or a trenta? If you haven't noticed, there's a line behind you."

Oh, really? Do you know what fottiti *means in Italian? I assure you it's not forty . . .*

A minute later, venti coffee in hand, Elizabeth reached for a carafe of nonfat milk at the end of the counter.

"It sure looks like a large to me," said a man with a thick Middle Eastern accent. He grabbed a Splenda, tearing it open.

"I know," said Elizabeth. She figured he'd been right behind her in line. "Forgive me for not speaking Starbucks, right?"

The man laughed. "That's funny," he said. "I was told you were funny."

Elizabeth immediately put down the carafe and turned toward the man. His sunglasses were as dark as hers. Maybe even darker. He was also impeccably dressed in a gray suit and blue tie with a matching pocket square that had just the right amount of puff to it.

"Do I know you?" she asked. Translation: *How the hell do you know me?*

"Here," he said, handing her the open yellow packet. "That's how you like it, right? Light with one Splenda?"

If this guy was trying to creep her out, he'd succeeded. Quickly, Elizabeth looked around. Was he alone? It seemed that way.

More importantly, was he a threat?

Through her sunglasses, Elizabeth focused on his hands. For the moment, both were where she could see them. The split second that changed, she'd be reaching for her Glock.

He knew it, too.

"I assure you there's nothing to fear from me, Agent Needham," he said. "I'm here to help you."

"Good," she said. "You can start by telling me who you are."

"I'm a friend of a friend."

"You're going to have to do better than that."

"Actually, I don't," he said. "That's not how this works."

"How what works?" asked Elizabeth.

"Take the Splenda, Agent Needham."

"Why?"

"So I can reach into my suit pocket," he said. "Slowly, of course."

Elizabeth thought for a second. *If he wanted to kill me, he would've done it already . . .*

She took the Splenda.

The man reached into his pocket—slowly, as promised—and removed an envelope, handing it to her.

"You'll be asked by people where you got this information," he said. "You can tell them anything, except that you got it from me."

Elizabeth glanced at the plain white envelope. "I don't even know who you are," she said.

He nodded, satisfied. "Exactly." He then pivoted on his heel, heading straight for the door.

Poof, he was gone.

CHAPTER 35

ELIZABETH GAVE another quick look around, her eyes darting, making sure the guy didn't have a wingman. If he did, the disguise was excellent. The entire Starbucks held either people rushing in and out on their way to work or wannabe screenplay writers getting an early jump on hogging all the tables.

Ping!

Never mind. Her Uber was out front.

In the back of an old Ford Taurus in desperate need of an air freshener, she opened the envelope. Inside was a photo—old-school, three-by-five glossy—of a young man wearing a taqiyah, the traditional Muslim cap. Even more traditional was its color: white.

On the back of the photo, written in pen, was presumably his first name. Gorgin. There was also an address up in Pelham in Westchester County, about a half hour's drive from Manhattan.

Finally there was this, her instructions: *Ask him what he knows about the Mudir.*

Elizabeth knew the word. *Mudir* was Arabic. It meant a local governor or someone who holds sway over a group of people. She didn't recognize the young man in the photo, though.

Of course, that was the whole point. This guy, "Gorgin," was supposed to be a lead. *Supposed* to be.

According to whom, though? And why the mysterious middleman back in Starbucks? Was she really supposed to trust this stranger with a Middle Eastern accent?

There were too many questions, with even more to come once she followed protocol and brought Pritchard up to speed. After his briefing, she'd show him the photo. If he didn't know the young man in the taqiyah named Gorgin, there was probably a computer somewhere in-house that did.

But before that could happen, Pritchard would want to know something else. She could practically hear his booming voice, prodding her. *Why you, Needham? How come you were the one he approached? Huh?*

"Here we are," said her Uber driver.

Elizabeth didn't hear him. She was still listening to Pritchard in her head. "Excuse me?"

"This is your stop, right?" asked the driver. "Where you wanted to go?"

Elizabeth stared out the window at the granite facade of the JTTF building. Pritchard's briefing would start in a couple of minutes. She'd have to hustle if she wanted to make it up to the conference room in time. She reached for the door handle.

Seriously, why you? What makes you so special, Needham?

Elizabeth's hand suddenly froze. "Change of plans," she told the driver.

Twenty blocks south and a $5.60 surcharge later, Elizabeth was at City Hall standing face-to-face with Beau Livingston, the mayor's chief of staff, who had his back up against the door to his boss's office. He was literally blocking her way.

"You can't just show up unannounced, Elizabeth," he said. Livingston's arms were folded, his feet spread. The only way she was getting past him was through him.

No problem.

"If you don't move, I'm going to kick you in the balls, Beau," she said.

Livingston didn't need his Phi Beta Kappa Harvard education to know she was serious. As for Mayor Deacon's secretary, she might as well have had a bucket of popcorn in her lap while tilting back some Jujubes. She was watching from behind her desk, transfixed.

Of all things, though, Livingston started to laugh.

"What's so funny?" asked Elizabeth.

"The mayor bet me five bucks that you'd figure it out by lunch." He glanced at his watch. "Nicely done. It's barely even breakfast."

He turned and opened the door to Deacon's office. As he did, Elizabeth could hear Pritchard's voice in her head one last time.

What makes you so special, Needham?

CHAPTER 36

"WELL, IF it isn't my favorite agent," said Mayor Edward "Edso" Deacon, looking up at Elizabeth from the sprawl of morning papers on his desk. He managed to punch the word *agent* enough to underscore that she was no longer just a detective, thanks to him. He waved her in. "To what do I owe the surprise?"

"Nice try," she said. "You know you could've just called if you wanted to see me."

Deacon cocked his head. "Really? Because I distinctly recall our last conversation, when you were so adamant about not being my eyes and ears over at the Task Force."

"Is that what this is about?"

"The opposite. I'm the one doing you a favor," said Deacon.

"Do you mean this?" she asked, removing the photo from her inside blazer pocket.

The mayor squinted. He was nearsighted, albeit not politically. "I don't know. Is that what he gave you?"

Elizabeth stared, incredulous. "You don't even know?"

"No, and I don't want to."

"Why not?"

Deacon pointed at the chair in front of his desk. "Have a seat, Needham."

"I'd prefer to stand."

"Duly noted. *Now sit the fuck down.*"

Elizabeth sat down. Edso Deacon was still the mayor of the largest city in the country, after all. He giveth and could taketh away. Namely, Elizabeth's job.

Meanwhile, Livingston was about to make his usual walk to the couch by the window, where he always sat during his boss's meetings.

"Actually, Beau," said Deacon, "give us a couple of minutes alone, will you?"

Livingston tried his best to hide his surprise, but his smile was as fake as a street-corner Rolex. "Of course," he said, and out he went.

"Was that for my benefit or yours?" asked Elizabeth once he was gone.

"More yours," said the mayor. "Call it a goodwill gesture, proof that you earned your promotion and that every conversation with me doesn't need a buffer."

Elizabeth appreciated the sentiment but still hadn't forgotten how she'd ended up in his office. "Why the cloak-and-dagger?" she asked. "Better yet, why not pass along any info you have directly to the FBI?"

"Because it's not my info."

"Whose is it?" But no sooner had she asked than she realized the answer. "You can't tell me. *You can't tell anyone.*"

Deacon nodded. "Now you've got it."

Yes, she did. The mayor had an intel source he could never reveal—not only to protect the source but to protect himself.

Suffice it to say, whoever the guy was who'd approached her at Starbucks, he wasn't a Boy Scout.

Still, "How do I know this is for real?" she asked, holding up the photo.

"The short answer is you don't," said Deacon. "That's why you'll check it out on your own first. Something tells me, though, it's legit."

Elizabeth stood. "I won't be able to update you directly," she said. "You realize that, right?"

"I wouldn't have it any other way." Deacon leaned back in his chair, stretching his long frame. "You know, there's a perverse irony to all this. When it comes to street crime and the murder rate, it's always the mayor's fault. But, God forbid, a terrorist attack? Not only is it not my fault, I become the great unifier."

"That's not perverse. It's just human nature," said Elizabeth.

"Believe me," said Deacon. "There's no difference."

CHAPTER 37

A HALF hour out of Manhattan, Elizabeth pulled up slowly to the address in Pelham she'd been given for the young man named Gorgin. She was driving a Honda Pilot from the JTTF lot. Honda Pilots don't say gun-toting special agent. They say soccer mom.

There were two possibilities when no one answered her knocking on the door. Either no one was home or someone was choosing not to answer. Before she could settle on the latter, she had to wait out the former. Parking a few houses down the street with an eye on Gorgin's driveway, Elizabeth settled in.

As towns go, Pelham and the word *ritzy* were never going to be used in the same sentence unless that sentence happened to be that Pelham was far from ritzy. Compared to Jersey City, however, it was a major step up. Gorgin's house, a small, vinyl-sided colonial, might as well have been a mansion compared to the shit shack she had descended upon with Pritchard and company. A good sign, thought Elizabeth.

Better still was the black BMW that pulled into the driveway less than an hour later. In terms of wait time, she'd hit the stake-out jackpot. Even from fifty yards away, there was no doubt that the guy who got out from behind the wheel and headed into the house was Gorgin. He was alone.

Not for long. Elizabeth sprinted as soon as the front door closed behind him. He barely had time to put down his car keys before she was knocking again.

"Who is it?" he asked from behind the door. There was no peephole.

"My name is Agent Needham from the JTTF," said Elizabeth, standing off to the side with her back to the vinyl siding. "I'm looking for Gorgin."

She had one hand alongside her holster. With the other she reached for her badge, the ink on her new ID barely dry.

She fully expected Gorgin to ask what the JTTF was. But, nope, he was apparently familiar with the Joint Terrorism Task Force. That may or may not have been a good sign.

He opened the door.

Elizabeth remained off to the side, waiting for him to poke his head out to look for her. Instead he came all the way out, stepping onto the small landing at the top of the steps. She could see both his hands as he turned to her. They were empty.

"Are you Gorgin?" she asked.

"Yes, that's me," he said.

Elizabeth flashed her badge even though he didn't ask to see it. "Do you have a couple of minutes? I'd like to ask you a few questions."

"Sure," he answered. He didn't hesitate. He also didn't move. It was as if he were blocking the door.

"Can we talk inside your house?" she asked.

"Actually, do you mind if we do this outside?"

That was *definitely* not a good sign, thought Elizabeth. As red flags go, it was the equivalent of a Chinese military parade. What didn't he want her to see?

"As a matter of fact, I do mind," she said. "We need to talk inside."

CHAPTER 38

THIS TIME, Gorgin hesitated.

Elizabeth could practically see the wheels churning in his head. He glanced back over his shoulder into his house not once but twice. Finally he broke into a smile. Or was that a grimace?

"Okay, come on in," he said.

Elizabeth followed him inside. She was still watching his hands. *Always watch the hands.* But now there was everything else, an entire house he seemingly didn't want her to see.

What are you hiding, Gorgin? Who are you? Tell me why I'm here...

He looked to be in his late twenties. He was clean-shaven. The English was near perfect, but there was a lingering hint of a Middle Eastern accent. He probably came to the States as a teenager. Best guess, from Turkey. Backup guess, Jordan.

The prayer mat facing east in the corner of the living room took any of the guesswork out of religion. Gorgin was a prac-

ticing Muslim. But he was also very Westernized. If the BMW
didn't give it away, the skinny jeans, zip-up hoodie, and gelled-
back hair did.

"Do you own this house?" asked Elizabeth. She assumed he
didn't.

"No, this is a rental," he said. "I wish I could afford it, though.
One day."

"What do you do for a living?"

Gorgin was still walking; Elizabeth was still following. He
stopped suddenly, turning back to her at the entrance to the
kitchen.

"I'll answer all of your questions, Agent Needham, but first I
have one for you," he said. "Would you like some tea?"

Tea? "No, thank you," said Elizabeth.

"Are you sure? I was just about to make some."

"No, really, that's—"

"It's excellent tea. Very special. My uncle sends me boxes of it
from overseas. You really should try some."

There was no change in the tone of his voice. No punching
of any particular word. The inflection was normal. That's because the conversation wasn't about what Elizabeth could hear.
As Gorgin was talking he was also nodding. He was signaling
her. *Say yes to the tea, Agent Needham. Trust me.*

"In that case," said Elizabeth, "I'd love some tea."

Gorgin turned and went to the stove, grabbing a kettle from
one of the burners. As he filled it with water from the sink, Elizabeth took a seat at a small table in the corner.

"Sales," said Gorgin.

"Excuse me?"

He returned the kettle to the stove, turning on the burner. "I
sell commercial-grade cutlery to restaurants. That's my job."

Great. The guy handles knives for a living.

Gorgin opened a cabinet, removing two teacups. From another cabinet he removed a box of tea bags. Elizabeth eyed the label. It was Lipton.

Lipton? That's the special tea your uncle sends you?

Of course it wasn't. He'd obviously made that up on the fly. It was the only thing Elizabeth was sure about. Everything else was still unclear, including her next move. Should she start asking her questions or just make small talk and wait?

Wait for what, though? Gorgin wasn't giving any more signals. All he was doing was making tea. At least she could still see his—

No sooner had he pulled out a couple of tea bags than he shifted his body, his back suddenly facing Elizabeth. She couldn't see his hands anymore, but his arms were definitely moving. He was doing something.

Something he didn't want her to see.

Elizabeth edged forward in her chair and dropped a hand to her side, slowly tucking her blazer back behind her Glock. Her fingertips tap-danced on the grip as if keeping time. Any sudden move. That's all it would take.

How long can someone go without blinking?

"What's that?" she asked.

Gorgin had said something. She didn't hear him.

"I said, you're awfully quiet over there, Agent Needham."

He began to turn. There was something in his hand.

No. Both hands.

CHAPTER 39

TEACUPS. HE was holding the teacups.

He walked over, casually placing them on the table. One for her and one for him. Elizabeth didn't look down at hers. She wasn't about to take her eyes off this guy, not for a second. Not until she knew what the hell was going on.

The answer was right in front of her.

"The water should be ready in a minute," said Gorgin, returning to the stove. He was talking over his shoulder. "My uncle says it's best to pour from the kettle directly onto the tea bag."

Again, there was nothing in Gorgin's voice. Nor was there any head nodding this time or anything approaching a signal.

Still, Elizabeth heard him loud and clear. His instructions. She looked down inside the cup and literally read the tea leaves.

They're listening.

Gorgin had written the two words on the tea bag in her cup. That's what he'd been doing when he turned his back to her. Clever. If she'd seen him taking a pen to a tea bag, she would've asked what on earth he was doing. Not a good thing if someone was listening in—someone who probably didn't want Gorgin talking to an agent with the JTTF.

Elizabeth looked up from the cup, locking eyes with him as he leaned against the counter next to the stove. She nodded. Message received.

Only who's listening? Why the hell is the house bugged?

Elizabeth quickly replayed the last few minutes in her mind. She'd told Gorgin who she was, but that was outside on the steps. Still, he'd referred to her as Agent Needham once she was inside. That couldn't have been by accident. He wasn't trying to pass her off as the Avon lady or a neighbor looking to borrow a cup of sugar.

So now what?

Elizabeth was about to motion for the pen. She would write out her questions, hopefully on something bigger than a tea bag. She wanted to ask how to play this out—should she inquire about the Mudir as intended or instead make up an excuse for her being there?

It was as if Gorgin could read her mind.

"So let me guess," he said. "In the wake of the Times Square bombings, every Muslim in the tristate area is getting a house call."

"That would be a lot of house calls," said Elizabeth.

"You're right. Make that young single men of a certain age who just happen to be practicing Muslims. I believe the word is *profiling*."

"That's your word, not mine. It's also not a word that the JTTF would use."

Gorgin gave her a thumbs-up. They were ad-libbing the script, but she was sticking to it perfectly. So was he. Whoever was listening needed to think that Gorgin would never crack under pressure. That he could take the heat. It was only fitting they were in a kitchen.

Elizabeth still had no idea who this guy was or even what information she could expect to get from him, but there was no doubting the sense that he was someone she could trust. That was the point, right? It was why she'd been sent his way. Gorgin could help her.

For a moment, she even stopped watching his hands.

Oh, shit. No!

No-no-no-no-no!

CHAPTER 40

EVERYTHING HAPPENED at once. The worst things usually do.

The sound of the kettle whistling suddenly pierced the room, drawing Elizabeth's eyes to the stove just long enough that she didn't immediately see Gorgin's right hand reach under the dish towel by the sink. He was already whipping his arm around toward her before she could reach for her holster.

There was no catching up; he'd outdrawn her. There was no getting out of the way; he was too close.

This is how I die.

Elizabeth watched the barrel of his gun line up with her chest. All that was left for him to do was pull the trigger.

But the barrel kept moving.

She hadn't heard the front door opening down the hallway. She hadn't heard the footsteps. And she definitely hadn't seen the man with the thick black beard entering the kitchen with an AK-47 trained at her head. But Gorgin had.

Now he pulled his trigger.

He got off two rounds. Maybe three. He only needed the first. It was a perfect kill shot to the carotid artery.

The bearded man spun from the impact, his neck wildly spurting blood as he shifted his aim off Elizabeth and onto Gorgin. He was falling to the ground, his legs collapsing underneath him. Maybe he squeezed his trigger. Or maybe his finger just twitched. Either way, his AK-47 sprayed a line across the kitchen as he came crashing down with a thud.

Elizabeth looked at him by her feet and then up at Gorgin, their eyes locking as they'd done before. His stare said it all. She didn't need to see the two holes in his chest, the dark redness oozing and spreading across the front of his hoodie. She knew how badly he was hurt.

Elizabeth sprang from her chair as Gorgin fell to the floor, gasping for air as he rolled onto his back. He was losing too much blood, too quickly.

Grabbing the dish towel from the counter, the one that had concealed his gun, she tried to clamp the entry wounds, only the blood kept coming. It wouldn't stop.

Gorgin could barely speak but he wanted to. He *needed* to.

"The house," he said, his lungs wheezing. There was more to the sentence, only he couldn't finish it. He blinked a few times as if trying to gather his strength. "The house . . . it's wired."

"I know," said Elizabeth. "You told me. They're listening."

Gorgin reached up, his hand flailing as he tried to grab her arm. "No," he said. "The house is *wired*."

CHAPTER 41

WHAT GORGIN meant hit Elizabeth almost as fast as the smell.

She first thought a stray bullet had pierced the stove and somehow triggered the gas. Except the smell wasn't coming from the stove.

She looked up. *Oh, Jesus.* It was so thick she could literally see it. The gas was pouring out from the air duct in the ceiling.

Chemistry 101. The bomb ignites the gas, which levels the house and everything in it. There's no evidence to be had. Or witnesses.

"We need to get the hell out of here," said Elizabeth. She started to slide one hand under Gorgin's back, another under his legs. Could she even lift him? She had to try.

"Don't," he said. "There's no time."

"I'm not leaving without—"

"Go."

Elizabeth coughed, her lungs burning. She could barely breathe. It was now or never.

He had saved her life. There was no way she wouldn't try to save his.

"Okay, here we go," she said, steadying herself to lift him up. "We can do this. Just stay with me."

She was so focused on his body, so consumed with mustering the strength to carry him, that she didn't see his eyes. They were still staring at her, but it wasn't the same. There was nothing behind them. He was gone.

"Go," he'd told her. The last word he would ever speak. *Go.*

Elizabeth pushed herself up off the floor, stumbling as she began to run. She sprinted from the kitchen, the front door straight ahead down the hallway. On a dime, though, she stopped and looked back behind her. There was no time, she told herself. She did it anyway.

Are you crazy? Are you insane? What are you doing?

Elizabeth raced back to the bearded man in the kitchen. His gun would have his fingerprints. Better yet, was he dumb enough to have ID on him?

She riffled through his back pockets. He was wearing cargo pants. There was no wallet. There was no anything. One pocket, then the other, came up empty as she continued coughing from the gas, her eyes stinging and tearing so badly she could barely see.

Flipping him over in a pool of his own blood, she tried both of his pockets in front. Still nothing. She was about to give up when she spied another pocket—a small one on his T-shirt— with the slightest hint of a folded piece of paper sticking out. She grabbed it, checking to see if there was anything else with it. There wasn't.

Instinctively, Elizabeth began to unfold the paper to see what it was when she caught herself. *Now, you really are insane. Get the hell out of here!*

She scooped up the AK-47 and raced down the hallway again. She could hear a siren off in the distance. A neighbor probably called 911 after hearing all the gunshots.

Oh, crap! The neighbors.

Flinging the front door open, she bolted down the steps and out to the street before turning back to see which neighbor's house was the closest. It was no contest. There was a split ranch to the right less than twenty feet away from Gorgin's house. If anyone was inside, she had to get them out of there. She was about to run.

"Freeze!" came the man's voice. He was behind her.

Elizabeth froze. She had to. She literally had blood on her hands and was wielding an AK-47 in the middle of the street on the heels of shots being fired.

Still, she tried to explain. "I'm an agent with—"

"I don't give a fuck if you're the pope," he barked. "Lower your weapon and lie down on the ground!"

"There's no time," she said, pointing. "That house is about to—"

BOOM!

And, like that, they were both flat on the ground.

CHAPTER 42

"I THOUGHT this only happened in the movies," I said.

"What's that?" asked Landon Foxx.

"A couple of operatives meeting secretly in a Chinese restaurant."

"First of all, I only count one operative, and it's not you," said Foxx. "Second, the Chinese know how to do something that Americans don't. *Mind their own damn business.*"

Sure enough, the CIA's New York section chief and I were standing in the back of a crowded kitchen during lunchtime in Chinatown, and not a single cook, busboy, or any passing waiter or waitress even glanced our way. As for Foxx's jab about my no longer being an operative, I sort of leaned in on that one. Best to just take it on the chin and get to the point of my wanting to meet with him.

"Is this woman with the Agency?" I asked, holding up a picture of Sadira Yavari on my phone.

Foxx stared at her for a moment. He shook his head. "Not that I know of."

"Would you actually tell me if she was?"

"Probably not," he said. "In any event, this is the part where you tell me what you know about this woman and, more importantly, why I should know it."

Fair enough. "Professor Jahan Darvish," I said. "Ring a bell?"

Foxx nodded. "The MIT guy who died with a liquor bottle up his ass." He said it so matter-of-factly you would've thought Darvish had died from something typical, like cancer or a heart attack.

"This woman—Sadira Yavari—was with Darvish when he came back to his hotel the night of his death," I said.

"Was she his girlfriend?"

"No."

"Escort?"

"Nope."

"How can you be sure?" asked Foxx.

I swiped left on my phone to a screenshot from the hotel's surveillance footage. "That's how," I said.

Foxx blinked a few times, taking it all in. I could see the questions lining up in his mind like planes on a tarmac. "Let's start with this," he said. "How are you even involved in this, Reinhart?"

"It's a long story," I said.

"They always are." He stared at the picture again, the glow around Yavari's face. "How were you able to identify her if she was using Halo?"

"That's an even longer story," I said.

"Is there *anything* you want to tell me about this woman?" he asked. "Besides her name?"

Yes, there was. Plenty.

"Sadira Yavari was born in Iran—parents also Iranian, both deceased. Now a US citizen. Lives in Manhattan. Pays her taxes,

clean record, never even jaywalked. She's a philosophy professor at NYU."

"How many years?"

I knew that would be his very next question. On the surface,
it confirmed that Yavari wasn't CIA—at least as far as Foxx
knew, and Foxx knew most everything within the Agency.

"Seven," I said. "She's been teaching at NYU for seven years."

"Who else knows she was with Darvish at the hotel?" he
asked.

"That depends."

"On what?"

I cocked my head and stared at Foxx without saying anything. For a moment it was as if the entire restaurant kitchen
had gone silent, all the banging and clanking of pots and pans,
all the sizzling of oil, just fading away.

He got the hint.

I never liked the official motto of the CIA. Few people even
know what it is. *The Work of a Nation. The Center of Intelligence.*
It reads like it came from a junior copywriter on Madison Avenue. For sure, it didn't originate from anyone who actually
worked in espionage. But mottos are for flags and plaques. If
you ever really wanted to summarize the work of the Agency—
how critical information is actually gathered—there's a far better expression.

To get trust you have to give trust.

Foxx was holding back. He wasn't telling me something, and
until he decided to spit it out, I was keeping my mouth shut.
There'd be no more information from me. No more intel. Hence
my long stare at him and, ultimately, his nod in return.

"Okay, here it is," he said finally. *"Professor Darvish was an
asset."*

CHAPTER 43

I KNEW IT.

Okay, maybe it was more like a gut feeling. It had to be *some-thing* like that, though. Foxx tipped his hand with the regularity of a solar eclipse, but the questions he had been asking—the *way* he had been asking them—it was as if he'd intended all along to bring me into the fold regarding Darvish.

The Iranian nuclear physicist from MIT was an informant for the CIA.

"We had the same surveillance footage from the hotel, but Halo prevented us from identifying the woman, although we sure as hell still tried," said Foxx. He nodded with what felt like begrudging respect for me. "Well done, Reinhart."

Forget a solar eclipse. Foxx complimenting me? That was hell freezing over.

"When was Darvish recruited?" I asked.

"The summer of 2015."

"During the Iranian nuclear deal, in other words."

"Exactly," said Foxx. "Among the working theories was that the Iranians would try to further their program in our own backyard while we were busy snooping around in theirs. Sure enough, they leveraged Darvish by threatening his parents and brother back in Iran."

"What about money?" I asked. "Did they also pay him?"

"Handsomely, from what I understand."

I literally scratched my head. "Safety for his family and financial security to boot," I said. "Why would Darvish risk that to become an asset?"

"Because the even bigger risk was running an underground nuclear lab in the middle of Cambridge, Massachusetts. That, and maybe he had a conscience," said Foxx.

"What did he want in return?" I asked. "His family out of Iran?"

"We offered that, but he was smart enough to know it still wouldn't guarantee their safety or his. Turns out, he had something else in mind."

That meant only one thing. "To be a double agent, right?"

"For lack of a better term, yes," said Foxx. "Darvish would make periodic progress in his lab, except not quite at the rate he was fully capable of. Tehran remained satisfied, and meanwhile we were able to monitor his handlers and learn what else they were up to. It had been working extremely well for us."

"And then along came a pretty woman," I said. "Sadira Yavari."

"Darvish must have thought he'd hit the jackpot at first," said Foxx. "He didn't exactly look like Brad Pitt, in case you didn't notice." He chuckled to himself before turning to me. *"What?"*

"Nothing," I said.

"Bullshit."

He was right. I was trying to get a read on him. Was Foxx telling me the whole truth? "I was just wondering," I said.

"I know. How did she have access to Halo? I'm telling you, though, it wasn't an inside job. Halo has been around for over a decade. Word was the Russians had gotten their hands on one of the necklaces and reverse engineered it about three years ago, and as you know, the Iranians get all of Putin's hand-me-downs." Foxx paused as if to stress the point. "This Yavari woman is not one of our operatives."

"Are you sure?"

"Positive," he said. "But don't just take my word for it."

"What does that mean?"

"I think you know."

Unfortunately, I did. In Tony Soprano terms, Sadira Yavari was about to get whacked. "When?" I asked.

"As soon as possible," he said. "Newton's Third Law. It's the only thing the Iranians are capable of understanding."

"You're right," I said. "Only that's the part that doesn't make sense. The Iranians discover that Darvish is an informant and they try to make his death look like an accident? They'd want you to know it was them, loud and clear."

"What are you suggesting?"

"I'm not sure," I said.

Foxx shook his head. "You're going to have to do better than that, Reinhart. Speak now or forever hold your peace."

CHAPTER 44

YOU CAN never fully rely on what any operative tells you, even if he is the section chief of the entire New York region. The reason I know this is because I was once an operative, too. It was my job to lie.

But in the words of the British philosopher John Stuart Mill, *There is no such thing as absolute certainty, but there is assurance sufficient for the purposes of human life.*

Meaning, I was as convinced as I could be that Foxx was telling me the truth. The CIA hadn't had Darvish killed.

Now I just had to convince him that it might not have been the Iranian government either.

Once again, I swiped left on my phone. "Here," I said. Instead of a picture, this time it was a video. I pressed Play.

"What am I looking at?" Foxx asked.

"That's Sadira Yavari giving a lecture at NYU about six months ago. And that guy there in the third row, second from the right," I said, pointing, "is the same guy who came to my apartment posing as Ahmed's lawyer."

Foxx tapped my screen, pausing the video to take a better look at Benjamin Al-Kazaz, or whatever his real name was. "You're telling me there's a connection between Professor Darvish and the Times Square bombings?"

"There's at least something," I said.

"You mean, someone."

"Yes, and if you kill her, whatever she knows dies with her."

"So instead we bring Yavari in," said Foxx. "Have a conversation."

"And if she doesn't talk?"

"Then you're right. Whatever she knows dies with her," he said, folding his arms. Foxx could be as cold-blooded as they come when need be. "Why, you've got a better idea, Reinhart?"

"As a matter of fact, I do," I said.

BOOK THREE

I SPY A KILLER LIE

CHAPTER 45

"SPREAD YOUR legs, honey," said the Mudir.

"Excuse me?" she asked.

"You heard me," he said, stepping out from behind the concrete pillar.

Sadira Yavari had followed the Mudir's every instruction up until that point. She'd parked her car on level 3 of the underground garage in Tribeca and taken the stairs down one more flight to level 4 to meet him. She'd brought the passports mailed to her NYU office from Tehran. She'd also left any and all weapons at home.

Still, he wanted to frisk her. Or was he testing her?

"Why would I ever spread my legs for you?" she said.

The Mudir walked straight at Sadira, the heels of his Bruno Magli shoes scraping hard against the pavement. Reaching into his suit jacket, he removed his pistol, an MP-443 Grach, and raised it out in front of himself with his elbow locked. He didn't stop until the barrel was pressed firmly against her forehead.

"Are you questioning me?" he asked.

Sadira didn't answer. Nor did she move. She just kept staring straight back into his black-as-tar eyes. Right up until he pulled the trigger.

Click.

The Mudir smiled. He liked what he saw, which was nothing. This woman didn't flinch. The chamber was empty and she was still alive, and yet she didn't even let out a sigh of relief, not the slightest noise or peep. Her life was nothing. The cause was everything.

"*As-salāmu ʿalayki,*" he said, lowering his pistol. *Peace be upon you.*

"*Wa ʿalaykumu s-salām,*" Sadira replied.

None of her contacts back in Iran had described the Mudir to her. So few people knew what he actually looked like. He wore disguises. He'd had plastic surgery. Multiple times. Most of all, he knew how to move in the shadows. This was how he'd evaded intelligence agencies around the world. He would show up on their radars, yes, but only as a blip here and there. The key was making sure the blips never connected. They never did.

Sadira continued to stare back at the Mudir. He was taller than she'd expected. Leaner. And the more she looked at his eyes, the darker they seemed to get. They were soulless.

"Do you have them?" he asked.

Sadira removed the folded envelope from the pocket of her slacks, handing over the three British passports that would provide him with three new identities. He checked each one carefully. They were perfect forgeries. Satisfied, he tucked them away inside his suit jacket, followed by the pistol.

"We have mutual friends," said the Mudir.

"We have mutual interests," said Sadira.

"How much have you been told?"

"You were infiltrated," she said. "He was Muslim."

"He was CIA. He learned of our attack an hour before it happened."

"Are there others?"

"No," he said.

The Mudir looked confident. He sounded confident. But they both knew he couldn't know with absolute certainty if any other cells had been infiltrated.

"Do you need my assistance?" Sadira asked.

He wasn't expecting the professor to offer her help. "Maybe," said the Mudir. "We had a setback this morning. You'll see it on the news. A house in Pelham."

"Will this change your timetable?"

"No, the next attack will happen as planned."

The Mudir waited for her to ask the location, but she didn't. That was good. This woman was smart. She understood how things worked. "You know how to reach me," she said instead.

Sadira turned to leave. The Mudir wasn't finished.

"I saw you speak," he said. "A lecture."

"When?"

"Some months ago. The Great Thinkers Summit, it was called." The title obviously amused him. He was shaking his head, smiling. "Americans," he said. "All they do is think."

"Worse," said Sadira. "They always think they know best."

The Mudir nodded his approval. "We will teach them otherwise, won't we?"

"Yes," she said. "Every last one of them."

CHAPTER 46

IT WASN'T easy, but I got Foxx to buy into my plan. It wasn't Foxx I was worried about, though.

"Now *this* is what I'm talking about," said Tracy, cutting into a twenty-four-ounce bone-in rib eye that was literally bigger than his plate. Native Iowans don't do fillets. "This was such a great idea, Dylan. Thank you."

Don't thank me yet . . .

We were at the Palm on West 50th Street, one of our favorite steak houses in the city. I'd made the reservation and called Tracy to meet me for an early dinner, but not before making sure Lucinda was available. She's Annabelle's babysitter, although we hardly ever use her.

That's what I was leveraging with Tracy. We needed a night out together, just the two of us.

"I'm glad you were good with this," I said. "I wasn't sure you would be."

Tracy smiled knowingly at the subtext. *A baby changes everything.*

He and I had caught the homebody bug after Annabelle's arrival. Going out on a Sunday night — or any night — was tantamount to abandoning her. We both felt it, although Tracy felt it more. He knew it, too.

"Our friends with kids are always telling us, right? How important it is to still make time for each other? But for some reason —"

"Not just some reason," I said. "The best reason in the world."

"I know. Annabelle is the greatest thing that ever happened in our lives, but we can't forget about *us*. You and me."

"I agree."

"I know you do," said Tracy. "That was my way of saying I'm the one who needs to do a better job of it."

"Hey, you're here, aren't you?"

"Only because you got me here."

"What's the difference?"

"That's true," he said. "You've got to start somewhere, right?"

Good point. *So why the hell am I still stalling?*

"Speaking of you and me," I said. "There's something I need to talk to you about."

I couldn't stand it any longer. I'd requested a quiet table and was planning to tell Tracy before we ordered. Then I was going to tell him before our steaks came. At this rate, it was never going to happen.

I had to tell him. *Now.*

"Uh-oh, that sounds a bit ominous," said Tracy, tongue in cheek. "At least I'm already sitting down for this."

How do you tell someone who thinks he knows everything about you the one thing that changes everything he thought?

The answer is, I don't know. For better or worse, after nearly a decade of keeping it a secret, I simply blurted it out.

"I used to work for the CIA," I said.

Tracy didn't even look up from his rib eye. "Ha-ha, very funny," he said. "Can you pass the creamed spinach?"

I didn't pass the creamed spinach. I didn't do anything except wait for Tracy to realize that I wasn't kidding around.

Finally he looked up at me. "Wait, *what*?"

There was no turning back now.

CHAPTER 47

"IT'S TRUE," I said.

Tracy still didn't believe me. Or was it shock?

"Did you really just say that? You actually used to work for..." He couldn't even finish the sentence.

"The CIA, yes."

"Like, as an analyst? Behind a desk?"

"I was an operative," I said. "I was in the field."

Tracy couldn't stop blinking. "How? Where? *When?*"

He thought he had me with the timing. He'd known me since college. We hadn't always been together, though.

"It was after I was at MIT and before we started seeing each other again," I said.

His eyes narrowed. He was running it through his mind. "That's when you were at Cambridge. Your fellowship."

"The fellowship was actually my cover."

"Your cover? You mean, you lied to me?"

"Technically, I lied to everybody."

"I'm not everybody, Dylan."

He was right. *This isn't going so well, is it?*

"I'm truly sorry," I said. "The last thing I wanted to do was keep this from you. But it was really for your—"

"Don't say it!" He laid down his fork and knife, and folded his arms angrily. "Don't give me the bullshit line about it being for my protection."

"It's not a bullshit line. It's what it is," I said. "Leaving the CIA didn't erase my past with the Agency. There were risks. There *still* are risks."

This was the only part of my confession that I had specifically worked out in my head beforehand. It was my pivot. The segue. The point at which I would put it all out on the table and tell him that I was about to get involved again, after all these years, with another CIA operation—one of my own making, no less.

But Tracy had a pivot of his own.

"You say you wanted to protect me, but what I want to know is what you were required to do," he said.

"What do you mean?"

"You know exactly what I mean."

Again, he was right. Tracy, the Yale Law School grad, had shot a giant hole in my defense. I was simply procrastinating with my answer. I didn't want to lie to him again. Not ever. I couldn't.

"Just hear me out, okay? Let me explain."

The scenario I feared most when I left the Agency had happened. My past had caught up with me. In fact, he'd literally shown up at my front door. *Our* front door, I told Tracy.

The man who called himself Benjamin Al-Kazaz was a threat to our family and God knew how many others. One way or another he was linked to the death of Professor Darvish. He had to be—I was convinced. His being in the audience at Sadira Yavari's lecture was no coincidence.

I explained it all to Tracy, including how everything started. My old friend and fellow operative, Ahmed, who had saved my life in London, had died while trying to prevent the Times Square bombings.

"You and Annabelle were supposed to be there in that Disney Store," I said. That had to help him understand.

Eventually, though, there was nothing more for me to tell him. I'd done all the talking. It was Tracy's turn.

"Say something," I implored him. "Please."

He'd sat there stone-faced the entire time while listening. The usual glint in his eyes was gone. This man didn't look at all like Tracy. It was as if he were a total stranger.

I could only imagine how I looked to him.

"What are you doing?" I asked.

Tracy had pushed back from the table and stood up. "I'm leaving," he said.

"I understand. It's a lot to process," I said. I motioned to the waiter for the check. "We can talk more about it at home."

"No," he said. *"I'm leaving."*

It hit me. He didn't just mean the restaurant. "Tracy, please don't . . ."

But he was done listening to me. He was done with me, period. "Don't come back to the apartment for at least an hour. I need to pack."

"Where are you going?"

"I don't know yet," he said. "But I'm taking Annabelle with me."

CHAPTER 48

MY GOD, what have I done?

Tracy wanted an hour to pack. He could've taken all night, or at least until they kicked me out of the Palm. Even if I wanted to move from my chair, I couldn't. It wasn't numbness or paralysis. That's when you can't feel anything. I was feeling *everything*. And it hurt like hell.

"Would you like another, sir?" asked the waiter.

I was staring down at the only thing remaining on my table, every dish and plate having long since been cleared. It was a Macallan 18. My third. Or was it my fourth?

"Sure," I said. "Why the hell not?"

"My sentiments exactly," came Elizabeth's voice over my shoulder. "Make it two, and make 'em doubles."

I looked up to see her loop around the waiter and sit down across from me. There was no need to ask how she knew where I was. Tracy had surely told her when she arrived at our apartment.

"Is he really packing?" I asked.

"I'm afraid so. He was actually just about to leave when I got there," she said. We both knew my next question, but I couldn't even get the words out. She answered me anyway. "Yes. He had Annabelle with him."

I reached for the Macallan and downed whatever was left in the glass, every last drop. "Did I make a mistake?" I asked. "Should I have not told him?"

"Not telling him in the first place was the mistake, Dylan. That's why he's so upset. Tonight, though, you did the right thing."

"*Really?* Because it sure doesn't seem that way."

"I know," she said. "But I also know Tracy. He'll eventually understand."

I wanted to believe her. I needed to believe her. The alternative was too hard to imagine. Still, even if she was right . . . "What am I supposed to do in the meantime?" I asked.

I would've bet a gazillion dollars on Elizabeth's answer as the waiter returned with our double Macallans. She was going to tell me two words. *Be patient.*

Thankfully, I didn't have a gazillion dollars on me.

"The first thing you're going to do is enjoy your drink," said Elizabeth. "Because I fully intend to enjoy mine."

"Is there a second thing?" I asked. It definitely felt like it.

"As a matter of fact there is," she said. "But first, cheers."

The overall lighting in the Palm could best be described as an indoor solar eclipse, but as Elizabeth leaned forward out of the shadows to clink my glass I got a much better look at her face. "What are those from?" I asked, pointing.

There were two butterfly bandages along her hairline. As opposed to the other bandages from her heroics in Times Square, these were new.

"Oh, this," she said, pointing up at her forehead. "I think it was from one of the shingles."

"Shingles?"

"Yeah, from when the house blew up."

"What house?"

"The one where a bearded guy with an AK-47 tried to kill me this afternoon."

"What the hell are you talking about?"

Elizabeth stopped deadpanning and started to explain, beginning with the man who approached her in Starbucks, which ultimately led her out to Pelham to meet a young Muslim named Gorgin, who was going to help her until the bearded man with the AK-47 showed up. Now Gorgin was dead and the house was leveled, blown to smithereens by a one-two punch of C-4 and piped-in gas, which she managed to escape with only seconds to spare.

"And I thought I was having a bad day," I said.

"Oh, and I almost forgot. That mystery man in Starbucks? He's a friend of the mayor."

"How do you know?"

"I made a stop at City Hall before heading out to Pelham," she said. "Deacon admitted the guy was an informant for him."

"Did he give you a name?"

"Of course not," she said. "Which brings me to the second thing you're going to do after we enjoy our drinks. You're coming with me tonight to find Deacon."

"To do what?"

"Hold him steady while I punch him in the face."

"Oh, is that all?"

"His informant nearly got me blown up today," she said. "You should've seen the flames."

Hell hath no fury like a woman scorched. Still, "Deacon's never going to tell you who the guy is," I said.

Elizabeth let out a defeated sigh. "You're right."

Whoever said *Misery loves company* never saw anything like the look on her face. As bad as I was feeling, I felt even worse for her.

"C'mon," I said, signaling for the check. "Let's get out of here."

"And go where?"

"You'll see," I said.

CHAPTER 49

ELIZABETH KEPT asking me where I was taking her, and I kept answering that she'd find out soon enough. It was hardly helping her mood, but I knew what I was doing. Had I actually told her where we were going, she would've turned right around.

"For the last time, who lives here?" she asked.

We were standing outside a townhouse on East 84th Street, off Third Avenue. It was a decent building but nothing out of the ordinary. At least from the outside.

"Just do me a favor, will you? Stand right over here," I said, pulling her arm.

I'd positioned her in front of the door and directly in line with the overhead security camera.

"Wait," she said. *"Why are you hiding?"*

I'd peeled off to the side, directly *out* of line with the security camera. Again, I knew what I was doing.

"Just look up so he can see you," I said, pointing.

"Who?"

I didn't have to answer. By then, the snapping sound of multiple locks had Elizabeth spinning back around. He'd opened the door.

"Jesus Christ, Needham, what the hell are you doing here?" asked Evan Pritchard. "If this is about your fiasco up in Pelham this afternoon, I don't want to hear it, not tonight. *How'd you even know where I live?*"

"Trick or treat," I said, stepping forward.

"Oh, shit," said Pritchard. "You've got to be kidding me, Reinhart."

Elizabeth's head whipped back and forth between me and her new boss. "You guys know each other?"

"We've crossed paths once or twice," I said.

It was an obvious understatement. Elizabeth rolled her eyes at me. "Is there anyone you *don't* have history with?" she asked.

I shrugged. "What can I say? I tend to make an impression on people."

"Actually, I should've known," said Elizabeth. "You both knew about Halo."

Pritchard glared so hard at me I thought his eyes might pop out. "What the fuck did you tell her, Reinhart?"

"It's more like what you told her," I said. "Apparently, you flinched or something when she showed you that hotel surveillance footage. You really ought to work on that."

Never mind that Elizabeth caught me doing the same thing when I saw the footage. I conveniently left that part out. But Elizabeth already knew about my past. Now she was learning about Pritchard's.

He shook his head. "If I'd known it was you, Reinhart, I would've—"

"I know, I know. You would've never opened the door," I said. "Now that you have, are you going to invite us in or what?"

"That depends. What do you want?" he asked.

"Peace on earth and a brand-new Ferrari. *What do you think I want?* I need your help."

"You're still as charming as ever, Reinhart," he said.

"Yeah, and you still owe me," I shot back.

Pritchard mumbled something about my being the male off-spring of a female dog. He then turned and walked back into his townhouse, leaving the door open for us. It wasn't the warmest invite, but the result was the same. We were heading inside. Though not before I quickly whispered in Elizabeth's ear.

"Brace yourself," I said.

"For what?" she whispered back.

I didn't have to answer. With only one foot inside Pritchard's door she saw what I was talking about.

CHAPTER 50

IMAGINE IF Mike Tyson, Norman Schwarzkopf, and T. E. Lawrence from *Lawrence of Arabia* had all been interior designers. Now imagine Pritchard having hired all three at the same time.

We walked in. Every inch of his floor was covered with sand. Actual sand. Like from an actual desert.

As for interior walls, there weren't any. There was no second or third floor either. The townhouse had been hollowed out and fitted with an angled glass ceiling for a roof. You could see the night sky.

To the left of us were a standing punching bag and a full-size boxing ring. Behind the ring was a large military tent from Operation Desert Storm. It was the exact same tent Pritchard slept in as a land component commander.

That of course leads to the question *How do I know that?*

Meanwhile, Elizabeth was looking at me with her own question. *What the hell did we just walk into?*

The short answer was Pritchard's happy place.

After the liberation of Kuwait, Pritchard returned to the States as a warrior without a war. He cashed in as a bodyguard for a Saudi prince attending Columbia Law School. Thus, he was able to afford a Manhattan townhouse. He then joined the CIA with a fast-tracked application courtesy of a four-star general. It was a brief stint, followed by what's been a long tenure with the FBI and the JTTF.

But at no time was Pritchard more "alive," as he put it, than when he was on a battlefield. So instead of returning to a Middle Eastern desert, the terminal bachelor decided to install one in his Upper East Side townhouse.

Had it been anyone else, the word *crazy* would've come to mind. For Pritchard, it somehow made sense.

"All right, Reinhart," he said, folding his thick arms as he turned around to face us. "What do you want?"

"I need your file on the mayor," I said.

He laughed. "What file?"

"The one you compiled after Elizabeth was assigned to your unit." I glanced at my watch. "When you're done pretending it doesn't exist, let me know."

So much for his fake laugh. It was as if Pritchard had suddenly remembered my PhD from Yale wasn't in the field of classical banjo or underwater basket weaving. I was inside his head. I knew how he operated. There's a fine line between paranoid and protecting your ass, and Evan Pritchard walked it every day like a Flying Wallenda.

"Okay, let's pretend for a second—hypothetically, of course—that this imaginary file on the mayor somehow exists," he said. "What specifically would you want to know?"

"Deacon has a guy feeding him intel," I said. "I imagine it's not happening at City Hall, and wherever it is happening it's probably one-on-one. He's Middle Eastern. That's all we know."

Apparently, that's all we needed to know. "Give me a minute," said Pritchard.

He walked off, disappearing into his commander tent.

Elizabeth turned to me. "How long ago was he in the CIA?"

"The less you know about that, the better," I said.

"Why does he owe you? At least tell me that."

"Okay, but you'll need to wait until after."

"After what?"

"Eighteen more years," I said. "That's when it gets declassified."

That earned me an epic slow burn that would've probably lasted for days were it not for Pritchard returning. He had a black-and-white photo in his hand, courtesy of a super-long lens.

"Is this him?" he asked, holding it up.

"Yes!" said Elizabeth. "Who is he?"

"He's former Mossad," said Pritchard. "Goes by the name Eli these days."

"Where can we find him?" I asked.

"Good question," said Pritchard.

Huh? "You were able to find out his name and that he was former Mossad, but—"

"But exactly," said Pritchard. "No known address or phone number. The agent I had tailing the mayor saw him only one time. He was entering Deacon's limo early in the morning. When he got out, it was as if he'd turned into a ghost. After two blocks my agent lost him."

"So we know who he is. We just don't know *where* he is," said Elizabeth. "We can work with that."

Pritchard shook his head. "You're not working with anything, Needham."

"What does that mean?" she asked.

"You know exactly what that means," he said.

CHAPTER 51

ONE SECOND, they were talking. The next, they were screaming at each other.

It was only fitting that we were next to a boxing ring, as I practically had to separate the two and send them to neutral corners. Pritchard was laying into Elizabeth for "going rogue" and not bringing any backup to the house in Pelham, as well as avoiding him and his repeated calls after she "nearly blew up the damn neighborhood."

Elizabeth was countering with how she couldn't know if the tip from this guy, Eli, at Starbucks was for real. The mayor couldn't even fully vouch for it, after all. "And it was his goddamn source!"

The bottom line was that Pritchard wanted to suspend Elizabeth until further notice. He couldn't trust her. Sure, she'd saved his life, but he was convinced she'd also gotten the kid, Gorgin, killed. Gorgin could've been the key to eliminating the cell responsible for the bombings. Now they had nothing to go on, said Pritchard. Everything and everyone was reduced to ash in the blast. Forget dental records. "And that AK-47 you grabbed? It came back clean from the lab. We don't even have one fucking fingerprint!"

"Yeah, but we do have this," said Elizabeth, reaching into her pocket. She pulled out a folded piece of white paper, handing it to Pritchard. "This was on the guy with the AK-47."

I craned my neck to look. It was an ATM receipt from Chase Bank.

"Do we know the branch?" asked Pritchard.

Elizabeth knew that and then some. "Penn Station, main concourse," she said. "I've spoken with their security office already. We should have footage matching the time stamp by tomorrow morning."

Pritchard nodded. It was definitely a step up from his yelling at her but well short of anything approaching a compliment. *Nice work,* for instance. After all, it's not like the guy with the AK-47 *handed* her the receipt before trying to kill her. I figured the least I could do for Elizabeth was to point this out.

I turned to her. "So with the house about to explode at any second you still stayed behind to search this guy's pockets?"

"Shut up, Reinhart," said Pritchard.

Mission accomplished. I shrugged. "Just saying."

"It doesn't change anything," he said.

"Actually," I replied, "it could change everything."

"I'm not talking about the investigation," he said. "You know what I mean."

I did. So did Elizabeth. Pritchard was talking about her suspension, and she was about to take the reins back from me to argue it. We all understood what she wanted—the chance to track down the mayor's informant, Eli, and find out how he's connected to Gorgin and what else he knows. It made sense.

Still, Elizabeth had barely gotten her first word out when I interrupted her. She wasn't going to win this battle with Pritchard. He was stubborn. He was pissed. Plus, he had home-field advantage. *Who the hell turns his Manhattan townhouse into Operation Desert Storm?*

A guy who lives to fight. That's who.

Elizabeth could've either fallen on her sword or waved the white flag. At least, that was the conventional way to look at it.

Screw conventional.

CHAPTER 52

"WHAT THE hell was that?" asked Elizabeth.

She was hopping mad. Literally. The second we reached the sidewalk outside Pritchard's townhouse she was right up in my face, rocking up and down on the small heels of her flats so fast she actually got airborne a few times.

"That was a compromise," I said. "Pritchard doesn't have to look at you for a few days, but you're not actually suspended."

"I was standing right there. I know what you said."

"Then what's the problem?"

"You shouldn't have done that," she said. "That's the problem."

"This isn't going to be a gender thing, is it? I know you can fight your own battles."

"Then why didn't you let me? And where do you get off promising Pritchard that I won't go hunting for this Eli guy? That's exactly what I'm going to do."

"No, you're not," I said.

"Why?"

"Because I promised you wouldn't."

Elizabeth raised her hands up like she was squeezing a basketball really hard. Or my neck. She officially wanted to strangle me now. "For Christ's sake, how many of those whiskeys did you have back at the restaurant?" she asked.

Not nearly enough.

"The reason you won't be tracking down Eli is because that's what I'm going to be doing," I said.

"So why can't I help you? We'll do it together."

"Sure, like old times," I said. "Except you're going to be too busy doing something else. I need to borrow you for a couple of days."

"Borrow me?"

"It's a figure of speech."

"You're right," she said. "This is going to be a gender thing."

Elizabeth folded her arms and stared at me, waiting for my witty retort. There wasn't one. I was too preoccupied with going over the checklist inside my head, the things I could and couldn't tell her. I was having a hard time. This from a guy who memorized pi out to fifty digits when he was eleven. Just to see if I could.

Yeah, I know. I was a weird kid.

Elizabeth had been assigned to investigate the death of Professor Darvish. She was then officially taken off the case, only to unofficially continue the investigation on her own with me in tow. We had narrowed down to five the possibilities for who that mystery woman was with Darvish, and then I went off to get Julian's help. I had assumed the woman was CIA, which meant Elizabeth couldn't know her identity. I had assumed wrong, though. My meeting with Foxx in Chinatown had convinced me as much.

Now it gets tricky.

I could tell Elizabeth about Sadira Yavari. I just couldn't tell her about Darvish. *He* was CIA. An informant, at least. An asset. No matter how much I trusted Elizabeth, there were some secrets I simply couldn't tell her.

Of course, that's what got you into trouble with Tracy, isn't it? You ruined everything, you genius. What are you going to do?

"Earth to Dylan," said Elizabeth. "Are you there?"

I snapped out of it. "I'm sorry. What was I saying?"

"That you needed to borrow me."

Again, no witty retort. In fact, no anything. I simply stared at her until she was done doing what she always does in her head: figure things out.

Three, two, one . . .

"You know which woman was with Darvish!" she said.

I nodded. Yes, I did. "Her name is Sadira Yavari," I said. "And she's about to be your new best friend."

CHAPTER 53

DIVIDE AND conquer. Or as the Romans first said it, *Divide et impera.*

I beat Elizabeth out the door the next morning by a couple of hours. Mayor Edso Deacon sleeps even less than Trump. His Honor's always up before the sun.

Of course, the ancillary benefit of that was that I didn't have to sit around and wallow in the absence of Tracy and Annabelle. It was so stupid of me to look into Annabelle's room before going to bed. Her empty crib was all I could see, even when I closed my eyes.

Okay, Deacon, what's on your agenda this morning? Surely you want a face-to-face with your guy Eli after his tip nearly got Elizabeth killed. Lucky for me you don't trust phone calls. Who knows who could be listening in?

If the meeting was going to happen, it wasn't going to be at City Hall or anywhere else requiring an official log of the mayor's whereabouts. Deacon would never be so sloppy. Not a chance.

No, I was looking for a meeting that no one was supposed to see.

First decision? Whether I stake out the mayor's residence at Gracie Mansion or the Excelsior Hotel on the Upper West Side, where Deacon hunkered down during his reelection campaign. The Excelsior was also where he met up with his mistress, the woman Elizabeth unwittingly provided cover for when she was first brought in as a member of his security detail. The guy had no shame. Of course, that's job requirement number one of any successful politician.

"Start with the hotel," Elizabeth told me. Then she told me what to look for. "He never uses the front entrance. Always the back. If you see his limo, he's there."

I saw the limo.

It was parked by an unmarked door next to the loading dock used for deliveries. The engine was off. The driver looked to be sleeping. That made things a little easier.

Perched on my bike in an alley near the back of the hotel, I watched through the visor of my helmet and waited for that unmarked door to open. A half hour became an hour. The sun was officially up. *Could you actually be sleeping in, Deacon? Of all days?*

I didn't care. I was prepared to sit there on my bike for as long as it took. That was the plan. It was all about finding Eli. One way or another the mayor was going to lead me to him.

One way. Or another.

The more I kept staring at that unmarked door, the less I could hear of the city. The traffic, a plane overhead—every noise was fading into the background. That's when something strange happened. My phone rang.

It shouldn't have. That was the strange part. The ringer was off. But it still rang.

I glanced at the caller ID before quickly removing my helmet. It was Elizabeth.

"Hi, there," I said. "How'd you sleep?"

I knew right away from the laugh that it wasn't Elizabeth. "I slept like a log," he said with an Israeli accent.

"Who is this?" I asked, although I already knew. He must have air-swiped the IMEI from Elizabeth's phone at Starbucks. He was now piggybacking on her line. This guy was Mossad, all right.

"I'm the guy you're looking for," he said. "Now say 'Cheese.'"

And like that, I was Al Pacino and his fellow detectives in *Heat*. I'd been made. Eli had gotten me to take my helmet off. He was probably now clicking away nearby with a long-range lens.

On second thought, I should've been so lucky.

CHAPTER 54

FUNNY THING about the mind. You get a certain idea stuck in it and then all other thoughts funnel through like lemmings. That is, until it turns out you had the wrong idea.

I looked everywhere in front of me, trying to spot Eli. Was he on a rooftop? A terrace? In a window nearby? If he wanted to identify me, he had to be able to see my face. That was the idea.

I had my helmet in one hand, my cell in the other. Eli was no longer on the line. *Say "Cheese"* was the last thing he'd said.

I'd taken the bait.

He wasn't taking my picture. He was just making sure I kept looking in front of me.

"Nice bike," came his voice behind me.

I turned to look. It was pure reflex and exactly what he was banking on. He was tall, wore dark sunglasses, and never broke stride in his black blazer and turtleneck as his left hand went up. *Pzzzz!*

The spray hit my eyes like a thousand tiny needles, the sting nearly knocking me to the ground. It was mace. Military grade. The kind that could stop a grizzly dead in its tracks, never mind a person.

My helmet and phone hit the ground as I reached up to my eyes. Again, pure reflex. I was all but blind, blinking furiously to try to keep seeing—if only for a split second at a time. The Glock holstered above my ankle was useless.

That's when he raised his right hand.

I could just make out the movement. The grip. The steel. The suppressor attached to the end of the barrel. *Pffft!*

The muffled sound pierced the air with barely a wake. Once, then twice. He'd shot my back tire followed by the front. It was all happening frame by frame, like clicking through one of those old View-Masters. My mind was desperately trying to fill in what my eyes couldn't see.

He could've killed me if he'd wanted to. He didn't want to. All he was looking for was a captive audience. He had it.

"Is the girl okay?" he asked.

Is the girl okay? You just maced me, my eyes are burning like hell, and you want an update on Elizabeth?

The mere question told me plenty, though. He truly had been trying to help her with the tip about Gorgin and his house up in Pelham.

"She's okay," I said.

Two words were pretty much all I could manage. I was bent over in agony, out of breath from the pain. Fine by him. He was there to talk, not listen.

"You don't know me, and the mayor doesn't know me. Do

you understand? I see everything, Dr. Reinhart, and you clearly don't. Not any longer. Not these days."

He obviously knew who I was and what I used to be. He just wasn't giving me enough credit for it.

All I needed to do was muster three more words.

"Look behind you," I said.

CHAPTER 55

I WISHED I could've seen his face. Hell, I wished I could've seen anything.

But I saw enough.

Eli had turned to find the business end of a SIG P226 pointing straight at him. The man doing the pointing was only a set of eyes beneath a John Deere cap, the rest of his face covered by a red bandana. Old school. Like the Old West. Or, more likely, the best he could manage given such short notice. Either way, it worked.

Eli didn't need instructions. He knew the drill. He laid down what looked to be a Remington R1 Tactical, given the raised sights to accommodate the suppressor. He then spread his arms slightly away from his body. No monkey business.

"About time you showed up," I said to my cavalry of one. I immediately regretted it. Josiah Maxwell Reinhart suffered sarcasm even less than fools.

"That's a damn funny way of saying thank you," he snapped back.

"I could've done without the mace, that's all," I said. Slowly, I was getting my vision back. If only the pain would go away. "And how did you know he wasn't going to kill me?"

"Who maces someone before they shoot him?"

Decent point, Dad. Still, "There's always a first time."

I walked over and frisked Eli. He had no other weapon. In fact, he had nothing else on him except a pack of Marlboros and a money clip stuffed with hundreds inside his blazer. No credit cards. No ID of any kind.

As soon as I scooped up his gun, my father lowered his. I could tell the old man was exhausted, although he'd never let on. He'd left Concord, New Hampshire, immediately after I called around midnight, arriving in his old, beat-up Jeep Commando at about four thirty in the morning.

"So now what?" he asked. I couldn't blame him for wanting to keep the show moving. He'd been up all night.

"Now I talk to our friend Eli here," I said. "It is Eli, right?"

I wasn't expecting him to answer. What was I going to do, shoot him if he didn't cooperate? We both knew that wasn't going to happen.

No, I needed another form of leverage. Fast, too. The sun was beginning to peek over the building tops. Our dimly lit alley was turning into broad daylight. Last I checked, New York still wasn't an open carry state.

Eli raised a hand, although not to ask a question. He was motioning to the breast pocket inside his blazer. "I'm going to smoke."

That settled why Elizabeth couldn't originally peg his accent. His voice was so gravelly in person it sounded as if he'd been born with a cigarette in his hand.

The hell you are, I was about to say. He was no longer in charge.

Turns out I wasn't either.

"Jesus Christ," said my father. "Is that you, Elijah?"

My father lowered his bandana. Eli—make that, Elijah—lowered his sunglasses. They both smiled.

"It's me," said Elijah.

"I thought you were retired," said my father.

"Yeah, and I thought you were dead, Eagle."

CHAPTER 56

HE CALLED my father by his old code name, the Eagle. They obviously had history. A somewhat complicated one, I was about to learn.

My father casually walked over to Elijah. The way the two were still smiling I thought they were going to hug.

Nope.

The very second my father was within range he delivered a roundhouse punch to Elijah's gut. I mean, hard. I could literally hear the wind getting knocked out of the guy.

"That's for macing my son," said my father.

Elijah was now bent over and gasping for air, but I figured not for long. He was bound to retaliate, and I was ready to jump in between the two to make sure he didn't. Instead, Elijah didn't do anything. Not in terms of fighting back. He simply waited to catch his breath, straightened out his spine, and gave my father a slight nod as if to say he knew he'd had that coming.

When he proceeded to reach into his blazer, I figured he was finally having that cigarette. Nope again. Out came his money clip.

"Are those Dunlop Elites?" he asked, pointing to the tires on my bike.

"They *were,*" I said.

Elijah peeled off five one-hundred-dollar bills and handed them to me. "That should cover it."

I took the money. Apparently all debts were settled because, of all things, *now* my father hugged Elijah, and Elijah hugged him back. *What the hell is going on?*

There's always been a weird unspoken code among operatives, no matter which flag they saluted, but this was even beyond weird.

"I take it you guys worked together?" I asked.

"Not really," said my father.

"Let's just say we didn't work against each other," said Elijah.

That was actually the first thing that sort of made sense in a screwed-up-world kind of way.

"Son, meet the Prophet," said my father.

And like that, I was shaking the hand of the guy who only minutes earlier had maced me and shot out my tires. I didn't think twice about it, though. The guy was a legend. Now he was officially real, too. Up until that moment, I'd never been fully convinced he actually existed.

Remember when President George W. Bush was assassinated at the Red Sea Summit in 2003? Of course you don't. It never happened. It almost did, though. The story goes that the Prophet took out not one but two would-be suicide bombers in Sharm El Sheikh, Egypt. What made that all the more incredible was that the Prophet was known to be a Mossad agent. He saved not only Bush's life but also the lives of the leaders of Egypt, Jordan, Saudi Arabia, Bahrain, and the Palestinians. Give

that a moment to sink in. It was a Who's Who of Israeli antag-
onists, if not outright enemies, and this guy saved them all in
order to save Israel's strongest ally. *And you wonder why we always have their back?*

The Prophet saw coming what no one else had. Hence, his
nickname in the intelligence community from that day forward.

Clearly, he hadn't lost his touch. He knew that someone
would be staking out Mayor Deacon. If not Elizabeth, then
someone who was working with her. I never saw him coming,
but at least I thought enough to bring backup. Who knew they
would know each other?

Do I call him the Prophet? Mr. Prophet?

"I need your help," I just said instead.

He nodded. "More than you even know. The Mudir is only
getting started. It's all coming."

"Another attack?"

"Yes, and another after that. A series of them. And if I'm right,
the finale will make everything else look like child's play."

I wasn't sure where to begin. *What kind of attacks? When? And
how do you know?* I wanted everything, every last detail. There
wasn't enough he could tell me.

Until I realized something.

There was actually nothing he could tell me. Not here. Not
now. I had to let him know I understood that. This wasn't
checkers. It wasn't even chess. It was classic game theory. Whatever I gained from him could end up costing him dearly in ways
I couldn't even fathom. Sources. Contacts. Cooperating agents.
In short, his current livelihood. Or worse, his life. There was a
young man out in Pelham named Gorgin who had already paid
with his.

It was the Prophet's move, and it would have to come on his
terms.

"How much time do you need?" I asked.

He looked at me and then my father. "He's smart like you, Eagle," he said.

"Even smarter," said my father.

The Prophet let go with a quick smile, as if maybe he had a son of his own. "You'll see me again," he said.

He then turned and walked away, out the alley and toward the back of the Excelsior. I watched, along with my father, as he got into the limo. Immediately, it drove off.

Son of a bitch. The mayor wasn't even at the hotel. He never was.

The Prophet had set the whole thing up.

CHAPTER 57

I STEERED clear of the question while my father and I waited in the alley for the flatbed to arrive and tow my bike. We kept the conversation light, talking mostly about the happenings at Yale and my teaching. My father had pulled the lever for Republicans far more times than any Democrat in his life, but he could never understand the way some people saw fit to mock the so-called Northeast elites in their supposed ivy-covered towers. "Any of those morons would kill to have their kid go to Harvard or Yale," he would say. He was right.

Finally, in the elevator up to my apartment, I got around to the question. He knew all along it was coming. "Were you there?" I asked.

"Yeah, I was there," he said. The Red Sea Summit in 2003. "I almost died there, too."

"What happened?"

"It's all about what didn't happen, of course. The assassination of six world leaders including a US president. The intel said that a rogue Israeli agent was about to forever change the Middle East—and the rest of the world—all in a day's work."

"Elijah, you mean."

"Yep. It was a mad scramble trying to find him. All we had was one grainy black-and-white. An outdated photo, no less."

"So, what happened?"

"I found him. Or, I should say, he found me first. Kind of like what happened to you today. I thought I had him cornered, and the next thing I knew there was a pistol pressed against the back of my head. He told me to close my eyes and count backward from ten. By three, he was gone. An hour later, the two suicide bombers were found dead in their hotel room, all bombs intact. I don't know how he knew where to find them, but I was sure he was the one who did. He was a rogue agent, all right. The right kind of rogue."

"You got some seriously bad intel," I said.

"Let's just say there was a lot of that in the wake of 9/11."

We stood in silence for a few moments as I stared at the elevator's buttons for each floor lighting up, one after another. It dawned on me. There was something my father's story didn't explain. "He knew your code name," I said. "He called you Eagle."

"Yes, he did." My father paused as if choosing his next words very carefully. "We met a few years later, this time face-to-face. I even managed to return the favor somewhat."

I was about to ask how when the elevator opened. My father stepped off first. He promptly turned around and did the thing he always did when he was done talking about a subject. It was a quick slice through the air with his hand. A karate chop to the conversation. *No more questions.*

I let it be. My father always had his reasons, and there was only so much you could push him. Besides, I was thinking of pulling the same move when we got into the apartment. *Where's my granddaughter?* he was surely going to ask.

The concept of Tracy and me was still a work in progress for my father, but he was all in on Annabelle. Completely smitten. In fact, he'd already made two trips down from New Hampshire just to see her. Now he was going to wonder where the hell she was. Maybe I could just chop away all his questions.

I was so consumed with having to explain what happened with Tracy that I barely even glanced at the man in the Mets cap who passed us in the hallway. He could've been anybody. I didn't have a clue who he was. Right up until the moment when I reached the door to my apartment. That's when I realized.

He'd been sent to kill me.

CHAPTER 58

IT WAS barely there—a smidge, a notch, a sliver above a dog whistle. But I could hear it.

That metallic hum, the sound of the automatic lock on the door having been engaged only seconds before. He'd been inside the apartment. He'd just left.

No, wait. *He's coming back.*

I knew it even before I turned my head. I didn't need to see it. I could feel it. Instinct. Killer instinct.

Once he'd passed the corner leading to the elevator bank, he'd turned around to look. I saw his head peek out as he spotted us in front of my door. He was ten yards off with nothing in his way. He had a clean shot.

But only if I let him take it.

There was no time to even yell *Gun!* as I reached for mine while all but slamming my father to the ground. I fired once, rolled, then twice—neither with any aim. Just direction.

Enough to force this guy back around the corner, if only for a few seconds.

"Silver one," I said, tossing my key chain to my father. He was now closest to the door. The two other keys, copper colored, were for a storage unit and my office at Yale.

Having a former CIA operative for a dad has its drawbacks, but it sure comes in handy when taking fire. He knew what to do. More importantly, he knew what not to do. As in, try to open the door to my apartment at the wrong time.

We were crouched on the tight pile carpet, spread on either side of the hall with our guns drawn, waiting for the next rounds to come our way. It wasn't a matter of if, only when. *C'mon, bring it...*

We kept staring at the corner, waiting for movement. Amateurs always go for speed, trying to outdraw you. This guy wasn't an amateur.

The first thing we saw was subtle, a hint of blue from the brim of his Mets cap. It was sticking out no more than an inch, about six feet off the ground. He was decoying us. I could practically picture him holding the cap above his head, trying to draw our eyes.

Instead I gave a quick glance to my father, who nodded back. Enough said. My father was no amateur either.

The Mets cap—and only the cap—suddenly came flying out from behind the corner like a clay pigeon, but my eyes stayed focused below it. Sure enough, his hand came whipping around the edge, the barrel of his semiautomatic leading the way only a few feet up from the floor. *Nice try, asshole...*

We traded shots. My father and I were pinned down, but the guy had no time to square either of us up. He was quick, though. Good reflexes. No sooner did he lunge forward than he immediately pulled back, although not before I nicked him. A small burst of blood splattered against the wall, probably from the meat of his forearm.

Now!

My father sprang to his feet with the key, finding the cylinder on the first try. With a twist and a shove, he threw open the door. All I had to do was follow him in. That's all I had to do.

Take it away, Robert Burns.

The best laid plans of mice and men often go awry.

CHAPTER 59

ALL AT once came a cacophony of sounds I didn't want to hear. Not then. Not there. *What are you doing, Mrs. Jones?*

The sliding of the security chain on her door. The snap of the dead bolt. The squeaking of a turning doorknob that probably hadn't been oiled since the last time the Mets actually won the World Series.

The hallway was about to have company.

Our next-door neighbor, Mrs. Irma Jones, had just submitted her application to the infamous Darwin Awards by hearing gunshots outside her apartment and somehow deciding that the smartest move for survival's sake was to get a closer look. Then again, she was in her eighties. Who knows what she thought she heard?

She sure didn't hear me. As soon as her door opened, I tried to tell her to go back inside. I couldn't yell, though. Yelling would've been the same as grabbing a bullhorn to announce to the shooter that I was distracted. In other words, fire away.

After looking down the hall, Irma turned and saw me flat on the ground behind her. She was about to do the one thing worse than peeking her head out. She was about to come all the way out.

"Are you okay, Dylan?" she asked, squinting.

Irma had maybe an inch on Ruth Bader Ginsburg, if that. She was tiny. And she was about to get body-slammed.

I pushed up off the carpet, launching myself toward her like a sprinter out of the blocks. I had one eye on her and the other over her shoulder, and before I could even blink, it went from bad to worse.

There was no decoying us this time. No trickery with the Mets cap. He jumped out from around the corner with a two-handed grip. He had no intention of missing me twice.

Irma screamed.

Irma never saw him. She had her back to him. She was screaming because of the gun I had pointed at her head while charging at her. At least, that's what it surely looked like to her eyes. Her neighbor, one of those *two nice gay men* from next door, was about to kill her. That had to be against the co-op board's rules, right?

My move was straight out of Ringling Bros. I dove for Irma, leaping through the air while getting off one shot over her head, my other arm wrapping around her shoulders so I could spin and hit the ground first to break her fall.

One bullet whizzed by my ear. There aren't enough words to accurately describe the terror of that, except to say that it could always be worse. You could hear the bullet hit you instead.

Not today, though.

He got off two more shots. There wasn't a third. My father made sure of that. He returned fire from my apartment, buying me just enough time to pull Irma into hers. Was I trying to kill her? Save her? She had no idea as we fell into her foyer.

Shit. What's that noise?

My head whipped back to the hallway. Irma's door was still wide open. The sound heading our way was the worst one yet. It was the sound of a good idea.

The clever bastard had grabbed a fire extinguisher, removing any sight line we could have on him. He wasn't going to be denied, which meant he wasn't a contract killer. If he were, he would've fled. *Catch you on the flip side.* He'd simply wait for a more opportune time to hold up his end of the deal.

No, this guy wasn't a hit man at all. He was a soldier. Not military, but terrorist. A guy who had been given his orders. Kill or be killed.

He was firing again as he continued spraying the hallway with the extinguisher, moving toward us through a cloud of white. I could see the edges of it reach the doorway as the shots got closer.

There was only one word for this. Chaos.

And there was only one way to respond.

CHAPTER 60

CIA OPERATIVES aren't given an official how-to handbook. But if we were, the section dedicated to getting your ass out of almost any jam could be summed up with one sentence.

When chaos reigns, create more chaos.

I scooped up Irma in my arms and carried her behind the counter in her kitchen. My telling her not to move as I put her down would've been redundant. The poor woman was still in shock.

Everything I needed was in my eyeline. The gas stove. The dish towel on the counter next to it. The bottle of vodka on the credenza near the window. Good thing Irma wasn't a teetotaler.

The secret of a good Molotov cocktail is saturation. It's not enough that the fuse—a.k.a. the dish towel—is in contact with the alcohol. It needs to be soaked from top to bottom. Of course, that takes some time. Time was the one thing I didn't have.

To hell with saturation.

I flipped on the front burner of the stove, grabbed the vodka, and jammed the dish towel as far as I could into the bottle before giving it a couple of quick shakes. I was staying low, keeping my head clear of the top of the counter. The shots outside the hallway had stopped. That's because he wasn't in the hallway anymore. The sound of his closing the door behind him was all I needed to hear. He was inside Irma's apartment.

C'mon, asshole, reach for that lock . . .

It wasn't about keeping me in. It was about keeping my father out. This guy wanted a fair fight, one-on-one. I could practically feel his eyes scanning left and right, waiting for me to make my move. But he still had to lock that door behind him. He had to look away if only for a split second.

I glanced at Irma, my forefinger pressed against my lips—*Shhhh*—as my other hand reached for the now red-hot burner, the edge of the dish towel leading the way. Could he already smell the gas? He'd for sure see the flame. I had to time this just right.

The blink of a human eye takes between 300 and 400 milliseconds. A normal heartbeat is upward of 900 milliseconds. I figured my window was somewhere between two blinks and a murmur.

But not until you turn to lock that damn door. What's taking you so long?

I lit the dish towel, my ears tuning out everything except the sliding of that dead bolt. The streets below us ceased to exist. The entire city had gone quiet. Dead.

Then. *Snap!*

I sprang up from behind the counter as he locked the door, launching the bottle where it would do the most damage. Not at him but at his feet. He never saw it coming.

The glass shattered as he turned back around, the flames igniting straight up his legs. He didn't care, at least not yet. He wildly shot in my direction as I ducked behind the counter. The irony, though. He was holding a fire extinguisher while on fire.

I was about to pop up again. I wanted this guy alive if at all possible. The things he could tell us. Names. Locations. Who sent him to kill me and from where? That fire wasn't going to put itself out, and it was only going to spread unless he did something about it. That's when I'd have him. Score another one for more chaos.

Before I could even push up off the floor of Irma's kitchen, however, I heard the shots from outside in the hallway. My father was taking a page from that same nonexistent handbook. He was breaking down the door with bullets, shooting out the locks. It was full-on crazy in every direction.

But I still wanted this guy alive.

I rose up from behind the counter as my father kicked his way in, the door flying open. He fired off two shots, one at each shoulder. That's how you level a guy without killing him. My father knew I'd want this guy alive, too.

That made three of us.

My star informant was on the ground and in flames, his blood sprayed all over Irma's living room carpet. He'd dropped his gun, along with the fire extinguisher, and he was rolling around in agony.

Still, my father was taking nothing for granted. "Watch him," he told me, tucking away his Glock to pick up the extinguisher.

In the blink of an eye, faster than the beat of a heart. That's all it took.

The guy now had his own window.

Literally.

CHAPTER 61

THE COPS, the two detectives, the EMTs—they all kept referring to him as *the deceased* since there was no ID to be had on his half burned, fully mangled body, which had literally cracked the sidewalk in half outside my apartment building thirty stories below. No surprise the guy would end up being a John Doe. I could've told them as much.

Then again, I was too busy having to tell them everything else.

"Wait, let me just repeat that back," said the junior of the two detectives, who had introduced himself to my father and me as simply *Miller*. Not Joe or Bob Miller or even Detective Miller. Just Miller. "So after getting shot, the deceased sprang up and proceeded to run at the window glass, shatter it, and then jump to his death. Is that right?"

"It was actually more of a leap," said my father. "A swan dive, really."

My father was now going on twenty-four straight hours without sleep and was officially beyond punchy. Miller was barely even acknowledging him at this point, content instead to look only at me or down at his notepad. He was taking a lot of notes.

"Yes, that's what happened," I told him.

As for why it happened, I kept that to myself. The police didn't need to know, at least not yet, that the guy pancaked on the sidewalk with his entrails splattered was part of a terrorist cell. Point being, his getting caught was absolutely, positively not an option.

I glanced at my watch. This was taking too long. The news vans were beginning to line up along the curb. My father and I needed to exit stage left in a hurry.

"Just a few more questions," said Miller.

"Actually, no more questions," he was told instead.

I turned—we all turned—to see Elizabeth flash her badge to Miller, who seemingly could not have cared less.

"You can have Dr. Reinhart when I'm done with him," the detective told her, almost shooing Elizabeth away with the back of his hand.

The poor guy. I almost felt sorry for him as Elizabeth blinked in disbelief. She was about to give him a quick refresher about the pecking order among badges, and while she had her subtle moments from time to time, I knew immediately this wasn't going to be one of them. Sure enough, she grabbed the notepad right out of Miller's hand and heaved it to the other side of the street.

"Congratulations. You're now done with Dr. Reinhart," she said.

With that, my father and I followed her inside my apartment building, never once looking back.

"I like her already," my father said as we walked.

He knew of Elizabeth from what I'd told him back when she

and I were hunting the serial killer the Dealer, but this was the first time they were meeting face-to-face. I made the formal introduction in the lobby.

"Normally, I'd ask what brings you down to Manhattan," she said, shaking my father's hand.

"Normally, I'd tell you," replied my father.

Enough said, at least about my father's former life as an operative.

I was prepared to tell Elizabeth all about my morning. Meeting Eli. The fact that I now had a target on my back courtesy of some very impolite terrorists. But first there was something I needed to know.

"What are you even doing here?" I asked her. "You're supposed to be out following—"

"Yes, I know," said Elizabeth. "I was supposed to learn her entire routine. Everything she does. Everywhere she goes."

"In other words," I said, "tailing her *for days*."

"Or maybe just hours," she said. "I found out everything you need to know about Sadira Yavari. But we don't have much time."

CHAPTER 62

ELIZABETH WAS right, twice over. A beautiful little thing called serendipity had intervened in her reconnaissance mission. I no longer needed to know Professor Sadira Yavari's daily routine, what her regular haunts were, or the particular park bench where she liked to go to read. Engineering my "chance" meeting with her had already been taken care of courtesy of the United States District Court for the Southern District of New York. In short, Sadira had jury duty.

Right now.

There was barely any time for the things I needed to do, let alone wanted to do. I wanted to head back up to the apartment, pack a suitcase, and say good-bye to the place. I'd be back, but I'd never live there again—not as long as the Mudir, or whoever was posing as Benjamin Al-Kazaz, knew the address. *Can those two guys be one and the same? It definitely feels like it.*

I also wanted to visit Irma in the hospital, whichever one the ambulance had taken her to. I think she was more shaken up than actually hurt, but the EMTs had wisely decided to play it safe. A night of observation made even more sense given her apartment was currently a crime scene, not to mention a complete shambles.

I had to put a pin in all those plans. Everything that could wait had to wait. Instead, I had to get downtown to the courthouse on Pearl Street and join the jury pool.

"How do you know Yavari's name hasn't been called yet?" I asked.

"It hasn't," said Elizabeth. "And it won't be. I've made sure of it."

"So you were actually there? At the courthouse?"

"Yeah. She's wearing a white blouse with a gray skirt. Reading a book."

"What's the book?"

"I didn't get *that* close to her," said Elizabeth. "Forget about her book. More importantly, what's your plan?"

I didn't have one. Not yet. "Charm and charisma?" I offered.

"In that case, we're doomed," said my father, chiming in.

That got a chuckle out of Elizabeth. "I just got a glimpse into your childhood."

"Yeah, nothing's changed," I said.

"If this Yavari woman is who you say she is, she's hardly going to cozy up to any stranger," said my father. "You need a Tebow."

"Did you say a T-bone?" asked Elizabeth. "Like the steak?"

"No. Like the football player," I said.

"Tim Tebow," said my father, which did nothing to help Elizabeth. She looked at me, lost.

"A distraction," I said. "Tim Tebow probably could've played a few more years in the NFL as a backup quarterback, but he was too much of a media distraction for teams, so they didn't bother." I turned to my father. "And I don't need a Tebow."

Elizabeth, who only ten seconds earlier didn't even know

what the hell my father was talking about, suddenly seemed intrigued. "What do you have in mind, Mr. Reinhart?" she asked.

"Please, call me Max," said my father. Josiah Maxwell Reinhart never did like the shortened Joe for Josiah. Come to think of it, he didn't much like Josiah either. He always thought it made him sound like a character in a Mark Twain novel.

"Okay," said Elizabeth, obliging him. "What did you have in mind, Max?"

"That depends."

"On what?"

"How fast we can get our hands on a flask, a flannel shirt, and a pocket copy of the Constitution," he said.

CHAPTER 63

IT WAS like Renée Zellweger to Tom Cruise at the end of *Jerry Maguire.*

"You had me at flask," said Elizabeth.

Even I had to admit, it was all just crazy enough to work.

The second I gave my blessing, Elizabeth was on the phone to a staffer at the JTTF named Freddie. She told him he had forty-five minutes to hit a Barnes & Noble and an REI store or "any other flannel-and-flask-loving outdoorsy place" to gather the necessary props and meet us at the courthouse. JTTF staffers aren't accustomed to questioning their marching orders, but surely Freddie had to be wondering what on earth he was doing and why.

I feel you, Freddie . . .

Forty-five minutes later on the dot, my father was getting into character in an empty conference room at the courthouse. A sweaty and out of breath Freddie had delivered. No sooner had he handed off the goods to Elizabeth than she was scuffing them all up, making them looked used. Or, in the case of the flask, abused.

Meanwhile, through an open crack of the conference room door, I was watching everyone still remaining in the jury pool return from their lunch break. One after another they were filing back into the waiting area. Everyone except Sadira.

"Where the hell is she?" I asked.

"Are you sure she didn't already go in?" asked Elizabeth. "You could've missed her."

Elizabeth was still busy behind me with my father's wardrobe. I looked back to see her actually ripping off a button from the flannel shirt. She kept glancing up at his old, beat-up John Deere cap as if it were the template for his overall look. The cap was probably how he got the idea for this in the first place.

I returned to staring through the crack in the door, waiting for a gray skirt and white blouse. The thought that Sadira had decided not to return to the courthouse crossed my mind like a wrecking ball. *C'mon, c'mon, c'mon—where are you?*

There she was.

She was almost hidden among a small group of other potential jurors. They were all returning at the same time. Most were talking to one another, surely commiserating about having to spend a perfectly good day waiting in an overcrowded room, all in the name of a nebulous concept that most New Yorkers tend to put in air quotes or utter with an eye roll: civic duty.

Sadira, on the other hand, wasn't talking to anyone. Moreover, her body language was all but screaming, *Keep your distance.* Not exactly a good sign for what we were about to attempt.

Still, all that mattered for now was that it was her. It was definitely her. Sadira Yavari. Our mystery woman. Forget the gray skirt and white blouse. I'd know that walk anywhere.

I turned back to my father and Elizabeth. "It's showtime," I said.

CHAPTER 64

PLACES, EVERYONE.

Elizabeth went first. She walked out into the courthouse lobby, flashing her badge and prepping two security guards who were manning the door. They were nodding like a couple of bobbleheads. So far, so good.

I went next, walking straight past them and into the waiting room, where I took a seat with a clear view of Sadira. Not once, though, did I even glance in her direction.

A minute later, my father entered as a last straggler from the lunch break. If Simon & Garfunkel had written a song about how he looked, it would've been called "The Only Living Hick in New York." Then again, that's the beauty of the city. The diversity is so truly diverse that everyone ends up blending in. Until, for some reason, they don't.

Exactly what we were banking on.

The Birthday Paradox is seemingly a mathematical improbability based on how many people would have to be in the same room before the odds were 100 percent that two of them shared the same birthday. The paradox is that the number of people is surprisingly low. Only twenty-three people are required in the room before the odds are fifty-fifty. At only seventy-five people, the odds of two sharing the same birthday jump to 99.9 percent. How can that be right when there are 365 days in a year?

But it is. The math proves it.

As for the Jury Pool Paradox, there was no math. Just instinct. How many people had to be in the room before no one noticed that two extra people had joined them after the lunch break?

Sure enough, no one seemed to give my father or me a second glance as we took our seats. Good thing. Because as fast as you can say *Tim Tebow* the entire room was about to notice us. Big time.

Whenever you're ready, Pops...

Fittingly, it started with a fumble. Under the guise of trying to sneak a swig from inside his flannel shirt, my father dropped the flask to the ground. It landed with a metallic thud against the tile flooring, the sound echoing throughout the entire waiting room. Naturally, everyone looked. Their faces said it all. *Oh, great. Some drunk guy.*

Worse, a red-state drunk guy, given how he was dressed.

"Mind your own damn business, you liberal lookie-loos," my father barked. He wisely didn't go for the full-blown Barney Gumble and tack on a belch, but he did appear to lose his balance as he leaned over to pick up the flask.

Right on cue, someone nearby snickered.

"What are you laughin' at, baldy?" my father asked, jabbing his finger at a follicularly challenged man, who immediately regretted the snicker, as well as not wearing a hat to jury duty. He dipped his eyes back into his magazine, hoping this nutcase would let it be. Fat chance.

"Do you think you're better than me? 'Cause you're not," my father continued, slurring a word or two. "Hell, you're probably not even an American. A real American, that is. *Born here.* In fact, I'm lookin' around this room and I hardly see any real Americans at all."

Sadira Yavari was a philosophy professor with an epistemological focus. A bigoted rant was right smack in her professional wheelhouse, and she had a front-row seat.

C'mon, Sadira, look up from your book and stare at the crazy lunatic. How can you resist?

She couldn't.

Now, let the real show begin.

CHAPTER 65

"GREAT, SOMEONE else who can't mind their own damn business," said my father, his jabbing finger swinging over to the attractive woman in the gray skirt and white blouse. "Oh, and look, she's another foreigner. I bet you're a Muslim, aren't you, lady? It doesn't matter how American you dress. You can't hide it."

That was my cue. *Muslim.*

"That's enough," I announced from a few chairs over. "You're out of line."

Heads whipped back and forth now between my father and me, anyone within earshot waiting to see how he'd respond. But my father was only getting started with Sadira, as was the plan. I was merely setting the table.

"What are you reading there, Muslim lady? *The Koran?* Do you want to see what I read?" He stood and reached into his back pocket, pulling out the copy of the Constitution and all but shoving it in Sadira's face. "See? This is what real Americans read."

"Then why don't you sit back down and read it," I said, "and leave the woman alone. In fact, leave us all alone."

"I wasn't talking to you!" barked my father.

"I'm pretty sure I speak for everyone—you shouldn't be talking at all."

"This thing here says I have the right to speak my mind," he said, pointing. Elizabeth had wrinkled, rolled, and dog-eared his pocket copy of the Constitution so much there was no doubting he'd been carrying it around with him for years, if not decades.

"You have the right to speak, and I have the right to tell you to shut the hell up," I said.

"Oh, yeah? Just try and make me, you commie-loving bastard."

Damn, my father was good. Almost too good. *Commie-loving bastard?* I was ready to spring out of my chair and pop him one.

But no. I couldn't be the guy who threw the first punch. Everyone loves a hero, only this wasn't the movies. This was manipulation. Human psychology. Pavlov's dog. We needed a precise reaction from Sadira, which meant there could be no doubt about what she was witnessing. It had to seem real.

"Yeah, I didn't think so," said my father, smirking as he watched me now try to ignore him. Most anywhere else in the country I would've been chickening out. But in Manhattan it was called living to fight another day. Ninety-nine percent of the time, it worked.

Hello, one percent.

My father neatly placed his flask and pocket Constitution on his chair. By the time he turned back around, he was already lunging for me. I had just enough time to stand up so he could knock me down.

The secret to a fake fight? Real punches. As I rose to my

feet, my father landed the first one as required, a haymaker that would've caught my chin were it not for a quick turn of my shoulder. Everyone began to scramble, scream, or gasp. Not Sadira, though. She'd barely budged in her chair. From the corner of my eye, I saw her simply staring at the spectacle, taking it all in.

Duly noted: the woman has seen her fair share of violence.

From the corner of my other eye, I could see the guards rushing toward us. Elizabeth had released them like hounds. I had only a few seconds before they would break up the fight, just enough time to seal the deal.

Sympathy is a powerful emotion, but it makes a lousy aphrodisiac. I couldn't merely be the victim in Sadira's eyes. Nor was it enough to be the guy who came to her defense. I had to be able to take a punch and, more importantly, be able to land one. A really good one at that.

Brace yourself, Pops...

It was no haymaker or roundhouse. In the trade, it's called a stunner: a quick, sharp jab to the xiphoid process, otherwise known as the small extension of the sternum.

Suddenly, the drunk old man with a lot to say was rendered silent as he bent forward, the wind knocked clean out of him. It was the last thing Sadira saw before the guards swooped in and grabbed us. Before anyone even had a chance to say the old man started it, they were dragging the two of us out of the room.

All the while, I didn't risk sneaking a peek at Sadira. I didn't have to. I could feel her gaze. Would it be enough, though? Had she bought in?

CHAPTER 66

APPROXIMATELY A half hour later, a court clerk read off a list of twenty names in the jury-pool waiting room. The pool was being pared down for the day, the clerk explained, the twenty names having been chosen randomly. Of course, Sadira was one of them.

I was pacing outside the courthouse, pretending to be looking at my phone. I had my back to the doors, waiting for the signal from Elizabeth, who was watching from the side about twenty yards away. She was pretending to eat a hot dog. It would've been more convincing if she'd actually taken a bite of the thing.

Never mind. She gave me the nod.

I turned around, my eyes still glued to my phone. The rest of me, however, was clearly visible to Sadira. I continued pacing, a human lure.

She took the bait. I could hear the clicking of her heels heading my way. "Excuse me," she said. I looked up. "I just wanted to thank you for what you did in there earlier. Coming to my defense the way you did."

"You're welcome," I said. "It was nothing."

"It certainly wasn't nothing to that old man. He didn't like you very much."

"He wasn't a big fan of yours either."

She smiled. "Please tell me they arrested him."

I smiled back. A sheepish grin. "And it's not even Christmas," I said.

She rolled her eyes while running a hand through her long brown hair. Sadira Yavari was truly even more stunning up close. "You didn't press charges, did you?" she asked.

"What can I say? I'm a sucker for drunk old bigots. The only thing I insisted on was that he drink some coffee." I motioned inside the courthouse. "He's doing that right now in their holding area."

"That's good," she said. "Although I've read that's a myth."

"What is?"

"Coffee doesn't sober you up any faster."

"You're right. I've read the same thing," I said. "Although that's only in a medical sense."

"As opposed to?"

"Psychological. The human brain can be tricked into sobriety if it buys into the myth."

Her eyes lit up with a flash of recognition. "I knew you looked familiar," she said. "You're the psychology professor who tracked down that serial killer last year."

"That's me, all right."

"No wonder you let the old man off the hook," she said. "Compared to a serial killer, everyone else is merely having an off day."

"Dylan Reinhart," I said, extending my hand.

"Sadira Yavari."

I could tell she was still sizing me up as we shook hands. "I remember reading about you after you saved the mayor's life," she said. "I actually spent a fair amount of class time talking about the Dealer's motivations after he took his own life."

"Class time?" I asked.

"It turns out we have more in common than jury duty," she said. "I'm a professor as well. NYU."

"No kidding. What do you teach?"

"Philosophy. Epistemology, to be exact."

"From the Greek *epistēmē*, meaning knowledge," I said. "Ironic, don't you think?"

"What's that?"

"The word for the study of knowledge—epistemology—is a word that most people don't know."

"And to think I've dedicated my life to it."

"You know what Kierkegaard said, right?"

"Well, I am a professor of philosophy, so I probably do."

"Truth always—"

"Rests with the minority," she said, finishing the quote. She raised a hand to her chin, giving me a quick up and down. "You're an interesting man, Professor Reinhart."

"Flattery will get you everywhere."

"How about dinner tomorrow night? Will it get me that?"

"I don't know," I said. "I'll have to ask my wife."

Sadira blinked. She literally took a step back. "I'm sorry. I didn't see a wedding ring, and the way we were talking I sort of assumed that—"

"I'm just kidding. There's no wife," I said. "And I'd love to have dinner with you."

BOOK FOUR

THE ENEMY OF MY ENEMY

CHAPTER 67

"I CAN think of a dozen foreign governments that would give their collective left nut to blow up this table," said my father.

Julian chuckled. "Maybe we should move tables."

"Maybe I should call Foxx again," I said. "Where is he?"

"He'll be here," said Julian. "And don't ask me what you're about to ask me for the hundredth time."

For the hundredth time, I asked him anyway. *"Julian, why are you here?"*

"Because Foxx wanted me here," he said. "Last I checked, he was still the New York section chief."

As usual, Julian had a point. There were only a few people on the planet who could force him to leave his proverbial bat cave against his will. Landon Foxx was one of them.

Now, if only Foxx would show up.

No sooner had I booked my dinner date with Sadira than Foxx called and asked me to meet him at O'Sullivan's Bar on the Lower East Side, the back booth. Word had already gotten to him that my father was in town. Foxx wanted him there, too. "Tell Eagle I look forward to seeing him," he said.

Lo and behold, there was Julian in the booth with a glass of whiskey when my father and I arrived. I'd spoken to him only an hour before to ask a favor. He hadn't mentioned the meeting. Why not, I wondered. Once again, Julian wasn't saying.

I let it lie and focused on the favor.

"So how many pages did you have to scrub?" I asked while we waited for Foxx.

O'Sullivan's had been around since Prohibition and smelled like it, too. It was the perfect Irish dive bar where everyone had their own problems.

"Not as many pages as you might have thought," answered Julian. "There was that story in *New York* magazine and a piece in the *Provincetown Banner* that referred to you as being rumored to be gay. All other mentions were in blogs."

"Are you sure you got them all?" I asked.

Julian looked at me as if I'd just asked Annie Leibovitz if she was sure there was film in her camera. "*Yes,* I got them all," he said. "When Sadira Yavari googles you, there will be nothing to dispel the notion that you're straight."

I glanced across the table at my father, who looked to be holding his tongue on a couple of punch lines to the point of dizziness. Or maybe it was the fatigue catching up to him. He still hadn't slept. If Foxx hadn't explicitly asked for him to join us, I would've insisted he crash at Elizabeth's apartment, as she'd offered. For the record, she was less than pleased that she couldn't come along to O'Sullivan's. She'd mumbled something about an all-boys club, but she understood the real reason. She didn't work for Foxx. She wasn't CIA.

That didn't mean she had to be happy about it. Whatever

the purpose of the meeting, she knew it had to be important. I knew it, too.

For the hundred and first time, "Just give me a hint," I said to Julian. "Amuse me. Why does Foxx want all of us here? What's it about?"

Julian tilted his glass of whiskey, motioning over my shoulder. "You can ask him yourself," he said. "Here he comes."

CHAPTER 68

FOXX SAT down in the booth. He nodded to me and Julian and then promptly forgot we existed for a couple of minutes while he caught up with my father, reminiscing about a couple of missions. "Company hasn't been the same without you, Eagle," Foxx eventually said, shaking his head. "Like it or not, you're a legend."

"Careful or I might just believe you," said my father. "Now go ahead and ask me what you really want to know."

Foxx wasn't one to play coy. Called out by my father, he normally would've been more than happy to cut to the chase. But he was also no dummy. When a man already knows your next move, you'll never get what you want from him.

"I was going to ask what brings you to New York," said Foxx, "but we both know you have no intention of telling me the real reason because you're not ready yet. So we'll leave it at that."

My father smiled, impressed. For a second, I thought he

might actually tell Foxx about our early morning encounter with Eli, the Prophet. Then I remembered. *This is my father.* As sure as Woodward and Bernstein, he would never burn a source.

"Okay, now that we've got that settled," I said. In other words, *Let's get on with things.*

I'd already briefed Foxx about Sadira when he called me at the courthouse. He was pleased that I'd made contact with her, although he still wasn't entirely comfortable with my plan.

"Sadira Yavari either killed Jahan Darvish herself or set him up for someone else," said Foxx. "Either way, he had to have been compromised. The question is how."

"That's what I'm working on," I said.

"It's what we're all working on," said Foxx. He gave a quick nod to Julian. That was his cue.

"Landon asked me to look at Darvish's file to see if there was anything the Agency had missed about him," said Julian.

"So what was missed?" I asked. It had to be something. Julian wouldn't be at the table otherwise.

"The Agency had presumably pulled all of Darvish's financial records, including a Caymans account that was receiving his payments from the Iranian government," explained Julian. "The professor was laundering rials into dollars through an offshore gambling site, exactly as he'd told the Agency when he became a double agent."

I really heard only one word of that. *"Presumably?"* I asked. "The Agency had presumably pulled all of his financial records?"

"We stopped at rials and dollars," said Foxx.

It was all he needed to say. I turned to Julian. "Cryptocurrency?"

Julian touched his nose. *Bingo.* "Only this particular crypto is new and a bit different. It's on the darknet and seems to be backed by hard currency."

That was new. Imagine being able to digitally print your own hundred-dollar bills. "But you don't know which currency it is yet, right?" I asked.

"No," said Julian. "I have my suspicions, but the whole setup is rather sophisticated."

That was Julian's way of admitting he hadn't fully hacked it yet. There were indeed limits to what he could do from behind a keyboard, at least under a time constraint. Not that he would ever wave the white flag. As he was fond of telling me, failure is just success that hasn't happened yet.

"So transmission-wise, how does it differ from the likes of Bitcoin?" I asked.

While Bitcoin and other cryptocurrencies are pseudonymous, a few hackers have been able to chart individual transaction flows, as well as figure out the real-world identities of both senders and receivers. In fact, Julian was the first.

"I can see where the crypto lands," he said. "I just can't see who sent it. There's an added layer in this case, an intermediary account that actually erases the trail a split second before the transfer is complete," said Julian.

"How is that possible?"

"I'm not sure yet. It's as if the currency intuitively knows where to go even after the transaction is canceled."

"You mean, like a snake that still slithers even after its head gets cut off," I said.

"More or less," said Julian.

I turned to Foxx. "So Darvish was receiving additional monies he didn't tell you about, and it wouldn't make sense that they were from the Iranian government since Iran was already paying him."

Foxx nodded. "I know what you're thinking, Reinhart."

"You got played," I said. "Darvish was feeding you misinformation."

"Maybe," said Foxx. "Maybe not. We'll never know for sure."

"I wouldn't go that far," said Julian.

"What do you mean?" I asked.

"Yeah," said Foxx. This was clearly news to him, too. *What do you mean?*

My father chuckled. Exhausted as he was, he was still listening to every word. Better yet, he was reading between the lines.

"He means he knows who the intermediary is," said my father. "He knows who the money is funneled through."

Julian grinned and put a finger to his nose again.

Bingo.

CHAPTER 69

"WHO IS it?" asked Foxx.

Julian took out his cell. The picture was already cued up. "Meet Viktor Alexandrov," he said.

We all stared at the photo. It came from the web pages of Viktor Alexandrov International.

"That's convenient, the guy has a website," I said. "Does it list an address?"

"No, just his phone. But it's a New York number," said Julian. "He lives in SoHo."

Foxx grabbed the phone for a closer look, his finger scrolling. "He's an art dealer?"

"A Russian art dealer," said Julian. "And if there was ever a country that would create a darknet cryptocurrency to counterfeit the ruble it would be the Russians. Black market weapons, money laundering, influencing foreign elections—and, of course, the occasional funding of terrorism."

"Who better to run cover for them than an international art dealer," I said.

"We need to get acquainted with this guy," said Foxx. "Quickly."

"He could be sitting in your lap right now, and it wouldn't make a difference," said Julian. "He's not going to know anything."

"What do you mean?" asked Foxx. "How would he not know where the money emanates from?"

Again, my father chimed in. "That's the whole point of the intermediary," he said. "He can never know."

Foxx was back to being pissed. "What the hell, Julian? So it *is* a dead end."

"I didn't say that. All I meant was that Viktor Alexandrov wouldn't be able to tell you the source even if you waterboarded him on a bed of nails," said Julian. "But there is a way to find out."

"How?" asked Foxx.

"I would need access to his computer."

"Easy," said Foxx. "I can have a search warrant by this afternoon."

"Are you sure about that?" I asked. "On what evidence, a hacked digital currency transaction?"

"You're both missing the point," said Julian. "Alexandrov can't find out that I've accessed his computer. Even if he doesn't know the origin of the transactions, he can still signal whoever it is."

"So we need to get you in front of his computer without his knowing," said Foxx.

"That's one way," said Julian.

"What's another?" I asked.

"I only need access to the computer. That doesn't mean I have to be the one in front of it," said Julian. "I don't need to be in the room."

"But someone does," I said. "Right?"

"That gives us some more options," said Foxx. "Any ideas?"

"Yeah, two," said my father. "Breaking and entering."

"Or maybe just the latter," I said.

"What do you have in mind?" asked Foxx.

I pointed at Julian's phone and the picture of Alexandrov. He had slicked-back hair and looked like a rich playboy standing in front of what appeared to be an El Greco, given the elongated, almost drippy-looking figures in the painting.

"What else do we know about this guy?" I asked. "His personal life."

"How much more do you need to know? He's Russian," said Julian. "He likes to drink and chase women."

"Exactly," I said. "All we need to do is give him a chance to do both."

"I'll ask you again," said Foxx. *"What do you have in mind?"*

I was already halfway out of the booth. "I'll let you know in one hour," I said. "Maybe even sooner if the mayor's in a good mood."

CHAPTER 70

EDSO DEACON stared at me in utter disbelief from behind his desk at City Hall. *"You want me to do what?"*

"I want you to throw a cocktail party," I said, handing him a folded piece of paper. "Here's the guest list."

Deacon took the paper, clumsily unfolding it. He looked. He squinted. He stared back at me again. "There's only one name on it," he said.

"That's the only name I care about. The others you invite are entirely up to you," I said.

"Really? I get to choose the rest of the guests at my own party? That's awfully kind of you," said Deacon.

As if his sarcasm weren't enough to convey his annoyance, the mayor looked over at Beau Livingston and rolled his eyes. Livingston, sitting on the couch along the wall, let loose a sycophantic laugh.

"Yeah," said Livingston. "That's real generous of you, Reinhart.

Do you have another piece of paper with the hors d'oeuvres you wanted served?"

"Caviar, for starters," said Deacon. "The guy's Russian. Viktor Alexandrov."

"Are we supposed to know who that is?" asked Livingston.

"He's an art dealer," I said. "That's why he's getting the invite. The mayor is interested in diversifying his financial holdings by purchasing a major piece of art as an investment. He's heard Alexandrov is the man to talk to."

"Is he actually?" asked Livingston. "The man to talk to?"

"He will be once you tell him he is," I said. "He's hardly going to disagree with you, Beau. It's called an ego. Not that you Harvard boys know anything about that."

Livingston had his snappy comeback all lined up, I could tell. Probably something about my alma mater, Yale, being his safety school. But Deacon cut him off. "Just for shits and giggles," said the mayor, "if I did host this party, what's the real reason you want this Alexandrov guy there?"

"I can't tell you," I said.

If looks could kill. "You've got a lot of balls, Reinhart," he said.

"No, just one big chit I'm cashing in."

I'd saved Deacon's life, and he knew it. He also knew the reason I couldn't tell him about Alexandrov, or at least he had a pretty good idea.

"Does it involve your previous employer?" he asked.

"It might," I said.

"Then at least tell me it's a matter of life or death, or whatever they would say at Langley."

"I wouldn't be asking if it weren't extremely important," I said. "How's that?"

The mayor nodded. He was gradually buying in.

Livingston, meanwhile, couldn't believe it. *"Are you seriously considering this?"* he asked his boss.

Livingston was only doing his job. He got paid to be the devil's advocate. There were only two words ricocheting around in his mind: *Russian collusion.* The last thing the mayor needed was a subpoena from Bob Mueller.

"If I do you this favor, Reinhart, are we square?" asked Deacon.

Powerful men don't like owing anything to anyone.

"Square as a checkerboard," I said.

"Okay, then. When do you want to do it? A couple weeks?"

"Actually, it needs to be a little sooner."

"How much sooner?"

I put my hands over my ears and smiled. *If you think I had balls before, Deacon . . .*

"It has to happen tonight," I said.

Ten minutes later, with the sound of the mayor's screaming still ringing in my ears outside City Hall, I called Elizabeth.

"Remember those brand-new Louboutins you thought you'd never wear? Get ready to strap 'em on," I said.

CHAPTER 71

IT'S GOOD to be the king. It's even better to be the king of New York. Everyone wants to have a drink with you, no matter how last-minute the invite. I was banking on it.

Livingston called me within the hour to tell me that Alexandrov had said yes, no questions asked. Correction. *One* question asked. Alexandrov wanted to know if he could bring a date. It figured. He probably wanted to show off to her. *Look at me, babe, I'm buddy-buddy with the billionaire mayor...*

Livingston made it clear to Alexandrov that there could be no plus-one. That was key. Little did the Russian know I already had his companion for the evening all lined up.

"How do I look?" asked Elizabeth, performing a quick twirl in a little black dress outside the gates of Gracie Mansion. Deacon and his wife, Cassandra, only used the mayor's "official residence" for entertaining.

"You look positively stunning," I said. She truly did. Elizabeth had become so adept at concealing her attractiveness for the sake of her career that I almost hadn't recognized her when she arrived. "I wasn't sure you actually owned makeup."

"Ha-ha," she said. "The makeup is mine. The dress I borrowed from my neighbor. Remind me not to spill anything on it."

"There are too many other things I need to remind you about," I said.

"Don't worry. I've got this."

"Are you sure?"

"Sure I'm sure," she said. Elizabeth extended a leg through the thigh-high slit of her borrowed dress and smiled. "After all, I'm wearing my lucky new shoes."

Say no more.

We staggered our entrances. I went first. Earlier, Landon Foxx had sent an agent to my apartment to grab one of my suits and a tie, along with a clean shirt and a pair of loafers. The only thing lucky about the shoes he picked was that they matched my suit. Thankfully, the agent knew his way around a wardrobe.

Foxx was also providing temporary lodging for both me and my father, by way of the safe house in Brooklyn. At that very moment, my father was catching up on some much-needed sleep. His jury duty performance was Oscar worthy. One orchestrated ruse, however, was enough for him for one day.

"Nice to see you, Mr. Mayor," I said, after being led into a parlor off the foyer of Gracie Mansion by a member of the house staff. If there was one thing about this impromptu cocktail party that the mayor actually welcomed it was the cocktails. Comfortably ensconced in his second term, and with the press nowhere in sight, he was happy to throw back a few.

Not as much as the man of the hour, though.

Deacon shook my hand and immediately walked me over to Alexandrov, who seemingly had the mayor's wife cornered by the bar. Or maybe it was the bar he had cornered.

"Viktor, I want you to meet a friend of mine, Dr. Dylan Reinhart," said Deacon.

"Pleasure to meet you, Dr. Reinhart," said Alexandrov, sloppily moving a martini glass from his right hand to his left so we could shake. He already reeked of vodka and was about to slurp some more when he stopped and cocked his head. "Wait, you're that professor, aren't you? The Dr. Death guy!"

"Yes, he is," said Deacon. "This is the man who tackled me on the first-base line of Citi Field and saved my life last year."

"A real American hero," said Alexandrov. "In that case, it's even more of a pleasure to meet you. An honor, actually."

The guy was a charmer. I could give him that. Now with one step to my left, I was about to give him a perfect view of the entrance to the parlor.

Take it away, Elizabeth...

CHAPTER 72

ELIZABETH TAPPED the toe of her left Louboutin on the sidewalk outside Gracie Mansion as if keeping time. There was a window to staggered entrances, a sweet spot between too short and too long, and she'd know it when she felt it.

Here we go, she told herself. She'd felt it.

Beginning her walk up to the front door, she couldn't ignore the irony. Her job tonight was the one thing she'd promised herself she'd never do in her career. Exploit her looks. But if there was ever a night to make an exception, this was it.

Forget about all the research, the cramming she'd done only hours before as if she were back in college at Maryland during finals week. It simply didn't matter how fluently she now could speak about the ins and outs of the art world. None of that jibber-jabber would matter to a guy like Alexandrov unless she herself was a work of art. She needed to be something he absolutely, positively had to have.

Elizabeth stopped for a second and glanced down at the

plunging neckline of her dress, checking her cleavage. *Jeez, did I really just look to see if my boobs are straight?*

It would be a night of firsts, all right.

Part one of the plan went straight out the window when she was shown into the parlor. Playing it coy at the start and keeping her distance from Alexandrov was replaced by Dylan immediately coming over to her.

"Someone wants to meet you," he said, cracking a smile. "And he wasn't terribly subtle about it."

"Does he recognize me?" asked Elizabeth.

"That's the even better news," said Dylan.

There was a chance Alexandrov had seen the video of Elizabeth in Times Square on the news. Even if he had, the odds were slim that he'd make the connection. The Elizabeth in the video looked nothing like the dolled-up Elizabeth he'd seen walking into the parlor. Still, Dylan had made sure.

"I told him you were an interior designer," he said.

"I thought we agreed on lawyer," said Elizabeth.

"We did, but I called an audible. That dress doesn't say attorney. Besides, think of the money you saved on law school loans."

"Very funny," she said. "Now shut up and take me over to him."

"Actually, I told him to wait a bit before coming to us."

Elizabeth glanced over Dylan's shoulder. "So much for his waiting."

Seconds later, Alexandrov practically pushed Dylan aside. The only thing staggered about the Russian's entrance was his walking. "Are you going to introduce me to this beautiful woman, Dr. Reinhart, or do I have to do the honors myself?" he asked.

"Please, allow me," said Dylan. "Viktor Alexandrov, I'd like you to meet Elizabeth Johnson."

The first rule of fake names when working a mark is to keep your first name the same. The second rule? In the age of Google, make your second name as common as possible.

Not that Viktor was listening all that intently. He was too busy staring at Elizabeth's cleavage. Subtle, he wasn't. Even less so when he told Dylan to get lost.

"The mayor said he wants to speak to you, Dr. Reinhart. Right away, I believe."

"Of course," said Dylan. He gave Viktor a pat on the back and shot a wink to Elizabeth. "I'll leave you two to get acquainted."

CHAPTER 73

"WHERE HAVE you been all my life?" asked Viktor.

One cheesy line deserved another, thought Elizabeth. "I bet you say that to all the girls," she replied.

"Yes," he said. "But this time I actually mean it."

He was tall and handsome, although his Russian accent was straight out of a James Bond movie. And if that was cologne he was wearing, it was eau de Stolichnaya. *Is he already drunk?*

"So how do you know the mayor?" asked Elizabeth.

"He's looking to make a significant art purchase. That's what he and I were talking about. I'm an art dealer."

"*Really?*" said Elizabeth, feigning amazement. Eyes fluttering, she tried to look as if she were meeting a rock star. "You're an art dealer?"

"Does that turn you on?"

Did he really just ask me that? Yeah, he's drunk, all right. Drunk and horny . . .

238

"Well, art does excite me," said Elizabeth, playing along. "Especially modern."

Viktor grinned. "Modern is my specialty."

What a coincidence. Elizabeth proceeded to showcase the rest of her research, discussing trips she'd taken to various museums around the world. The way she talked about the time she got lost in the Louvre, she was almost starting to believe it herself.

"There's one museum still on my bucket list, though," she said. "I imagine you've been."

"I've been to them all."

"Given your accent, I mean." There were a lot of museums in Russia, sort of like there were a lot of guys named LeBron who play basketball.

"Ah, the Hermitage," said Viktor. "I was actually raised in Saint Petersburg. I know the museum like . . ." His voice trailed off as he showed her the back of his hand. He then lightly stroked Elizabeth's arm with it.

"That's awfully presumptuous of you," she said playfully.

"I'm only just getting started. What are you doing after this?"

"That depends. What do you have in mind?"

"Whatever you want. Dinner? Dancing?" He watched Elizabeth frown. "What? What did I say wrong?" he asked.

"I already told you what excited me," she said.

"You want to see some art?"

Elizabeth bit her lower lip and nodded as if the word *art* were code for the craziest, kinkiest sex act a man like Viktor could ever imagine.

He glanced at the gold Rolex on his wrist. "I can think of only one place that's still open at this hour," he said.

"A museum?"

"Actually, it's more of a gallery. At least it doubles as a gallery."

"What is it when it's not a gallery?"

"My apartment."

"We just met and already you're inviting me back to your place?"

"Like I said, I'm only getting started." Viktor leaned forward, whispering in her ear, "Do you want to see my Picasso?"

CHAPTER 74

ELIZABETH CRANED her neck as she stood outside the door of Viktor's penthouse apartment in SoHo while he fumbled with his keys. There was no hallway. It was more like an oversized foyer, which made little sense given there was only one other apartment on the floor. The rich really know how to waste space.

Quickly, she clocked the exits. The elevator bank, how she and Viktor arrived, along with the stairwell to the right of it. They were at six and nine.

Back at midnight, Viktor was turning off his alarm, tapping a keypad on the wall just inside his door.

"All clear," he said. "Welcome."

Elizabeth had faked everything with him up until that point. Walking in, though, her reaction was as real as it gets. "Wow," she said.

It clearly paid to be an art dealer—and whatever else Viktor Alexandrov was involved in. Never mind the floor-to-ceiling windows and the designer furniture. It was all about the walls in the living room straight ahead. The only things missing were the velvet museum ropes in front of all the paintings. Viktor wasn't kidding about his apartment doubling as a gallery.

"Would you like a drink?" he asked.

"Yes. But not before the tour," said Elizabeth.

"Of course." Viktor took a step toward the living room.

"No. I want to see the whole apartment. Where you eat. Where you work." She paused. "Where you sleep."

Viktor liked that. He liked that a lot. Maybe he didn't need to get her drunk first, after all. "Follow me," he said.

He began showing her every room of his massive apartment. The kitchen, the dining room, the den that served as his office. Next came his bedroom.

"What are you doing?" asked Elizabeth.

"Changing into something more comfortable," said Viktor, standing in front of his king-size bed and removing his suit jacket. "Would you like to do the same? You could borrow a robe."

"Maybe in a little bit," she said. "When we're done with the tour."

"Ah, yes, my artwork," he said. "I'll be sure to show you that after."

"After what?"

Viktor stepped toward Elizabeth, reaching for her shoulder and the strap of her dress. "After this."

"Not so fast," she said, putting a hand over his. "If you want to see what's underneath, you're going to have to earn it."

"Earn it?"

"Yes. You heard me." She cocked her hip, teasing him. "Do you think you're up for it?"

It was the daily double of male button pushing. The prospect of sex combined with challenging his masculinity. Viktor was suddenly putty in her hands.

"Darling," he said, "I'm up for anything."

"Good." Elizabeth took a step back and peeled a strap off her shoulder. "Follow me."

CHAPTER 75

I KEPT staring through the crack of the stairwell door, waiting for Viktor's door to open. *What's taking so long? Where are you, Elizabeth?*

"Any longer and I'll have to open another bottle of Scotch," came Julian's voice in my ear.

"Don't get hammered on me now," I whispered. "I need you sharp."

"Hammered is when I'm at my sharpest, old friend. You know that."

I did. I also knew it was weird to have Julian inside my head, courtesy of the earpiece he'd given me. It had GPS and cellular built in, too, and it was still no bigger than a raisin. Eat your heart out, Q.

"Should I do something?"

"Like what?" asked Julian.

"I don't know. Knock on the door maybe."

"You mean, ruin the whole plan?"

"You got a better idea?"

"Yes, and you're already doing it," he said. "Be patient. Elizabeth knows how to take care of herself."

"I know she does."

"It's not weird, in case you're wondering. Caring about her the way you do."

"Who said it was weird?" I asked.

"Exactly. You're just being human."

Jesus. Julian really was inside my head. I was about to tell him to cut it out when I saw Viktor's door open. Elizabeth appeared. Alone. Right according to plan. I quickly slipped off my loafers on the stairwell landing and made a beeline to her.

"You've got to be quick," she whispered.

"I know."

"No. I mean, you need to be really, really quick. I don't know how much longer I can hold him off. I'm only wearing so much."

"What does that mean?"

"I told Viktor I'd take something off for every shot of vodka he does. He's now chilling shot glasses while I'm supposedly in the bathroom."

I quickly looked her up and down. Two Louboutins, one dress, and whatever was underneath it. She was right; she wasn't wearing much. "I hope your jewelry counts," I said.

"And I hope it doesn't come to that." She stepped back and pointed. "Down the hall, second door on your left. There's a laptop on the desk."

"Wait. Where?"

"Viktor's office," she said. "It's—"

"No, I was talking to Julian," I explained, pointing to my ear. He was trying to tell me something. Suddenly, I was whipping my head around to look at the elevator.

"What is it?" asked Elizabeth.

"We've got company," I said. "Someone's coming up."

"What?"

As soon as the word left her mouth she knew she'd been loud. Way too loud.

"Did you say something, darling?" came Viktor's voice, calling out to her.

There was no time to think, and only two ways to go. In or out.

Elizabeth decided for me, pulling me inside the apartment. "The office," she said. "Go!"

CHAPTER 76

I TOOK off down the hall, racing in my socks so fast I nearly slid right past Viktor's office. I saw his desk. I saw his laptop. The problem was what I couldn't see.

"Julian, tell me that's Viktor's neighbor in the elevator," I said.

Julian was more than the voice in my ear. He was also the eyes in the back of my head. Once I told him where Viktor lived he was able to hack the building's security system by ghosting the IP address of the off-site monitoring company. He could see what every camera could see. The entrance and exits. The lobby and the elevators. Especially the lone elevator that serviced only the penthouse floor.

"No such luck," said Julian. "It's not the neighbor."

The way he said it, I knew it was trouble.

Julian told me who it was the second the doorbell rang. *Of all the gin joints in all the towns…*

The man who'd paid a visit to me as Benjamin Al-Kazaz was

now standing outside Viktor's apartment. Check that. He was about to be *inside* the apartment.

I listened as Viktor opened the door and greeted him. I couldn't make out their conversation all the way down the hall, but they definitely knew each other.

Then suddenly I could hear every word of what they were saying. Along with their footsteps getting closer.

"This way," said Viktor. "Let's go into my office."

I spun in my socks, looking for a place to hide. My heart was pounding, the panic setting in. There was no closet. No bathroom. No balcony. The one couch in the office was perpendicular to the door; I couldn't duck behind it.

I had only one choice. *The curtains.*

They were pulled back, bunched and long, the bottoms touching the floor. If they could hide my feet, they could hide the rest of me. Maybe.

Quickly, I slipped behind them doing a vertical limbo. All I could do was stand like a statue and hope that the first thing to see in Viktor's office wasn't a man trying to hide behind the curtains.

Don't swallow. Don't breathe. Don't even blink.

"What the fuck are you doing here?" asked Viktor.

Good question. Thankfully, it wasn't directed at me.

There was a pause—a long pause—before Viktor got a response. The voice was the same as I remembered from my apartment, but the tone was drastically different. "I'm sorry, what did you say?"

My gut had told me that Al-Kazaz and the Mudir were one and the same. Whatever doubt I still had disappeared in that very moment. I didn't need to see him. Hearing him was enough. It was the way he chillingly delivered the line, a simple question. *What did you say?*

Only it wasn't really a question. It was a reminder. No one talked to the Mudir like that. And just to make sure? He added his own special punctuation.

Click.

Sometimes it takes the cocking of a hammer to drive a point home.

Consider it driven. Viktor immediately apologized, his voice trembling. He was suddenly a guest in his own home.

"I know, I know. I should've returned your calls," said Viktor. "I was afraid to disappoint you."

"Then don't," said the Mudir. "Where's my package? What's the delay?"

"Please lower the gun."

"Answer the question. *What's the delay?*"

"It's customs," said Viktor. "It's being held up at customs."

"You said you had that covered."

"I do. Everything's going to be fine. I've been assured the shipment will be cleared by the end of next week."

"That's too long. The timeline has changed. Things will be happening faster," said the Mudir. "You've got twenty-four hours."

I had one ear trained on the conversation. In my other ear was Julian asking me if I was okay. If I had a third ear I maybe would've heard the footsteps out in the hallway.

"There you are!" said Elizabeth. I knew the second she saw Viktor, she'd also see his guest—and his gun. Her reaction was pure reflex. "Oh."

As in, *Oh, shit.*

The G42 is the smallest Glock there is, and I knew exactly where Elizabeth was hiding it. She had it strapped to the inside of her leg underneath her dress.

"My goodness. I can't imagine what this must look like," said Viktor. "Elizabeth, I want you to meet a good friend of mine."

I slowly reached inside my jacket, feeling for the grip of my own Glock. There was no telling how the Mudir would respond, but I could feel Viktor silently pleading with him to play along.

He did. "I'm Benjamin," he said. "Benjamin Al-Kazaz." As liars go, at least he was consistent.

He offered no explanation for the gun in his hand. Nothing more about himself. But he was very curious about Elizabeth.

"What's your last name?" he asked.

"It's Johnson," she said.

"What do you do for a living?"

"I'm an interior designer."

I waited for the Mudir's next question, but all I heard was silence. It was the loudest, most threatening stretch of dead air I'd ever encountered. The Mudir knew who Elizabeth really was.

"You're no interior designer," he said.

CHAPTER 77

ALL HELL broke loose. All at once.

I sprang from behind the curtains as the Mudir raised his arm to shoot Elizabeth. Viktor was screaming at him, "No!"

From the corner of his eye, the Mudir spotted me—a sudden distraction enough to shift his aim a couple of clicks to the left of Elizabeth as she dove clear of the doorway.

I closed the gap fast, bull-rushing him before he could swing his gun my way. I wanted him down but not dead. He knew too much. Too many secrets. The Mudir was more than a terrorist; he was *the* terrorist, the one behind the Times Square bombings and whatever else he was planning.

Had we hit the floor clean, I would've owned all the leverage, but my momentum carried us onto the back of the couch. As we careened into a bookcase, he was able to break free.

"Freeze!" yelled Elizabeth.

As fast as she was with her G42, the Mudir was even faster. By the time she was back in the doorway with him dead in her sights, he'd grabbed Viktor.

"Think again," said the Mudir, his gun pressed hard against the side of Viktor's head.

I didn't know if I was more relieved or impressed. The Mudir could've killed me instead of going after Viktor, but he knew Elizabeth was surely packing as well. If he pulled the trigger on me, he would've been a dead man, too.

The Mudir was smart, all right. But how smart?

"Go ahead," I told him, pointing at Viktor. "Kill him."

The look on Viktor's face. As if he weren't scared shitless enough. The look from Elizabeth, too. She knew what I was doing. It was one thing she couldn't do because of her badge.

But the only look that really mattered was the Mudir's. I needed that grin on his face to go away. I needed to see a flash of fear, the sudden realization that maybe he hadn't thought this all the way through.

Instead, he simply smiled wider. *Nice try,* he was telling me.

It didn't matter whether I gave a shit about Viktor Alexandrov or not. As long as the Mudir had his gun jammed against the Russian's head, he was walking out of that apartment. Alive.

With a couple of choice thoughts for me, as well.

"You're out of your depth, Dr. Reinhart," said the Mudir. "What brought you here tonight will only get you killed."

"I'll consider myself warned," I said.

The most unsettling thing about the Mudir in that moment wasn't the fact that he was threatening to kill Viktor. Or that he didn't seem to care that there were two Glocks aimed right at him.

No, the most unsettling thing was that he seemed to be enjoying himself. He was relishing the moment. It was as if he lived to be this close to death. His and everyone else's.

I had too much history with this. Too many encounters. Standing in that room, there was no shaking the feeling. One of us was about to die.

CHAPTER 78

JULIAN HAD been listening the entire time. I knew he didn't want to say anything, not even a whisper, lest he distract me for even a millisecond. But there was one question he had to ask. "Do you want backup? Clear your throat if you do."

I didn't clear my throat.

I was sure Julian understood why. That's why he asked. Otherwise he would've already made the call.

He knew the circumstances of how Elizabeth and I were in Viktor's apartment. As operations went, this was beyond unsanctioned. Even worse, I had involved the mayor. He was an unwitting accomplice.

So, no. Elizabeth and I would take our chances. Roll the dice on our own.

"We just need to grab one thing," said the Mudir, dragging Viktor a few steps back toward his desk. He winked at me. "You don't mind, do you?"

"We already know where the payments are coming from," I lied.

The Mudir didn't ask *What payments?* It was maybe the first mistake he'd made. Or maybe there was simply no point in his playing dumb. We all knew who everyone was in the room.

"Perhaps you do know. All the same, I think we'll take it with us anyway." The Mudir jerked Viktor toward his laptop. "Pick it up," he said.

Viktor's hands were trembling. He nearly dropped the laptop twice before securing it against his stomach. I could tell he wanted to say something, but he couldn't. It was as if he were drowning. A man suddenly realizing that he truly was out of his depth.

Elizabeth caught my eye, mouthing the word *No.* That's how well she knew me.

I had the shot. I could put a bullet through the middle of the Mudir's forehead, ten times out of ten. Eight of those times he'd die without even a twitch, never pulling his trigger. Those were pretty good odds.

But not good enough. Especially because I was nothing more than a civilian. The real reason Elizabeth was saying no was to protect me, not Viktor.

Still, something had to be done. A deal.

"You can't take him with you," I said. "We stay and you can go—*but only if you go alone.*"

The Mudir jammed the barrel of his gun even harder into the side of Viktor's head. "I'll do whatever I want."

"No. You won't," I said. "If you take him, you're taking all of us."

That seemed to get him thinking. "Maybe if you lower your guns first," he told us.

It was a lousy counteroffer and he knew it. He was stalling. He began moving for the hallway with his arm still wrapped around Viktor's neck.

"He stays," I repeated.

"After he shows me to the door," said the Mudir. "I am a guest, after all."

I joined Elizabeth in the hallway, but we stayed back as the Mudir headed for the front door of Viktor's apartment. He walked backward, his eyes never leaving us, and the sights of our guns never leaving him. When he reached the door, Viktor knew enough to open it for him, shifting his laptop from one hand to the other.

"Now let him go," I said.

Standing with one foot out in the foyer, the Mudir nodded. "As you wish," he said. But it was the way he said it.

Only by then it was too late.

CHAPTER 79

LIKE A magician, the Mudir made a show of reaching for Viktor's laptop while releasing him from his grasp. All eyes were where the Mudir wanted them to be. On the laptop. Not his gun.

By the time Elizabeth and I blinked, the Mudir had sidestepped out of the apartment. Now all we could see was the gun.

Viktor was staying, all right, along with everything he could tell us about the Mudir. It was all staying with him forever.

Bam!

The shot was so clean, so straight, that the blood didn't splatter. It gurgled. Then poured.

Viktor's right temple turned into a spigot of red as he spun downward, his legs collapsing beneath him. It was impossible not to watch, and again the Mudir was banking on it. We were frozen. Only for a few seconds, but it was all the time he needed for his head start. That and the length of the hallway that separated us.

"Me!" I said to Elizabeth, finally taking off. Me, as in, not you. As in, the one with the badge stays with the body.

"I can't see him," came Julian's voice in my ear. He was checking all the security cameras. He didn't need to be told what had happened. "Watch your front."

The Mudir could've been right by the elevator waiting for me. Only he wasn't. By the time I slid to a stop—*damn these socks*—and peeled around Viktor's front door, the only thing to be seen beyond the barrel of my gun was the door to the stairwell closing shut. As much as the Mudir wanted me dead, he wanted out of that building more.

"Shit!"

"What is it?" asked Julian.

I'd reached the stairs only to suddenly stop on the landing. "He took my shoes."

I could practically hear the Mudir laughing. It wasn't that I couldn't chase him without shoes, it's that he knew I'd come to a stop once I saw they were gone. That's just the way the mind works.

The Mudir's racing footsteps floors below were echoing all around me now. There was still a slim chance I could catch him. But I didn't budge.

Instead, I sat down and simply exhaled. Shoes or no shoes, I realized that ultimately catching the Mudir would have nothing to do with my feet. It was all between the ears. I'd have to out-think him.

"He just hit the lobby," said Julian. "Elvis has left the building."

I didn't say anything.

"You still there?" Julian finally asked.

"Yeah. Still here."

"You okay?"

"I will be."

"That's the spirit," he said. "Okay, say it with me now."

I knew what was coming. Of his many eclectic pursuits and interests, World War II held a special place in Julian's heart. Most people fixated on the musings of Winston Churchill. Julian, however, was more partial to quoting Charles de Gaulle. Go figure.

"C'mon, don't leave me hanging," he said before switching to his horrible French accent. "France has lost a battle . . ."

It was the accent that got me every time. "But France has not lost the war," I said.

Julian was reminding me that we'd been here before. The setback. The bump in the road. But this time felt different. The word *war* had always been a metaphor. Now it was literal.

"How much time do you figure?" asked Julian.

"Forty-eight hours," I answered.

That's how long we had to stop the Mudir before his next attack.

CHAPTER 80

TWO LARGE blackboards had been wheeled into the window-less conference room at the JTTF field unit, along with a mini fridge filled with sodas and waters. Four pizzas had been ordered, delivered, and eaten.

"Go home and get some sleep," Evan Pritchard told his assistant, Gwen, at almost three in the morning. She declined by quoting Warren Zevon.

"I'll sleep when I'm dead," she said. Then she announced to the room that she was making another pot of coffee. "Raise your hand if you want some."

Everyone's hand shot up.

We were redefining the meaning of *joint* in the Joint Terrorism Task Force. In fact, the non-agents outnumbered the agents. Elizabeth and her boss, Pritchard, were the only ones with proper JTTF field unit IDs. Landon Foxx, my father, and I were their SIGs, special invited guests. SIGs who just happened to be current and former CIA. Last but not least, on the two-way encrypted speakerphone, was Julian.

In the light of day, this ad hoc gathering of the minds would've never happened. Egos aside, there'd be too much bureaucratic red tape to slice and dice through. But under the cover of night, with the red tape asleep or at least looking the other way, here we were.

Waiting.

"I like the sound that chalk makes," Pritchard had told us, explaining his preference for blackboards in strategy sessions. "That's all we use here. It makes everything you write more emphatic."

Emphatically written across the two blackboards was everything we knew so far. And *everything* included a few things only some of us in the room should've been allowed to know. But there was simply no time for parsing security clearances. The clock was ticking. The Mudir had literally said as much.

My old friend and operative Ahmed Al-Hamdah had infiltrated one of the Mudir's cells. He gave his life trying to prevent the Times Square bombings. In doing so, he spooked the Mudir to the point of thinking there could be other moles in his cells. In his effort to find them, the Mudir somehow found a path that led directly to me. He literally knocked on my front door.

Only days before that, Professor Jahan Darvish's corpse had been discovered in his Manhattan hotel room. His toxicology report, filed by a city coroner, was initially viewed under the pretense of an accidental death. A second—and secret—report, issued by the CIA, had no such pretense but still couldn't prove foul play. While the combination of drugs in Darvish's system may have precipitated his cardiac arrest, two of the three had been prescribed for him.

Now, in reexamining the report, what appeared to be an inadvertent overdose was most likely anything but. As for the mini bottle of Jim Beam in his actual butt, well, that was just clever to the point of genius. Classic misdirection of the mind.

Professor Darvish just *had* to be the only person in the room given something like that, right?

Wrong. Sadira Yavari either killed him herself or paved the way for someone else. Because she'd used Halo to conceal her identity, my initial thought was that she was CIA. Foxx, as the Agency's New York section chief, would almost certainly know if she was an operative. But he swore up and down that she wasn't. And while the first rule of being with the Agency is *Trust no one,* I had no reason not to believe him. Especially when he revealed that Darvish had been a CIA informant.

There you have it. A terrorist attack and a murder in a hotel room. Two seemingly unrelated events that would've stayed unrelated were it not for a certain Russian art dealer, Viktor Alexandrov. Professor Darvish had been receiving additional money beyond what the Iranian government was paying him, and Alexandrov had been the cryptocurrency point man. Turned out, he also had been a point man for the Mudir on some type of shipment that had yet to clear customs.

Which, over the span of two rectangular blackboards, brought everything full circle. The Mudir and Darvish were somehow connected, courtesy of Alexandrov. Unfortunately, out of those three, two of them were dead.

So was a young man named Gorgin, as well as the guy with a pointed beard who killed him when it became clear that Gorgin was going to help Elizabeth. Gorgin, whoever he was, saved Elizabeth's life.

Now, with a little luck, he would end up saving the lives of countless others. That was why, at three in the morning, we were all still up and waiting.

The speakerphone on the conference room table suddenly crackled with the sound of Julian's voice. "Found it!" he said.

The waiting was over.

CHAPTER 81

HOURS EARLIER, Chase Bank had provided us with the security footage from its branch at Penn Station. Matching up the time stamp from the ATM withdrawal slip Elizabeth had taken from the shirt pocket of the guy in Gorgin's house with the pointed beard, we were able to see him enter and leave the branch.

What we weren't able to see—or learn—was his name. According to Chase, the account he withdrew money from belonged to a Priscilla H. McManus. Miss McManus had reported her card stolen one day after making an ATM withdrawal from a branch in Jersey City.

Suffice it to say, larceny was probably the very least of our guy's sins.

"So where did he go after the bank?" asked Foxx. "Did he catch a train? Was he meeting someone?"

Foxx was the only one in the room who had just learned of Elizabeth having the ATM receipt. We all turned to him. Damn. *Good question.*

There were a lot of sharp minds around the table, and we'd all been focused on who this guy was, not what else he might have been doing besides getting cash. Psychologists like to call that tunnel vision. I just call it a brain fart. Happens to the best of us.

Julian to the rescue.

We could've woken up the head of the Manhattan Transportation Authority, who, in turn, could've woken up his head of security, who then could've woken up whoever it was whose job entailed archiving all their daily surveillance footage on some MTA server. Even then, it would've taken hours. *Tick-tock, tick-tock.*

We didn't have hours. But we did have Julian.

"Give me a moment. I'm synching up all the timecodes," he said over the speakerphone. "How many monitors do you have?"

We all started looking around the room, but Pritchard already knew the count. He undoubtedly spent more time at the JTTF offices than anywhere else, including that crazy Operation Desert Storm townhouse of his.

"Seven monitors," said Pritchard, reaching over to a control panel built into the table. With the press of a few buttons the screens all lit up, flashing blue with the FBI logo. "Tell me when you want our password."

Julian chuckled. Which made me chuckle. Pritchard clearly didn't have a full grasp of Julian's hacking talents. *A password? Who needs a password?*

Not Julian. Not ever. Within seconds, all seven monitors were filled with different camera angles of Penn Station. Julian had assigned a letter to each piece of footage next to its time-code.

"Okay, here's before he went to the ATM," said Julian. "The

first up, A, is him entering the main entrance, western end of 32nd Street."

Like a play-by-play announcer calling a football game, Julian circled the guy with a telestrator. The man with the pointed beard was walking alone into Penn Station dressed in a pair of jeans and a zip-up hoodie. He had a backpack slung over one shoulder.

Our eyes darted to another monitor as Julian circled the guy again, moving through the main concourse. Then once more, heading toward the entrance of the Chase branch. A to B to C.

That was it. No detours. A direct path to the ATM machine.

"Anyone see anything out of the ordinary?" asked Pritchard. We all shook our heads. Pritchard nodded. "Yeah, I don't either."

"Okay, let's take a look at afterward," said Julian.

A new set of images appeared. Same angles. Just a couple of minutes later. Julian resumed telestrating the guy as he left the bank, as well as when he began walking back across the concourse to where he'd entered. Instinctively, we all turned to the next monitor, expecting to see the guy leaving the station.

"Wait. Where did he go?" asked Foxx.

We all leaned forward.

Good question.

There was no one for Julian to circle. The guy wasn't on the next monitor or any others. We whipped our heads around the room, looking at every screen once, then twice.

"Are you sure all the footage is synched?" I asked.

Of course Julian was sure, but he double-checked anyway. "Yep. All the timecodes match," he said. I could hear him pouring himself some more whiskey. "Occam's razor?"

"Yeah, probably a blind spot," I said. In other words, that

was the easiest and simplest explanation. Except there was one thing Occam's razor wouldn't explain. Julian knew it, too.

"Let me fast-forward," he said. "All eyes on the exits."

Julian sped up the footage. There was no way the cameras could cover every square foot of Penn Station. But there was also no way any of the exits could be among the blind spots.

"There!" said Elizabeth, bolting up from her chair. She headed straight to one of the monitors, pointing. "By the Hudson newsstand."

"That's him, all right," said Julian.

Suddenly, our guy with the pointed beard was back in frame and heading for the exit in his jeans, zip-up hoodie, and—

Oh, shit.

"Does everyone see what I'm not seeing?" I asked.

CHAPTER 82

WE IMMEDIATELY woke up the head of the Manhattan Transportation Authority, who, in turn, woke up his head of security, who then woke up whoever it was whose job entailed archiving all their daily surveillance footage on some MTA server. But not because we needed the footage. We already had that. We needed to know the areas of Penn Station the security cameras didn't cover. *Immediately.*

The backpack was missing.

Within an hour, a small army descended upon the station. Over fifty officers from the NYPD were called in to seal the perimeter. It was hardly rush hour at just past four in the morning, but there were going to be news vans for sure. If the busiest transportation facility in the country was about to be evacuated, it didn't matter what the hell time it was. The press would be there.

"Keep 'em outside," said Pritchard. "Them and anyone else. No one gets in."

The press would be told it was a bomb scare. Even if they weren't told, they'd ultimately see the arrival of the bomb squad. There was no hiding it. There was also no reason to. Staying far away from the building was for their safety, and they would have no argument.

But as I heard Pritchard bark that order down the chain of command, I had a feeling he and I were both thinking the same thing. There was definitely an argument coming, only it was going to be among ourselves. I could smell it. As sure as every bomb-sniffing dog that had been brought into the station.

"They're not all Vapor Wakes, are they?" my father asked as soon as a dozen of the dogs were led in.

"No, only half of them are," the chief handler answered. "That's what I figured made sense when I got the call."

My father nodded his approval. Years before Diamond, his cherished vizsla, was one of the world's best hunting dogs, he was one of the world's best bomb sniffers, deployed with US Special Forces in Afghanistan. After my father inherited Diamond, however, training for a majority of bomb dogs changed. This new breed was called Vapor Wake because they were trained to detect scents in motion, as in a moving suitcase in an airport terminal or a suicide bomber weaving through a crowd. In the modern age of terrorism, the change seemed like a necessity.

Tonight was a reminder, though. Embrace the future but never fully let go of the past. We needed the old-school dogs as much as, if not more than, the Vapor Wakes. Wherever that backpack was, it wasn't moving.

"Looks like the same tactics they used before Times Square," said Pritchard, staring at a schematic provided by the MTA's head of security, who introduced himself as Mac. "They methodically find all the blind spots before planting the bombs."

Mac was sporting some serious bedhead and a couple of missed belt loops, but other than that he was on the ball. He'd already highlighted the areas the security cameras in the station didn't cover.

But where there could be one backpack, there could easily be a half dozen. Just like in Times Square. While Pritchard was right about the blind spots, we needed to check every spot there was in Penn Station.

"Where's the bomb squad?" asked Foxx.

"They take longer than the dogs," said the police captain on duty for the Midtown South Precinct. He squinted at Foxx. "I'm sorry. Who are you again?"

"He's with me," said Pritchard, without looking up from the schematics.

"And you two?" the captain asked, pointing at me and my father. "Who are you?"

"They're also with me," said Pritchard, who finally looked up from the schematics to give the captain a death stare. "Any more fucking questions?"

And just like that, the captain suddenly had something else to attend to.

I turned to Elizabeth, fully expecting to see her fighting back a smile. Her new boss certainly had a way with words. *Isn't that right?*

Elizabeth? Wait. Where are you? Where did you—?

She was gone.

CHAPTER 83

ELIZABETH HAD walked away from the group. She turned to me the exact moment I spotted her. It was as if she could tell I was searching for her.

She didn't say anything. She didn't need to. The look in her eyes, even from fifty feet away, told me everything I needed to know.

I turned back to the group. "Hey, guys?"

My father had moved over to Foxx and Pritchard, who were staring at a tablet screen they'd just been given by an IT guy with MTA security that showed a live feed from every security camera in the vicinity. We could now identify every blind spot in the station simply by looking at the tablet and checking if we could see ourselves as we walked.

"What is it?" asked Pritchard.

"This way," I said, pointing.

I led them over to Elizabeth, who was standing in front of a large trash bin, the square kind with a door on one side so the actual bin could be removed to empty it.

Pritchard tilted his head. "What are you looking at, Needham?"

"Basic geometry," said Elizabeth.

It was all she had to say. The bin was a circle within a square, which created four hiding places, all about the size of a backpack. Pritchard glanced down at the tablet before holding it up for all of us.

Does everyone see what I'm not seeing?

We weren't in any of the security camera feeds. We were standing smack-dab in the middle of a blind spot.

"Dog!" yelled Pritchard. "DOG!"

His voice echoed throughout the concourse as the nearest handler came over with his German shepherd. Elizabeth pointed. We all pointed at the garbage bin. The handler never broke stride.

Within seconds, though, he was turning back to us and shaking his head. We could already tell. His dog wasn't picking up anything.

"Maybe it's the metal?" asked Pritchard, referring to the bin. "Is it trapping the scent?"

"Not at all," said the handler, pointing to the gaps along the side panels. "Plenty of places where air is getting through."

"And the smell of the garbage itself?" asked Foxx. "It wouldn't mask the scent?"

The handler thought for a second, which was clearly one second too long for Pritchard. "Dog!" he yelled again. "ALL OF THEM!"

It was shades of Westminster as a parade of canines made its way past the bin. Mostly German shepherds, a few rottweilers, and one Belgian Malinois. I knew for sure what my father was thinking, especially since there was no vizsla in the pack. He was wishing Diamond were here.

We all kept waiting for at least one of the dogs to sit—what they're trained to do when they smell an explosive. If there'd been any C-4, they would've all sat immediately. Of all bomb components, C-4 gives off the strongest scent. After that comes dynamite and Tovex. No dog could ever miss any of those.

But not a single dog sat.

"Screw it," said Pritchard, stepping forward. "Everyone clear the area."

CHAPTER 84

THE DOG handlers were as well trained as their dogs. They immediately pulled back, as told.

Foxx turned on his heel to Pritchard, staring at him sideways. "What do you think you're doing, Evan?"

"I'm seeing if the damn backpack is in there or not," said Pritchard.

"The hell you are. EOD will be here any minute."

It was typical of Foxx that he would choose *explosive ordinance disposal* over *bomb squad*. But it didn't matter either way what Foxx had said. Pritchard didn't care. "I don't feel like waiting," he said.

"I'm sure you don't," said Foxx. "I'm also sure you don't feel like dying."

We listened to them go back and forth a few more times. This wasn't the argument I'd been thinking about with Pritchard. That argument I knew was still coming—the kind of moral dilemma that haunts all law enforcement in the war on terror. The sooner we got to it the better.

Tick-tock, I kept hearing in my head. But not from any backpack.

"There's no bomb," I announced. Apparently not loud enough, though. Everyone was still tuned into the Foxx versus Pritchard jabberfest. I tried again. "THERE'S NO BOMB!"

That did the trick. Everyone turned to me. *Huh?*

"How do you know there's no backpack in there?" asked Pritchard.

"Yeah," said Foxx. "How do you know?"

"I didn't say there was no backpack. I said there's no bomb." That didn't clear anything up. Nor did this. "In fact, I'll bet the backpack is actually in there."

Foxx shook his head in disgust at me. I'd seen it before. Heard it, too. "You give your instincts way too much credit, Reinhart."

"Then you're *really* not going to like this," I said, walking up to the trash bin. "Ten seconds for anyone who feels like running."

The only one who didn't flinch was my father. I was sure he'd already worked it out in his head, probably a split second before I did.

It wasn't just that the dogs didn't smell anything. Or that the guy originally carrying the backpack would somehow think to hit up an ATM before depositing a bomb. It was that he allowed himself to be in front of the station's security cameras without making any attempt to conceal the backpack. That would've been the same foolish mistake those Al-Qaeda wannabe kids made with the Boston Marathon. They were smart enough to wait until the bomb-sniffing dogs had swept the area around the finish line but too stupid to realize there would be footage of them before and after they placed their backpacks.

Only we weren't dealing with kids here.

As sure as Sadira Yavari did reconnaissance at the hotel without using Halo, this guy with the pointed beard never thought anyone would be watching him after the fact. Why? Because this was only a dress rehearsal. A dry run. A way to see if the backpack would stay unnoticed until *all* of the backpacks were planted. Just as they did in Times Square.

"What do you think they'll ultimately use, Dad? A duffel or a carry-on?" I asked. In other words, how would they transport the backpacks with the actual bombs?

"Probably carry-ons," my father answered. "Two wheels, pop-up handles. Standard."

"Any chance they'll make the same mistake the Lashkar-e-Tayyiba did in New Delhi?"

"You mean, at the Karim Hotel?" My father grinned.

Lashkar-e-Tayyiba, the Islamic terrorist group that mainly attacks targets in India, had attempted to blow up the famous Karim Hotel but inexplicably used red suitcases. A half dozen of them, no less. The CIA, working in conjunction with India's Intelligence Bureau, already had been tracking the bombers, but the red suitcases made spotting them almost comically easy.

"So you're saying this cell is probably a little smarter, huh?" I said.

"That depends," replied my father.

"On what?"

"If there's actually a backpack in there with no bomb in it."

I turned to the rest of the group. "Okay, that was more than ten seconds," I said.

No one had moved.

Kneeling down, I slowly opened the side panel of the trash bin.

CHAPTER 85

THERE IT WAS.

The backpack was stuffed in the corner on the same side as the panel's hinges. The zipper was exposed, the pull tab at the top and right in front of me. All I had to do was reach for it.

I turned around again. "Anyone want another ten seconds?" I asked.

Except now there was an extra pair of eyes staring back at me. *"What the hell do you think you're doing?"* he asked.

If I didn't know better, it was Jeremy Renner from *The Hurt Locker*. He was certainly dressed like him with the full blast suit, head to toe. His visor was flipped up over his helmet. Even if the visor had been down and concealing his eyes I was pretty sure I would've still been able to feel his stare.

I was also pretty sure he'd asked a rhetorical question. He knew exactly what I was doing. Or was about to.

The Irish have a saying. A good retreat is better than a bad stand. I simply stood up and backed away.

Renner didn't ask who anyone was. He flat-out didn't care. As far as he was concerned, we all answered to the name Idiot. When Pritchard tried to explain, the guy raised a big padded arm with his palm out front. *Talk to the Kevlar hand...*

"I don't give a rat's ass who you are," he told Pritchard. "I need all of you to vacate the area, and not in ten seconds," he said. "I need you to do it *now*."

Behind him, far behind him, was the rest of the bomb squad, standing in various poses, none of them happy. These guys had enough to deal with—the threat of being blown up, for instance. They certainly didn't need the added headache of an abnormal psychology professor trying to explain himself. Or just as bad, someone else trying to do it for me.

"Of course," said Pritchard, motioning across the concourse. "We'll be over there if you need us."

"Make it way over there," said Renner.

To Pritchard's credit, he let the guy have the last word. Or maybe he was just saving up his ammo.

The argument I knew was coming had arrived.

We'd barely reached the middle of the concourse when Pritchard turned to my father, Foxx, and me as if we were some three-headed CIA monster. "I know what you boys are thinking, and it ain't going to happen," he said. "So get it out of your heads."

I couldn't speak for my father or Foxx. Nor did I need to. I had plenty of my own thoughts on what Pritchard was talking about. I cut right to the chase.

"If you close down this station, you'll kill our best chance of catching them," I said.

I stopped walking, thinking Pritchard would do the same.

"Keep moving," he said instead. "We're not far enough away, in case you're wrong about that backpack."

"I'm not wrong about it. I'm also not wrong about why you have to keep the station open as if nothing had happened here tonight."

"Oh, yeah? And what if we do keep it open and something does happen? Should we gather all the grieving families together at once so you can explain the CIA's ethical theory of utilitarianism or would you prefer simply going funeral to funeral?"

With that, Pritchard stopped. We all stopped. We were in front of a Zaro's Bread Basket. When was the last time I ate?

"If we close down the station, it's game over," I said. "They'll know we're on to them, and they'll just choose another target."

"Then we catch them before they do," said Pritchard.

"Yeah," I shot back, "just like you caught them before Times Square."

Me and my big mouth . . .

CHAPTER 86

I KNEW the moment I said it I'd gone too far. So did Foxx and my father. Before Pritchard had even raised his arm to clock me, they'd stepped in between us. They had to hold him back, and it was definitely a two-man job.

"I apologize," I said. "That was the wrong thing to say."

"You're damn right it was," said Pritchard.

"He has a point, though," said Foxx. "You know this is our best chance. You don't have to like it, but you can't deny it."

"You're the ones in denial," said Pritchard. "You're trying to rationalize the risk. How do you know this station doesn't already have a half dozen other backpacks planted?"

"The same way I know there isn't a bomb in the one in that trash bin," I said.

"We'll see about that," said Pritchard.

"You're right, we will. In the meantime, do you see a sitting dog anywhere?" I asked.

The handlers were working the far side of the concourse, where we were now standing. They'd yet to find anything.

"Even if you're right about the backpack and the station is clean, you're forgetting one thing," said Pritchard.

"What's that?"

"Outside," he said. "The press. All they'll be talking about later today is the bomb scare at Penn Station."

"No, they won't," I said.

"Of course they will. And as soon as that happens, this station will be the safest place in the city. They'll be choosing another target, just as you said."

"Only they won't. Because they're not going to know about the bomb scare," I said.

"Oh, that's right, I forgot," said Pritchard, rolling his eyes. "Terrorists don't watch the news."

"I told you. It won't be on the news. Or in the papers or any-where else." I turned to Elizabeth. *"Isn't that right?"*

It took her a moment. At first she was clearly wondering why the hell I was dragging her into the argument. She looked mor-tified. She was on thin ice with Pritchard as it was.

Then, as if logging into my brain, her eyes suddenly lit up. She and I weren't partners for nothing.

"That's right," said Elizabeth. *"Who knows what really happened in here tonight?"*

CHAPTER 87

PRITCHARD WAS listening. He wasn't sold on anything yet, not by a long shot. But he was listening.

All the more so when I was interrupted even before I could fully pitch the plan. Renner from the bomb squad had called out to us from across the concourse. He was standing in front of the trash bin, holding up the backpack. They were done x-raying it.

"You got lucky," he yelled out. "Some cans of soda and a few magazines. Nothing more."

"Yep, that's what it was. Dumb luck," I muttered under my breath, albeit loud enough for Pritchard to hear me.

He gave me a slight nod. It was as close to an acknowledgment as I was going to get from him. "As you were saying, Reinhart?"

It suddenly occurred to me to let Elizabeth tell him the idea. She'd be the one making the phone call, after all. This was originally her connection, not mine.

"Actually, go ahead," I told her. "You tell him."

Pritchard still wasn't sold on anything when she was done. But he was still listening. You want to change someone's mind? Start with their ears.

"Are you sure he'd even go along with it?" he asked.

"Go along with it? Hell, he'll thank us for it," said Elizabeth.

Pritchard thought for a moment. There was still time to decide on whether to close the station, perhaps as much as an hour, and he knew there was no harm in seeing if we could pull this off.

"All right," he said. "Wake the guy up and sneak him in here as fast as you can."

Elizabeth made the call, although she and I both knew it was highly doubtful we needed to wake the guy up. When people say Manhattan is the city that never sleeps, Allen Grimes and his crime column for the *New York Gazette* is one of the reasons why. The only real question was whether or not he'd be sober when he arrived.

Minutes later, by way of his being picked up and then being told to lie flat in the back of a speeding patrol car, Allen Grimes came walking toward us in the station. As soon as he saw me he shook his head.

"I should've known," he said, wagging a finger.

Elizabeth wisely hadn't mentioned my name when she called him. The last time Grimes and I "worked" together he nearly got killed.

"Glad you could make it," I said.

"Did I have a choice?" Grimes glanced around. "So what's with the bomb scare?"

"What bomb scare?" I said.

"Nice try. I peeked on the way in and saw the bomb squad packing up," he said. "The dogs, too."

Grimes folded his arms, waiting for me to come clean. When I simply stared back at him, saying nothing, he began looking around at each of us. First at Elizabeth. Then at the others— Pritchard, Foxx, my father—none of whom he'd been introduced to. We were all staring back at him, stone-faced.

"Did you ever do any acting?" I asked. "Drama club in high school? Summer stock?"

Grimes broke into a grin. We both knew his entire life was a one-man show. "Okay, but just promise me one thing," he said.

We also both knew he didn't need to spell it out. I knew exactly his one demand. "I promise," I said. "You get to be the hero in the end."

CHAPTER 88

WE STOOD watching from behind a window in a small station master's office on the upper level of Penn Station that acted as a one-way mirror once we turned off the lights.

Grimes was being "escorted" out to the curb, kicking and screaming, by two officers chosen specifically for the task based on having the kind of height and weight typically seen at the NFL Scouting Combine. To say Grimes was getting manhandled would be an understatement. He was being taken out like the trash.

All according to the plan.

"The guy has some lungs on him, huh?" muttered Pritchard.

Grimes was yelling so loudly it didn't matter that we were easily a hundred feet away and behind thick plate glass that had been designed to drown out street noise. We could hear him perfectly. Hell, there were probably people across the Hudson River in New Jersey who could hear him perfectly.

"I know what I saw!" he kept yelling. "I know what I saw!"

Grimes was selling it, and by the looks of everyone gathering around him, people were buying it. His fellow reporters especially.

Sure, they all mostly hated him. But there was also a begrudging respect. Grimes was good at what he did for a living. Very good. He got stories that they didn't, and his writing sold papers. A lot of New Yorkers bought the *Gazette* just for his Grimes on Crimes column. He was known for doing whatever it takes in pursuit of a story, and this seemed to be a perfect example. While the rest of the media accepted their fate—shut out from the station and relegated to the sidelines—Grimes had seemingly figured out a way to sneak in.

So what if he got caught and was now getting his ass kicked out to the curb? He clearly had discovered something.

"Cover-up!" Grimes now yelled. "It's a cover-up!"

As soon as the cops let go of him with a shove, the circle around Grimes quickly tightened so everyone could hear his story. He was no longer screaming; we couldn't hear him. But we didn't have to. He was surely sticking to the script.

It's never the crime. Always the cover-up.

The bomb scare was a ruse. The real story was far less sexy as headlines go but potentially a political house of cards. That's what Grimes was telling them.

The station had been closed down due to an asbestos find in an area that still contained remnants of the original Pennsylvania Station built by McKim, Mead, and White. The reason for the made-up bomb scare, Grimes would speculate, was because of the legal liability the city would face given how many people had been exposed to the asbestos on a daily basis. Someone very high up, perhaps as high as the mayor himself, had clearly given the order to see if the asbestos could be removed in secret.

"Do you really think they'll buy it?" asked Pritchard as we kept watching.

"That's the best part," I answered. "They *can't* buy it."

"I thought you told me—"

"I said they'd believe him. To buy it and, more importantly, for their editors to run it they'll need a second source. That's something they'll spend all day trying to get and never will. Without that second source, there's no story."

"I'll believe that when I see it," said Pritchard. "Or rather, don't see it."

Tick-tock. "We don't have that long," I said.

"He's right," said Foxx. He motioned out the window. "If Grimes pulls this off, nothing's changed. This station is still the next target, and we need to be ready."

I glanced at my watch. In less than an hour, the first commuter trains of the morning would be arriving, assuming the station was open.

Pritchard stared me straight in the eyes. I stared right back.

"It's now or never," I said.

CHAPTER 89

IT WAS NOW.

After Pritchard briefed the director of Homeland Security, immediate around-the-clock surveillance of Penn Station began. A horde of undercover NYPD and FBI was assembled faster than a New York minute.

At some point the soda cans and magazines in every backpack were going to be replaced by actual bombs. The trick was not only to spot each one but also to tail each courier back to the proverbial nest. This was about more than stopping an attack and apprehending some terrorists. This was about eliminating an entire cell, and with any luck, all the cells attached to the Mudir.

And the Mudir himself.

In the eyes of each and every civilian making their way through Penn Station, there couldn't be anything out of the ordinary. Everyone assigned needed to blend in seamlessly as commuters or employees of the station.

Backing them up would be additional surveillance personnel manning the cameras all around the station, including the new cameras that had been hastily installed to cover the blind spots. Nothing could be left to chance.

We controlled everything except the timetable.

"I have to admit, I was pretty tempted," Foxx said to me in the back seat of his bulletproof Ford Expedition as the sun began to rise over the East River. His driver, a young operative he called Briggs, was taking my father and me to the safe house in Brooklyn. Foxx needed to file a report immediately for the Agency's director, and I needed to finally catch up on some sleep. While my father could crash at Elizabeth's apartment if need be, the safe house was really my only option. Thanks to the Mudir, I was homeless and a marked man.

"What do you mean by *tempted*?" I asked.

Foxx chuckled. "Letting Pritchard take a swing at you."

"You'd like that, wouldn't you?"

"You do have a way of pissing people off, Reinhart."

"You say that like it's a bad thing," I said.

Foxx closed his eyes for a catnap, and in the silence that ensued, my thoughts turned to Tracy and Annabelle, and the mess I'd made of our family. I couldn't help it. As if things couldn't get any worse, they now didn't have an apartment to come home to—assuming they were ever coming home again. The idea that I had to call Tracy and warn him to stay away from the city was the ultimate irony. All I wanted was for him and Annabelle to come back. Even if Tracy wanted to, they couldn't.

Twenty minutes later, in the basement of the Agency's safe house, I set the alarm on my phone for four hours later. Turned out, I didn't need to.

After only two hours of sleep, Foxx woke me up.

"We have a problem," he said.

CHAPTER 90

FOXX DIDN'T bury the lede. He knew no other way.

"Your dinner with Sadira Yavari tonight? It's off," he said.

My first question would've been why were it not for what Foxx was holding in his hand.

"What's in the file?" I asked.

"Nothing I can show you," he answered.

I figured as much. I've always admired the almost comical paradox of US intelligence agencies. Everything has a code name and nothing is as it seems except for one thing, the files themselves. If something is top secret, it literally says so with a bright red stamp.

Just like on the file Foxx was holding.

"Okay. So what *can* you share?" I asked, rubbing my eyes. He'd obviously woken me up to tell me more than just the dinner was off. *At least you better have, Foxx…*

"Sadira Yavari has killed before," he said, "and the other victim was also a nuclear physicist."

I had to let that sink in for a few seconds. The implications. What it could mean. The questions it gave rise to.

"Was he also Iranian?" I asked.

"Yes."

"Was he tied to the Iranian nuclear program?"

"Yes."

"Was he the same as Darvish? A double agent?"

Foxx suddenly got hard of hearing. I didn't ask him where the hit on this other nuclear physicist had taken place, but that's the question he answered. "The guy was on holiday in London, three years ago," he said.

"Holiday?"

"Just go with it."

Foxx was more than walking the line on what he could and couldn't tell me. He was tap-dancing. "How about you just nod at the appropriate moment," I said.

Any agency can get burned once with a double agent, the CIA included. Getting burned twice takes a special set of circumstances, if not an extraordinary level of incompetence. Unless, of course, it was a separate intelligence agency getting burned. Foxx had made a point of mentioning London.

"This other nuclear physicist," I said. "He was doubling for MI6, wasn't he?" Foxx hesitated for a moment until deciding that, yes, this was the appropriate moment for him to do as I'd asked. He nodded.

"Just like Darvish, dead in a hotel room," he said. "A little different twist, though. Autoerotic asphyxia. He was found with a belt around his neck strapped to a clothes rod in the closet."

"Again, it was made to look as if he were alone," I said.

"Yes. An accidental death."

Only it couldn't be. The Brits had to know something was

amiss. Or maybe it was Foxx who just now helped them put it together. Otherwise, Foxx and I wouldn't be having this conversation.

"Did they know it was Yavari?" I asked.

"Not until about an hour ago," he said. "She didn't use Halo, just a good old-fashioned wig and glasses. They had surveillance footage of her in the hotel lobby with the guy. Back then, when it happened, she was thought to be Israeli. The decision was made to look the other way. They let it be."

The reason they thought Yavari was Israeli was because the only other real possibility was that she was CIA, and if she were, Langley would've at least given MI6 a heads-up, if not outright involved them.

"So you gave MI6 a photo of Yavari," I said.

"From her NYU bio, yes."

"And because she didn't use Halo they were able to confirm it was her."

"The match was 89 percent."

For facial recognition systems, especially given that she was wearing a disguise, that was as good as a lock.

My date with Sadira Yavari had always been a gamble, but the stakes had now changed. It wasn't just me who'd be taking a risk. There was now interagency intel involved. Documentation. *A file.* Stamped TOP SECRET, no less.

In other words, Foxx now had a lot on the line as well. Namely his job. That was for one reason and one reason only.

"Go ahead and say it," I told him.

He said it. "You're a civilian, Reinhart. You're just a goddamn civilian."

As long as that was the case, Foxx couldn't allow me to engage with Yavari. It didn't matter who or what I was in the past. No, as far as the Agency was concerned, my days as an operative entitled me to a pension and not much else. That was then; this is now. I was nothing more than a civilian. *A goddamn civilian.*

"But what if I wasn't?" I asked.

Foxx shot me a look. "Are you saying what I think you're saying?"

BOOK FIVE

STARING DOWN THE DEVIL

CHAPTER 91

"ARE YOU ready to kill?" asked the Mudir.

He'd assembled his team again in the basement of the mosque in lower Manhattan. He had news for them. The timetable had changed. The attack would now be sooner. There would be more attacks to come as well.

As always, the Mudir had chosen his words very carefully. The idea that there were more missions was essential to preparing his men. Generals fought wars; soldiers fought battles. The Mudir had read that in a book about Patton while studying at Princeton. Battles—and, ultimately, wars—are won by those soldiers who believe they are invincible.

The Mudir was a voracious reader. He'd read Darwin and understood the nature of survival. Adapt or die.

He'd read Adam Smith, too. He knew that one of the great ironies about Islamic terrorism aimed against the West was how beholden it was to the tenets of capitalism. When the demand for suicide bombers exceeds the supply, changes have to be made. And no matter how much ISIS recruited, no matter how vigilant its efforts, the demand was always destined to exceed the supply. Especially in America.

Martyrs were truly a dying breed.

Once more, the Mudir took the men through their positions in the train station, emphasizing their exit strategy as much as everything else they needed to remember. The only other change beyond the timing was that he himself would be joining them in the massacre. The Mudir wanted even more casualties. Even more suffering.

For this final meeting before the attack, he had arrived early, before any of the twelve. He had placed burner phones on each of their chairs assembled around his table. He'd also turned off the air-conditioning. Heat and sweat force the mind to focus.

The Mudir hadn't read that anywhere. He had lived it. Especially during his years in Islamabad. In the capital of Pakistan was where the Mudir had learned to focus. It was there that he had tried to get a message to Bin Laden. Bin Laden's trusted courier had been compromised, his pseudonym surrendered to an interrogator at Guantánamo Bay.

But the Mudir's message was never received. Two weeks later, Bin Laden was dead.

"Does everyone understand what their job is?" he asked the twelve, their faces shiny and dripping. The basement now felt like a sauna, but the men knew better than to wipe the sweat from their brows. Their only focus was the Mudir.

Above them were imams who had no idea what the Mudir was planning. They were so busy preaching peace and assimilation. They didn't see the West as a threat.

They were fools, thought the Mudir.

He dismissed the twelve with a final reminder to keep their burner phones close at hand. The call would come within the next day or two, but no later. They needed to be ready, weapons and ammunition packed.

"There can be no mistakes. There can be no loose ends," he warned them.

Again, the Mudir had chosen his words very carefully. The difference this time was the audience. It now included himself. There was something he needed to do, a piece of unfinished business. This was his own reminder.

There can be no mistakes. There can be no loose ends.

The Mudir had a very important appointment to keep.

CHAPTER 92

THE CROWDED restaurant was intentional. She wouldn't feel threatened. Not at first.

He arrived early and asked for a table in the corner but still with a view of the door. The Mudir wanted to see her when she arrived. He was sure he'd know in an instant, the first moment their eyes met, whether or not she could do what he needed her to do.

Only he was wrong. When she arrived, that first instant he saw her, he still didn't know.

All Sadira Yavari gave the Mudir was a look of recognition. Nothing more. She held his gaze the entire time she walked toward him and sat down, but again her eyes revealed nothing.

On second thought, it occurred to the Mudir, maybe this was exactly what he wanted. Could she be even more like him than he'd realized? Capable of giving nothing away, no signal or tip of the hand, until it was too late?

Sun Tzu. The element of surprise will always be your greatest weapon. The Mudir kept a copy of *The Art of War* by his bedside. He'd read it more times than he had the Koran.

"Do you know why you're here?" he asked.

She shook her head. "Should I?"

The Mudir waited a few seconds, continuing to stare. *No, you shouldn't know. Otherwise, I've been careless, and that's one thing I never am.* He folded his arms on the table, leaning forward. "How do you know Dr. Dylan Reinhart?"

Sadira's eyes collapsed to a squint as she put it together. Her. Reinhart. Outside the courthouse. "You've been following me?"

"For good reason, apparently."

"We both had jury duty," she said.

"No. You had jury duty. What he had was the need to meet you."

"Why?"

"You tell me," he said. "He's CIA. Or at least he used to be."

The Mudir studied Sadira in that moment more intensely than he'd ever studied anyone. It would've been near impossible for her to fake not knowing that Reinhart had been CIA. There were simply too many muscles around the eyes and mouth to control all at once.

No, this was pure reflex. Her expression. The way her head jolted back. He was convinced she didn't know.

"Are you sure?" she asked.

"Positive."

"Is that why you were following me? Because you knew Reinhart would try to make contact?"

"I was following you because I still don't completely trust you."

"There isn't a person on this planet that I trust completely," said Sadira. "I suspect you're no different."

She was right, and the Mudir let her know it with a smile. "Let's just say I don't trust you enough for what you need to do," he said.

"Which is what?"

"You need to kill Dylan Reinhart," said the Mudir.

"I'm only a courier," said Sadira.

"Not anymore you're not. Not after you take care of Reinhart and then help me with what comes next."

"What's that?" she asked. "What comes next?"

"After Reinhart," he said. He would tell her then. "Then I will know I can trust you enough."

"If you want him dead so badly, why is he still alive?"

"Because I made the mistake of trusting someone else to do the job. Now Reinhart is expecting me. But he won't be expecting you."

Sadira leaned back in her chair as if she were considering her options. But she'd already made up her mind when the Mudir told her about Reinhart's CIA past. "Okay," she said. "How soon do you need it done?"

CHAPTER 93

SADIRA HAD asked for my number outside the courthouse when we agreed on dinner. She was going to text me the restaurant and what time. There was a new Italian place on the Upper West Side she wanted to try but didn't know if we could get a reservation. "Stay tuned" were her last words to me.

By that afternoon, they were still her last words to me.

I hadn't heard from her. No text. No call. Nothing. *What changed? Did she figure something out? Is she on to me?*

I was about to call Julian to get her number when there was a knock at the door. Foxx was back for another visit.

He'd had his driver take me back into Manhattan that morning to one of the shell offices in midtown that fronted as a CIA station. After the New York headquarters at 7 World Trade Center was destroyed on 9/11, the Agency had opted to utilize multiple locations around the city. The conference room I was hanging out in belonged to a supposed international shipping company.

There was no file in Foxx's hand this time, but his expression left little mystery as to why he'd returned. He had more news, and it wasn't good.

"She's leaving the country," he announced. Sadira Yavari was skipping town.

"When?" I asked.

"Sunday. Turkish Air to Tehran via Istanbul."

"I'm gonna guess it's not a round-trip ticket."

Foxx shook his head. "One way. Non-refundable," he said. "The kicker? She only just booked it today."

"What about her recent calls?" I asked.

"Nothing to Iran, and no one we haven't already checked out," he said.

Foxx hadn't told me, but I'd assumed the Agency had been monitoring Sadira's phone records, both landline and cell, if not listening to the calls themselves. Of course, by law, the CIA is prohibited from collecting foreign intelligence based on the domestic activities of US citizens. Then again, the *C* has never stood for compliance.

I had one more question. "Did you put a body on her?"

There was a chance Foxx had tailed her without telling me, and there was also a chance that he still didn't want to. But he didn't hesitate.

"I was sort of counting on you for that," he said, "starting with your dinner tonight." He glanced at his watch. He knew Sadira hadn't been in touch with me. "But so much for that."

I grabbed my phone, checking for any new texts or voicemails even though I had my ringer on. Still nothing from her. It was time to face reality.

"Okay, I'm on board," I said. "Let's bring her in."

This time, Foxx hesitated. "We're not going to do that," he said finally.

I thought that's what you originally wanted, I would've said if I didn't already know what he meant. Sometimes it's all in the tone.

The Agency wasn't going to bring her in. No. They were going to take her down.

Permanently.

CHAPTER 94

"WAS IT your call?" I asked.

"It was my recommendation. Ultimately it was the director's call," he said.

"Same difference."

Foxx shrugged. "Maybe."

More like definitely. The director of the CIA is like the owner of an NFL football team. He might have final say on operations, but if he's smart, he defers to the coach, the one closest to the action, when it comes to play calling. Especially with a guy like Foxx. Foxx was basically the Bill Belichick of section chiefs. If he recommended having Sadira Yavari meet with an "unfortunate accident," then that's what was going to happen.

"Why, though?" I asked.

"You know why," said Foxx. "She's a case that can't go to trial."

"What about what she knows? *Who* she knows?"

"That's why I okayed your dinner with her."

"You can still bring her in," I said.

"Not after she stood you up."

That was Foxx's way of saying she would be less than cooperative under questioning. It was also a nod to the perverse irony of every piece of anti-torture legislation, especially in a world where the vast majority of information gathered at Guantánamo Bay and other dark sites around the globe turns out not to be actionable.

Bluntly put, killing terrorism suspects is far less of a headache for the CIA than waterboarding them.

I thought about trying to talk Foxx out of the decision. Plead my case. The reason I didn't was because all I could hear was Tracy's voice in my head. This wasn't Tracy, the idealist. This was the law school grad, the realist. My case was a lost cause. Without Sadira, there was nothing to argue. My lead witness had gone missing.

Ping!

Foxx and I turned to my phone, sitting on the conference room table. It could've been anyone texting me, but there was something about the way the sound broke the silence of the room—the timing of it—that had us both thinking one thing. It was her.

So sorry! Been crazy busy. Hope we're still on for 2night. Gramercy Tavern @ 8?

I read it once, then twice. Foxx did the same.

"Something doesn't feel right," he said.

He had a point. Her taking so long to follow up with me set off every alarm in my head. But as my thumbs hovered above the screen, all I wanted to do was type back and confirm.

I'd signed the contract with Foxx. I'd even borrowed a pen from him to do it. I was now an agent of the CIA. For all intents and purposes, an operative again. What Foxx was waiting for, though—what he needed to see and hear—was that I'd truly bought in. *Does Dylan Reinhart have that same killer instinct?*

There was only one way to convince him. "If I have to, I'll take her down myself," I said.

Foxx nodded as I texted Sadira and confirmed our dinner.

"Welcome back, Reinhart," he said.

CHAPTER 95

I WANTED to be the first to arrive at Gramercy Tavern. I showed up twenty minutes early. Twenty minutes wasn't early enough.

Sadira was sitting at the end of the bar, a book in one hand and a glass of red in the other. Only ten feet away, I froze as soon as I saw her. She would've easily noticed me, standing like a statue, were it not for the fact that the bar was three rows deep with people. Even if it weren't for the crowd, she seemed pretty engrossed in the book. I stared.

Not at her, though. If you ever want to fully appreciate how attractive someone is, simply watch the people around them. The furtive looks. The up-and-down glances. And that was just the other *women* in the room. The men were far less subtle. Many of them were flat-out gawking at Sadira.

"What are you reading?" I asked, walking up to her. Right away I noticed that she'd held a chair open for me with her purse and a wrap. Or maybe it was just a way to prevent some of those male gawkers from hitting on her.

"Well, hi there," she said, greeting me with a kiss on the cheek. Her scent was lavender. She turned the book so I could see the cover. It was a biography of René Descartes.

"Ah, yes. A little light reading while waiting for a table," I joked. There was nothing light about Descartes.

"Actually, I was thinking we could eat right here, if you don't mind." She put down the book and scooped up her purse and wrap from the vacant chair, hanging both on a hook by her knees. "I always find that the drinks come faster when you sit at the bar."

"I like where your head is at," I said, taking a seat. "Faster drinks can be a good thing, especially on a first date."

"Is that what this is?" she asked. For a second, she looked a bit put off by my calling it that, but I saw right through her. She was messing with me.

"Nice try, Professor," I said.

"Good for you," she replied, flashing a smile. "You don't fool easily."

"Not as easily as most."

Sadira motioned to the nearest bartender. "No more grape juice," she announced, pushing away her glass of wine. "I think it's time we take it up a notch."

I almost felt like one of the guys gawking at her as she ordered a couple of Blanton's for us, her just assuming that I would enjoy a bourbon. She was beautiful, smart, funny, and liked to throw a few back. A killer combination, you might say.

"No luck with a reservation at that new Italian you mentioned, huh?" I asked. "Not that I don't love this restaurant. Who doesn't?"

Gramercy Tavern was the very definition of iconic in Manhattan. It was synonymous with the city. The warm wood and earth-tone décor. The impeccable service. And, most of all, the food itself. Ninety-nine percent of all restaurants will open and shut down without ever winning a James Beard award. Gramercy Tavern has won nine.

"To be perfectly honest, I didn't even try that other place," she said. "With what's happened this week, the bombings, I suddenly realized the last thing I wanted was new and different."

"Taking comfort from the tried and true," I said as our bourbons were placed in front of us. "I get it."

"I feel ashamed to admit this, but I can't even watch coverage of it anymore. The funerals. Learning the life stories of all the victims. That's awful of me to say, isn't it?"

"Hardly," I replied. "I remember reading this article after 9/11. People who weren't from here couldn't fathom how quickly New Yorkers seemed to go about their lives again as if we were somehow less affected than the rest of the country." I motioned to the rest of the bar, everyone enjoying themselves. "But this? This is as human as it gets. When surrounded by death is when we most need to feel alive."

Sadira grabbed her bourbon, raising it toward me. "To feeling alive," she said. "To *being* alive."

"Yes," I said, clinking her glass. "Here's to being alive."

CHAPTER 96

SADIRA LED the charge. We were on our third round of bourbons before we even cracked the menus. By the time our entrées landed in front of us, we were five deep and heading for six. If Sadira was trying to kill me, she'd chosen a method I didn't see coming. Alcohol poisoning.

"Okay, so I have to ask," I said as the bartender cleared our dinner plates. Sea bass for her, the duck for me. "Did you google me after we met at the courthouse?"

She gave me a sheepish grin. "Why would I ever do that? I know who you are."

"That's a non-denial denial."

Sadira shot up straight on her chair, raising her right hand as if being sworn in. "I solemnly swear that I did not google Professor Dylan Reinhart before coming here tonight," she said. "How's that?"

"Better."

"Besides, I prefer to do my research in person."

"So what have you learned so far?" I asked.

"That the only person who did any googling after the court-house was you."

"Guilty as charged."

"And what did you discover?" she asked. "What does the in-ternet have to say about Sadira Yavari?"

"That you're a beloved philosophy professor at NYU and have been published numerous times," I said.

"Ah, but only one of us has written a bestseller involving ser-ial killers."

"Not that you've read it."

"What makes you so sure?"

"That's another non-denial denial," I said.

"I actually did read your book."

"Really? What did you think?"

"It was a little dry in places." She held a straight face before breaking into a laugh. "No, I'm kidding. I thought it was fasci-nating."

"For example?"

"Are you fishing for more compliments or trying to make sure I really read it?"

"Both."

"It's how you dispel the traditional notion of abnormal psy-chology, especially with most serial killers," she said. "The way they rationalize their behavior is that they don't rationalize at all. They're doing what they think is absolutely necessary. It's what they believe in to their very core."

"I thought you might say that. I imagine it dovetails with what you teach regarding epistemology."

"Yes," she said. "The role that justified belief plays in society, which these days is really about only one thing."

"Religion," I said.

She nodded. "And let's face it, only one religion in particular."

"Which happens to be your religion, I'm assuming."

She nodded again. "On the plus side, my being a Shia all but guarantees me tenure. A real live Muslim delving into the minds of terrorists for the so-called liberal elites? It's my gig as long as I want it."

"Cynicism *and* sarcasm, all in the same breath," I said. "You really are a New Yorker."

"Farther away from home than Dorothy, that's for sure."

"How often do you get back?" I asked.

"To Iran? It's been a while," she said. I waited to see if she would add anything about her scheduled flight to Tehran. She didn't. The pause turned awkward. "Was I supposed to keep talking?"

"No, sorry." *Think quickly, Dylan.* "That was me debating my next question in my head. I fear it might be a bit sexist."

"Ah," she said with a nod. "You want to know how I'm not married or even have a boyfriend."

"I'd never survive those liberal elites at NYU, would I?"

"Yale is hardly turning out many William F. Buckleys these days."

Good point. "Does that mean you will or won't answer the question, though?" I asked.

Sadira motioned to the bartender as she threw back the last of bourbon number six. "It means we now order one more round and then maybe, just maybe, we'll explore the subject of my sex life."

She placed a hand on my forearm for a brief moment, the sort of flirty gesture that lasts just long enough to blur the line between innocent and suggestive. Her beauty was her edge, and it was enough to make most any man lose his.

Of course, most men would've probably thought that was just a pretty necklace she had on.

Why are you using Halo, Sadira?

What are your plans for me?

CHAPTER 97

"LET'S GET out of here," I said.

I pulled out four hundred dollars in cash—welcome to Manhattan—and placed it under my empty bourbon glass.

"Thank you," said Sadira. "I've got the next one."

The next one? Irony.

I knew she couldn't say no to leaving with me. Besides, she wasn't about to kill me in front of all these witnesses. I'd probably taken the words right out of her mouth. *Let's get out of here.*

But where?

I held the door for her as we walked out of the restaurant. She never turned back to me once she hit the sidewalk. Instead, she made a beeline for the curb and a waiting taxi. You can always bank on one outside Gramercy Tavern.

"Jane Street, corner of Hudson," she told the driver.

We were going to her place in the West Village. Only I couldn't let on that I knew where she lived. "Is that your—"

"Yes, my place," she said. She turned to me, holding my stare. "I don't usually do this."

"Neither do I."

"That's good. Perfect," she said. "We can both not usually do this together."

I would've laughed at that line were it not for her suddenly leaning in to kiss me. She pressed her lips softly against mine, keeping them there for only a second, as if to tease me for what was to come. There was barely any time for me to kiss her back, and that was the point. I might have been the one to suggest getting out of here, but I was hardly in charge. She was.

That's good. Perfect. You keep thinking that, Sadira.

We rode in silence the rest of the way. After we passed Union Square, she reached over and held my hand. Only when we arrived at her place did she let go.

"At least let me pay for the cab," she said, taking out her wallet.

I would've bet the cost of dinner and then some that Sadira didn't live in a doorman building. That would've defeated the purpose of her wearing Halo. No, I fully expected to be walking into a brownstone. The surprise, though, was that it wasn't merely a brownstone. It was *her* brownstone. All of it.

"Just how much are they paying you at NYU?" I joked as she led me into the foyer. It opened into a massive living room beyond which was a kitchen that would've made Martha Stewart jealous. And this was only the first floor.

"Family money," she said without any hesitation.

It was possible. Or maybe it was just a straight-up lie. The point was, I couldn't tell. Not with anything about her. Was any of this real? I didn't think so, but damn, she was convincing in every way.

From the get-go I'd felt there was more to Sadira than met the eye, and nothing about that had changed. Until now.

Now it was more than a feeling. I was sure of it. One way or another, I was about to learn the truth.

As Sadira put down her purse and wrap, there was no doubt that she had me exactly where she wanted me. This was home-field advantage.

"Let's go upstairs," she said.

CHAPTER 98

SOME THINGS you simply don't need to be taught. For example, if someone wants to kill you, the last thing you should do is turn your back on her.

I extended my arm toward her staircase. "After you," I said.

We walked up to the second floor and down a short hallway to what was clearly her bedroom. The sheer size of it, for starters. Also the books piled up on her nightstand, most with dog-eared pages. This was definitely where she slept. Among other things.

Sadira slipped out of her heels and dimmed the lights. *What exactly are we about to do?*

It was hard enough playing it straight, so to speak, back in the cab when she kissed me. This was shaping up to be a little more than kissing. Or was that simply what she wanted me to think?

In poker, sometimes you wait for the bluff. Other times, you have to draw it out. "Come here," I whispered to her.

Never mind that the last time I'd been with a woman was my freshman year in college. It was a *Let's just make sure I'm gay* encounter and, as I barely recall, it involved about the same amount of alcohol as the bourbon merry-go-round back at Gramercy Tavern.

"Who, me?" Sadira playfully whispered back.

"Yes, you," I said. "All of you."

She slowly walked toward me, her eyes trained on mine. I could swear she never blinked. Then, only inches away, she spun around. "Can you unzip me?" she asked, pushing her long brown hair to the side.

I reached for the zipper, pulling it halfway down her back. "How about the necklace?" I asked. "Do you need help with that?"

"No, that's okay. I've got it," she said. "It's a little tricky."

You're telling me . . .

I waited for her to turn around to face me again. Instead, she headed for her walk-in closet. "I'll be right back," she said over her shoulder.

Sadira closed the door behind her. And like that, she was gone. So much for not letting her out of my sight. I couldn't see her or anything she was doing.

Of course, the same was true with me.

A minute later, she reappeared. She was standing in the doorway of her closet, wearing a plush white robe and seemingly nothing else. Gone was her Halo necklace.

"Take your clothes off," she said.

Only there was nothing sexy about it. There wasn't even a smile. At least, I'm pretty sure there wasn't.

I was too busy staring at the gun pointed at me.

CHAPTER 99

"I'M DEAD serious," she said, tightening the grip on a Russian-made Makarov with a suppressor attached. "Strip."

She'd hidden the gun in her closet. Now she wanted to make sure I wasn't hiding one as well.

"What the hell's going on?" I asked.

Nothing more, apparently, until I started undressing. Sadira just stood there with the gun aimed at my chest.

Okay, we'll do it your way. For now...

I removed my sport coat, tossing it on the bed behind me before motioning to my ribs. *Look, see? No holster.*

Next came my dress shirt. I intentionally fumbled with the buttons.

"Faster," she said.

I ignored her. "I know who you are. I know who you've killed," I said. "And I'm not the only one who knows."

"You think you have me all figured out, huh?"

"What more is there to tell?"

"Maybe nothing," she said. "You're right, I've killed before. I'll kill again if I have to." She jabbed the gun toward my shirt. *"Faster!"*

I stopped fumbling with the buttons. The shirt was off within seconds. *Look, see? I'm not wearing a wire...*

My belt came next, followed by my pants. Or so it appeared. The zipper came down only halfway. Ever so slightly I shifted my feet, widening my stance.

This had to look natural. The pants had to fall just right.

"That was a nice necklace you had on tonight," I said. "How did you get your hands on Halo?"

She smirked. "I have no idea what you're talking about."

"Not a clue, right?"

"Nope."

"What about my phone?" I asked.

"Your phone?"

"Yeah," I said. "The one sending a live feed to the van parked outside across the street."

That's all it took. I motioned to her dresser and my phone propped up against a jewelry box, the camera lens angled directly on her. Never mind that the camera wasn't even turned on or, for that matter, no surveillance van was parked across the street. All I needed was a moment's distraction.

The second her eyes locked on my phone, I let go of my pants. As fast as gravity, I lunged down to my Glock strapped to the side of my right calf. By the time she was looking back at me again, we were now both staring down the wrong end of a gun.

"I don't know about you," I said, "but this is some pretty funky foreplay."

CHAPTER 100

"DROP IT!" she said.

"That's not how this works. We either both lower the gun or we don't."

"Great, you first."

She clearly had limited exposure to Mexican standoffs. "Why do you want to kill me?" I asked.

"I don't," she said.

"All evidence to the contrary."

"I just wanted to make sure."

"Of what?"

"That *you* weren't going to kill me," she said.

"Why would I do that?"

"Because you don't know the truth."

"You mean, *now* that I have a gun pointed at you? That's when you want to tell me the truth?"

Sadira glanced at my phone propped up against her jewelry box. "That's not really recording, is it?"

"Nope."

All the same, she sidestepped over and dropped my phone in her top drawer. Not once did she take her eyes off me.

"Yes, I killed the MIT professor," she said. "Jahan Darvish."

"That's not bad for starters," I said. "Well, actually it was pretty bad for him. And the way you did it, too. Very kinky but very clever. What else you got for me?"

Sadira squinted, trying to read between the lines. "There was another nuclear physicist. Also an Iranian," she said.

"What about the third one?"

I was baiting her for intel I didn't have. She didn't bite, though. Or, more likely, she was actually telling the truth.

"There is no third one," she said. "Only those two. And both for the same reason. If you lower your gun, I'll explain."

"Again, not how it works," I said. "Ladies first."

"On one condition. You need to believe I don't want to kill you."

I suddenly did believe that. Still, I couldn't afford to be wrong. "I've never *wanted* to kill anyone, Sadira. But that hasn't stopped me when it was necessary."

"Me neither," she said. And with that, she knelt and placed her gun on the floor.

I met her halfway. I lowered my arm. But I wasn't quite ready to let go of my gun. "Okay, I'm listening," I said.

"Darvish? The other nuclear physicist in London? They weren't double agents."

"Who said they were?"

"MI6, for one. Your former employer, for another."

"How would you know that about me?" I asked. Except I already had more than a hunch.

"Ask me first about Darvish," she said. "What he was really doing."

"In other words, the reason why you killed him."

If she could explain that, I didn't need to ask about MI6's informant in London.

"Darvish was doing what my father wouldn't do," she said. "Develop Iran's first nuclear weapon."

"Who's your father?"

"You mean, who *was* my father. Farukh Rostami."

Okay, that I didn't see coming.

Rostami had once been Iran's top nuclear physicist. "You're kidding me," I said.

"Do I look like I'm kidding? When my father refused the Shah, the Shah had him killed."

"It wasn't the Shah," I said. "It was the Mossad. The Israelis only claimed it was the Iranian government so they could deny it."

"No. The Israelis were telling the truth," she said. "It wasn't the Mossad."

It's not every day that an Iranian takes sides with Israel. In fact, it's barely any day. "How do you know?" I asked.

"Because my father warned me."

"He could've been wrong. The Israelis were convinced he was leading the Iranian nuclear program. They desperately wanted him dead."

"Not as desperately as his own government," she said. "That so-called evidence Iran presented at the UN, the pictures that implicated the Israelis? They were fake."

"Back to my original question," I said. *"How do you know?"*

"The same way I know that Darvish was feeding the CIA bad information while working ever closer to developing the bomb. His allegiance was always to his homeland." She paused. "Just like mine would appear to be."

It wasn't just the pause. It was the words and the way she said them. *Just like mine would appear to be.*

Sadira Yavari was telling me that she was a double agent of her own. Quite literally. She answered to Iranian intelligence, but she was working on her own, for her own reasons.

"For how long?" I asked. *How long had she been working against her own government?*

"Since they first came to me after my father's murder to convince me it was the Mossad," she said. "Exactly as my father warned me they would. He said the counterintelligence arm would then try to recruit me."

"And as far as they know, they succeeded."

"Exactly," she said. "I'm an Iranian spy."

Only she wasn't. Sadira Yavari was an Iranian spy who had gone rogue. Seriously, dangerously, altruistically, full-on Machiavellianly rogue.

I knew there was more to her than met the eye . . .

CHAPTER 101

SADIRA WALKED me through it all. Her recruitment. How she seduced a member of the Iranian government and stole files from him revealing the work of Darvish and the other nuclear physicist she tracked down in London. Even the origin of her fake last name, which she used to become a US citizen. Yavari's had been an ice cream shop in Tehran that her father used to take her to as a child.

The Iranian government had tried to leverage her presumed rage against Israel and the West, and she had them convinced they'd pulled it off. But she had her own motive. A deeply personal one. In the name of her father, Sadira had become a one-woman army to prevent what he feared most. That Iran would possess a nuclear weapon.

"So what now?" I asked.

"Now I kill you," she said.

"Excuse me?"

"Remember how you asked how I knew you'd worked for the CIA?"

"Yes. Who told you?"

"The same person who told me I had to kill you tonight."

The one and only. "The Mudir," I said.

"I figured he was on your radar. You're certainly on his."

"If you've had access to him, then—"

"I didn't know in advance about Times Square, if that's what you're thinking."

It was. "So you're not in one of his cells?"

"No. I volunteered to be a courier for him after the attack. I told my handler with the Ministry of Intelligence that I wanted to help with the next one."

"In order to stop it."

"Yes," she said. "To stop it and to stop the Mudir. I want him dead. But first we need to convince him that you're dead."

"How do you propose we do that?"

"I have an idea," she answered. "But first, do you think maybe you could pull up your pants?"

I glanced down. Smiled. "Why? You don't like my boxers?"

After pulling up my pants, I walked over to Sadira and picked up her gun. She and I had come a long way in a very short period of time. But believing her was one thing. Trusting her was another. We weren't there yet.

The way she described it, neither was the Mudir.

She'd been a courier, delivering fake passports to him that had been generated back in Iran. Now he wanted her help with an impending attack.

But he needed to know first if he could trust her. Especially when he discovered that I'd orchestrated my jury duty introduction to her at the courthouse. It was obviously a major red flag for him. It was also, though, an opportunity. He wanted me dead, but there was a risk in coming after me. He knew I'd be waiting for him. But I wouldn't necessarily suspect Sadira. If she could eliminate me, she could be trusted. Two birds with one stone-cold killer in heels.

"What do you know about this next attack?" I asked.

"Not much," she said. "My getting any details is contingent on your being dead. The Mudir did let one thing slip, though. Something about it being safer to fly that day."

"It's Penn Station," I said. "That's the target."

I suddenly didn't have to wonder if everything Sadira had told me was true. Her reaction, the look of horror that crossed her face, could never have been faked.

"The fact that you know," she said. "It means you're already prepared to stop it before it happens, right?"

"That's the plan," I said. "Now tell me about yours. How do we convince the Mudir that I'm dead?"

"He's waiting on the proof tonight, and he won't trust a photo."

"In other words, we need to record something."

"Exactly. He needs to actually see you die."

She walked over to her chest of drawers. As soon as she pulled it out I was shaking my head. "You're joking, right?"

Sadira tossed me the bulletproof vest. "It's Kevlar with titanium plates," she said. "The best money can buy."

"Yeah, and 100 percent worthless if you miss."

"I won't miss," she assured me. "Just try not to move around too much for the second shot."

"The *second* shot?"

"You want it to be convincing, don't you?"

CHAPTER 102

DEAD MAN TALKING.

Hours later, I was telling Foxx everything. He listened to me without saying a word as he ate an egg-white omelet between sips of coffee. Even if his mouth hadn't been otherwise occupied I suspected he still wouldn't have interrupted. He wanted to digest every last detail of my date with Sadira before asking any questions. The floor was mine. Or, more specifically, the end booth of a twenty-four-hour Greek diner a few blocks away from the safe house. At 5:00 a.m., the place was nearly empty. There were more photos of Anthony Quinn on the wall than there were people. Foxx and only Foxx could hear what I was saying.

"Tell me that last part again," he said when I finally finished.

"You mean, my waiting with Sadira after we made the recording?"

"No, I got that. You wanted to be on hand if the Mudir contacted her right away."

Only the Mudir hadn't. I waited with Sadira most of the

night, but he never responded to the video of her killing me. Was he buying it? We still didn't know. But there was no reason he shouldn't have. Sadira was right: the second shot sold it — almost as much as I did. If there was an Oscar for faking one's death, I was a shoo-in. All done in one take, no less. For what we did, there were definitely no reshoots.

Meanwhile, I still didn't know what Foxx wanted to hear again. "You mean, the hotel part?" I asked.

"Nope. Got that, too," he said. "If she killed you in her house, the Mudir would have to ask how she disposed of your body. The hotel meant she could walk. The do-not-disturb sign would buy her at least two days before your body was even discovered."

Foxx had heard everything I'd told him, even filling in some of the things I hadn't. "Okay, I give up," I said. "What are you not hearing?"

He pushed away what remained of his omelet and crossed his forearms on the table, leaning in. Apparently what he had the hardest time believing wasn't that I allowed Sadira Yavari to shoot me at point-blank range. Twice, no less.

"I was waiting for your explanation," he said through a clenched jaw. "How the hell is Sadira not in our custody right now?"

"Our custody?"

"She killed two informants, one of them being ours."

"They were hardly informants," I pointed out.

"According to her."

"Yes, just like the fact that she's Farukh Rostami's daughter. That was according to her, too," I said. "And it checked out."

I had Julian confirm it before I met up with Foxx. No hacking required. Just a good old-fashioned LexisNexis search. An Iranian magazine had done a profile of Rostami when Sadira was in her late teens. The piece mentioned her and her sister.

"So one thing true about her makes everything true?" he asked.

"I think you're losing the forest for the trees here," I said.

"And I think maybe you've lost your mind. Or maybe just your edge after you left the Agency. You *volunteered* that we know about Penn Station."

"Only after she *shared* what the Mudir had said—his remark about it being safer to fly."

"She could've been feeling you out for what we might know. She could be playing you."

"Or, again, she could be telling the truth. And, for the record, you're the one who got played by Jahan Darvish."

"All the more reason why you should've brought her in."

"She wasn't about to do that."

"That was your instinct, huh?"

That wasn't a question. It was a jab. But I hardly minded it. I understood where Foxx was coming from. Knowing in my gut that Sadira was telling the truth provided only so much comfort to a guy like him.

Or his boss. After he and I were done, he'd have to brief the CIA director. He would have his own questions. Topping the list? *Why the hell don't we have Sadira Yavari in custody?*

"Since you still have your doubts," I said, "let's go talk to her together. If we spot anyone still watching her, I'll keep out of sight."

Foxx immediately signaled for the check.

His driver, Briggs, took us into Manhattan and over to the West Village, pulling up to Sadira's townhouse near the corner of Hudson and Jane.

Before we even reached the first brick of her front steps, though, I knew something was wrong.

CHAPTER 103

"SHE'S GOT company," I said, pointing.

There was no daylight between the door and the latch jamb, but I could tell the door was propped open ever so slightly. It wasn't by accident. Whoever was inside with her wasn't invited.

Foxx drew his Glock even faster than I did mine. I knew what he was thinking. It was the Mudir. The Mudir wouldn't have been invited, let alone welcome given the circumstances.

Only this didn't feel like him.

Foxx raised three fingers, then two, then one. *Now!*

He went high and I went low as we peeled around, moving inside. Scan left, scan right, scan back again.

There was no movement, but the place had been turned upside down. Closets had been riffled through, coats and jackets strewn all over the floor. Cabinets and credenzas, their drawers yanked out and emptied. As we made our way around the first floor, there were all the telltale signs of a burglary. Except the more it looked like one, the more I was convinced it wasn't.

Whoever did this was looking for something of value, all right. Just not anything having to do with money.

Foxx pointed to the stairs. *Up we go...*

The only thing we could hear was our own footsteps as we reached the second floor. Room after room looked the same. It was as if Mötley Crüe had spent the night. Even the mattresses had been flipped.

I took the lead at the end of the hall as we approached Sadira's bedroom. I knew the layout all too well. Step and listen, step and listen. There still wasn't a sound to be heard. It was dead quiet.

Then, suddenly, it wasn't.

The noise came from behind us. Downstairs. Panicked running, heading toward the front door. We'd missed a room, a closet, a basement—something on the first floor. *Damn! How? Never mind...*

Go!

We sprinted down the hallway, the next sounds coming at us from out on the street. We couldn't see it unfold, but we could piece it together as we flew down the stairs.

Foxx's driver, Briggs, had blasted his horn before jumping out from behind the wheel. He yelled, "Freeze," but got fired on instead. One shot, immediately followed by one of his own. Just one. Maybe that's all he needed. Or maybe we were too late.

Foxx and I bolted out of Sadira's townhouse. Briggs was lying in the street and grabbing his right shoulder, blood seeping through his fingers. Foxx went to him while I spun around, trying to catch a glimpse of the gunman.

"There!" said Briggs, his hand dripping red as he pointed down the street.

There were two of them, about thirty yards away. One had just swung open the large back door of a van; the other was loading their cargo. Even in the murky light of dawn, I could see her bound and gagged. Sadira was writhing, trying to break free. The only good news was that she was still alive.

I traded glances with Foxx. *What do we do?* Only I already knew. I was back in the fold.

"C'mon," said Foxx, helping Briggs to his feet. That's what we do. We take care of our own first. "We need to get you to Raborn."

Raborn was the underground emergency medical center run by the Agency for operatives or others who fit the bill due to special circumstances. Namely, the need to avoid police reports or the press.

"Hell, no," said Briggs. He glanced at his shoulder and shrugged the other one. "I'll call an Uber."

An Uber? He was serious. Kids these days.

He grabbed his cell, wincing as he reached into his pocket. He was in pain, but he was going to live. Sadira was an entirely different story.

Up ahead, the van pulled away from the curb. We watched as it sped off down Hudson Street, tires screaming. Sadira was literally disappearing before our eyes.

Foxx and I turned to each other again.

Say no more.

CHAPTER 104

FOXX TOOK the wheel. I grabbed shotgun.

The van had a big head start, but it was still in our sights. On an open road, we'd close the gap in no time. Except this was lower Manhattan. With its narrow streets and cross traffic, we might as well have been miles apart.

Not for long, said Foxx's right foot.

He jammed on the gas, throwing the Expedition into Drive so fast I was nearly knocked out by the headrest.

"Who are they?" I asked. Nothing about this fit the Mudir.

"Hell if I know," said Foxx as he swerved around a taxi, nearly clipping a parked Jeep. "But apparently she's worth more to them alive."

The van turned onto Bethune, a long block south of us, heading now on a straight shot west, but they would soon run out of real estate. Up ahead of them was the West Side Highway.

I turned to Foxx. "Are you thinking what I'm thinking?"

There was only one way for that van to go when it hit the highway. North.

We hadn't lost them, but we weren't gaining on them either.

"Do it," I said.

Foxx jerked the wheel to the right as he made the turn onto narrow West 12th going the wrong way. We hurtled over the uneven pavers and squeezed at full speed past the few oncoming cars, their horns blaring at us.

"Hold on," he said calmly. He was dialed in.

Yanking the wheel as he pumped the brakes, Foxx threw us into the next turn. We were somewhere between drifting and fishtailing around the corner onto the West Side Highway, now heading north. With three lanes to choose from, Foxx gunned it. I leaned over, glancing at the speedometer. Even while weaving through the morning traffic, we were soon pushing eighty, eighty-five, ninety—

"There!" I said, pointing. "There they are."

The van was on the highway almost right in front of us. We'd narrowed the gap. Now we had to close it.

Shit! We had company.

A cruiser parked up ahead hit its siren. We blew by them, Foxx not even giving them so much as a glance. He was fixed on the van, nothing else.

"We need them to take the bridge exit," he said. The highway would soon become my familiar Henry Hudson Parkway, well before the bridge.

"Why?"

Foxx didn't answer. The entrance to the George Washington Bridge was a few miles north, a peel off to the right.

"*Why?*" I asked again.

We were going a hundred and ten and closing fast on the van. Behind us, the cruiser was chasing us both. Foxx leaned forward as if squeezing every last horsepower from the engine. He still hadn't answered me.

"Wake up Julian," he said instead, handing me his sat phone. When I hesitated, it knocked the calm right out of him. He yelled. "Now!"

Another time, another car chase, I maybe would've held my ground. But there had to be a reason Foxx was keeping me in the dark, and only when he was good and ready would he let me in on it.

I called Julian, putting him on speaker. The guy never slept.

There were no hellos, no setup beyond Foxx stating that I was with him. He cut straight to what he wanted. "I need you to hack someone," he said, "and you've got only two minutes."

"Who is it?" asked Julian.

"Me," said Foxx.

CHAPTER 105

AS HE slashed back and forth between lanes, staying right on the tail of the van, Foxx told Julian his password. Of course, if it were only that easy. He wasn't exactly asking Julian to hack his Book of the Month Club account.

Even without Foxx saying it, I knew the server he was referring to. So did Julian. As the CIA's New York section chief, Foxx had access to the Agency's tactics and operations protocol, including standing counterterrorism measures—most of them having been created and implemented after 9/11.

But the Agency took extraordinary measures to ensure that Foxx was actually Foxx. In addition to a password, he needed a simultaneous fingerprint and voice match. With Foxx on the phone, the voice wouldn't be a problem for Julian. The challenge was the fingerprint.

"Your iPhone, Dylan. Give me the serial number. It's listed in the settings," said Julian.

I quickly found it, reading it off to him. He then asked for my IMEI number. As soon as he did, I knew what he was trying to do.

"I'm resetting my Touch ID," I said. "Tell us when you're ready."

The FBI was limited by privacy laws, not to mention the likes of Apple, when it came to unlocking the phones of suspects. The CIA, however, really hates to be told no. By anybody.

Julian was setting up my iPhone's Touch ID to take Foxx's fingerprint. "Okay, ready," he said.

I held out my phone to Foxx, trying to steady my hand as he whipped the steering wheel left and right. He was mimicking the van's every lane change, zigzagging between cars with only inches to spare. "Thumbprint," I said.

His thumb was on my phone before I'd even finished saying *print*.

"Got it," said Julian. "I'm in."

He now had access. The question was why.

"Homeland Security, DOT override," said Foxx.

I knew DOT was the Department of Transportation, but I still had no idea what Foxx was planning. Julian did, though.

"You want the exit ramp or before the bridge?" he asked.

"Exit ramp," said Foxx.

"The timing has to be perfect," said Julian.

"Tell me something I don't know," said Foxx.

"Or maybe tell me what the hell is going on!" I said.

Pushing over one twenty, Foxx slid in right behind the back bumper of the van in the middle lane. Like a NASCAR driver, he was drafting them. The exit for the GW Bridge was only hundreds of yards away.

For the first time, he glanced over at me. "You ever try to back out of a rental car lot?"

Before I could ask what on earth he was talking about, he

swerved into the left lane and pulled up alongside the van. We weren't just close. We were touching. Metal grinding against metal, as Foxx began forcing the van toward the exit.

"Tell me when," came Julian's voice.

"Not yet," said Foxx. "Not yet . . ."

The van tried to straighten out, but Foxx wouldn't let it. Like a battering ram, he kept pounding the side panels, riding it harder and harder off the highway. The van had two choices, crash into the median or take the exit.

"Now!" yelled Foxx. "NOW!"

CHAPTER 106

IT HAPPENED so fast. It was as if I hadn't seen it. I had to piece everything together in reverse.

You ever try to back out of a rental car lot?

The tires of the van exploded, all four of them, strips and chunks of rubber flying through the air. Followed by the van itself.

I whipped my head around as Foxx skidded to a stop in the breakdown lane by the exit. That really just happened, didn't it?

Right before the tires ruptured, right before the van crossed into the exit lanes, the row of spikes had popped up from the pavement like magic. Only it wasn't magic. It was real.

And it was why Foxx didn't want to tell me—until it was done.

The van landed with a horrific thud on its side, crashing into the far guardrail, before flipping over on its roof. What remained of all four tires were still spinning amid a cloud of smoke and dust as we started running toward it, guns drawn.

The cruiser, bringing up the distant rear the whole way, nearly hit us as it slammed on its brakes. The two cops had barely opened their doors when Foxx tossed one of them his ID.

"Two ambulances," he said. "Call it in."

I was pissed at Foxx. Not because he might have just gotten Sadira killed or that he'd kept me in the dark leading up to it. No. I was pissed because I knew he was right and there was nothing I could do about it. He did what had to be done.

Whoever wanted Sadira wasn't one of us. And if she wasn't in our hands, she couldn't be in anyone else's. It was as simple—and cutthroat—as that.

"I've got the driver," I told Foxx.

He nodded, sidestepping to the passenger side of the van as I hung by the taillight for a moment in case he needed backup. "Unconscious. Pulse, though," he called out.

I edged up to the driver's side door, what remained of it. The van had landed so hard upside down, the door was half collapsed against the road. Bending down, I could still see behind the wheel. Only there was nothing to see.

"Over here!" came a voice behind me.

It was one of the cops from the cruiser. Before I even turned around I knew what he'd found. The driver.

Foxx stayed with the van as I went over to look. The driver had been thrown. More like launched. He was on his back. No pulse. No face either. The impact and his sliding across the asphalt rendered the front of him a bloody mess of ripped flesh and exposed bone.

"Jesus," muttered the second cop, joining us. He quickly looked away while gagging.

"I need your cuffs," I told the first cop.

I hustled over to Foxx. He'd just pulled out the guy from the passenger seat and was giving him a quick frisk as he lay on the ground. He was now conscious, moaning. I could barely hear him, though, over the backdrop of honking horns. We'd turned the Henry Hudson Parkway into a parking lot. Right in time for rush hour.

"You recognize him?" asked Foxx, taking the cuffs.

"Not a clue," I said.

"What about his partner?"

"His own mother couldn't recognize him now."

"Any ID on him?"

But by then I was already on the move again.

There had been no thinking when Foxx and I first approached the van. Only training. First things first, eliminate any threat.

With one guy wearing cuffs and the other about to be fitted with a toe tag, I could think of only one thing now. The back of the van.

Sadira.

What would I find when I opened the door?

CHAPTER 107

IF I could open the door.

It was jammed shut, the hinges buckled and wedged against the frame. I tucked my gun and pulled as hard as I could on the handle, but nothing was budging.

Sadira had been bound and gagged when they loaded her into the van. All I wanted was some sort of signal from her. Any sound would do. I pounded my fist against the door. *"Sadira? Can you hear me?"*

Only I couldn't even hear myself. The car horns had been joined by a chorus of sirens off in the distance.

"What?" I said to Foxx.

He was still alongside the van. I couldn't make out what he'd said. He tried for a second time, yelling. *"We need to get out of here!"*

I heard him. Sort of. The words went in my ears, except they didn't register. I was only focused on Sadira.

Again, I pounded while calling her name. Was she conscious?

Was she even alive? I pressed my ear hard against the door, desperately trying to listen. I was about to keep pounding when suddenly I heard it. Her. Ever so faintly. The muffled sound of her trying to say something through whatever they'd used to gag her. It was one word. "Help."

I called out to Foxx. Maybe the two of us pulling could open the door. "Get over here!"

"No, you come here!" he said.

I stepped around to the side of the van to see him lifting the guy he'd pulled out. Foxx was putting him over his shoulder. He didn't have to explain why.

The smoke billowing up had turned into flames. The engine was on fire.

Cars only explode in the movies if the flames reach the gas tank, and it's near empty. Fire plus fuel plus compressed air equals boom.

"Go ahead, get him out of here," I said. "Get yourself out of here."

"Where's Sadira?" he asked.

"Still inside."

Foxx looked at me. It was all in his eyes. *Your call, Reinhart.* Only we both knew what I was going to do.

"I'll come back to help," he said.

"Don't you dare."

I ducked down and climbed through the passenger side window, the flames now shooting through the air vents. I didn't know what I had, seconds or minutes. The fire could rocket into the fuel line at any moment.

I called out Sadira's name yet again, the back of the van so thick with smoke I could barely see.

But I heard her. Even with her mouth gagged she was able to make enough noise.

Everything was upside down. I was climbing on my knees along the ceiling of the van when I found her lying against the far side, one leg clearly broken. The other was bleeding from a huge gash above the thigh. She could barely move, her hands still tied behind her back.

I pulled the gag off her mouth. They'd used a ripped bedsheet. She was about to say something, only there was no time for conversation. I cut her off. "We've got to get you out of here," I said.

There was no going back the way I came. The front of the van was now completely engulfed in flames. The blaze was coming right for us.

I turned to the back door. The same door I couldn't open. It was the only escape.

Reaching for my Glock, the dos and don'ts of point-blank firing echoed in my head. Aim completely straight to avoid ricochets. That's what you do.

But don't shoot what can't be shot.

That meant the hinges. Too much metal. Too thick. No, the best chance was targeting the latch where the door locked. If I could knock that out, my feet could do the rest.

Shielding Sadira, I emptied my clip in a half circle on the edge of the door. All I could do now was kick as hard as I could.

The fire was scorching my back as I angled myself as if doing the leg press at the gym. The way the door had buckled, I needed to aim low.

C'mon, feet, don't fail me now…

CHAPTER 108

I WAS just about to kick when I heard the sound. Even before I saw what it was, I knew *who* it was.

Foxx was back. With a crowbar. He'd jammed it in below one of the hinges, prying open the door with one massive pull. There was a reason he was a gym rat, and it wasn't so he could look good in front of a mirror.

"What took you so long?" I said.

"Maybe because you almost shot me?"

So much for the buddy-movie banter. The flames had over-taken the back of the van. Foxx made a beeline for Sadira, helping me lift her into my arms. She was in so much pain, and my running with her was only going to make it worse. But there was no choice. There was no time.

In that same buddy movie, the van would've exploded at the very moment we were out of harm's way. Only this wasn't the movies.

No, the moment I reached the ambulance came and went without any explosion. I gently placed Sadira on a waiting gurney, two EMTs immediately taking over.

I turned to Foxx, with a nod back at the van about a hundred feet away. I even cracked a smile. "Whatta ya know, the gas tank was full."

BOOM!

The van exploded into a fireball, the sky above it filling with a massive cloud of thick black smoke and flames. Score one for the movies.

I watched for a moment, briefly entertaining the thought of Foxx arriving with that crowbar a little later than he had. When I turned back to the ambulance, the EMTs were lifting the gurney to load Sadira. I figured I'd ride with her to the hospital. She was in bad shape, but she'd live to tell about it—something I was banking on. Who were those two guys who had taken her? And why?

Foxx had already returned to the one he'd pulled from the van. The guy's body language said it all. Dressed in jeans and a black sweatshirt, he wasn't planning on saying anything. Another EMT was tending to him as the two cops from our car chase stood guard. Not that the guy was going anywhere. Forget making a run for it. He couldn't even walk.

"Dylan."

Sadira's voice was so weak, but even with all the commotion around us I could somehow hear her. The way she said my name, it was as if she were whispering in my ear.

I climbed into the back of the ambulance. Neither EMT asked me who I was or gave me a hard time about my wanting to tag along. They'd seen me run out of the van with Sadira. If that didn't buy me some slack, nothing would.

"What is it?" I asked her.

I suddenly remembered she'd tried to tell me something in the van.

"I was...about..." She paused, swallowed. She was already out of breath. "I was about to...call you."

I could see how much it hurt for her to talk. The least I could do was fill in the gaps as best I could.

"You mean, before those guys broke into your apartment," I said. "You heard from the Mudir?"

She nodded. "Rent a car...meet the Mudir near the train..."

"Yes, the train station." The fact that he wanted her to rent a car most likely meant one thing. "He wants you to be a driver," I said. But when? "Before or after the attack?"

"After," she said.

This was good. Knowing where the Mudir wanted to rendezvous with her would be crucial if we stopped the attack without catching him.

"So what street around Penn Station?" I asked. "He must have told you an address, right?"

I waited for her to nod. Instead, she shook her head. "No," she said. It was the whole point of what she wanted to tell me. "It's not Penn Station."

CHAPTER 109

I JUMPED out of the ambulance and sprinted over to Foxx while yelling his name.

"What the hell is it?" he asked.

"It's Grand Central."

"What is?"

"The attack," I said. *"The target is Grand Central Station."*

Foxx let that sink in for a moment. The implications. The logistics. The sudden loss of our leverage. "Holy shit."

"It's worse than that," I said, looking at my watch. It was about twenty of eight. The Mudir had told Sadira to be in a white rental car at 46th Street and Third Avenue, right near the station, at 8:30 sharp. "Whatever's going down, it's all about to happen in less than an hour."

Foxx had to make calls. Immediately. But right in front of us was a guy who clearly knew things about Sadira. Did he also know about the attack?

With his cropped blond hair, he looked more like a Hitler

youth than a Middle Eastern terrorist, but that hardly meant there was no connection to the Mudir. He could've been Russian. He could've been anybody. What we couldn't afford was his being useless. We had to get him talking. Fast.

He'd been staring at me since the moment I came over. His head was cocked, his eyes narrowed to a squint. I knew that look. It meant the same in any country and any language. The guy was sizing me up, trying to figure out if I was baiting him by what I told Foxx. *I'm clever, but not that clever, dude . . .*

Foxx reached for his cell while giving me the nod. The plan was to divide and conquer. He'd get the word to Evan Pritchard, who was camped at Penn Station, and I'd go to work on our mystery man here.

As soon as Foxx stepped away, I stared at the EMT, who thankfully was fluent in subtext and knew enough to step away as well. The two cops standing guard would still do their jobs, but their stares made it clear they would neither remember nor repeat anything they were about to hear.

All right, du verdammtes Arschloch, *let's you and I have a chat . . .*

I knelt down, getting eye to eye with him. The key was letting him think he was in control. I'd ask the questions he'd never answer. He'd get into a rhythm. He'd get comfortable. Then, maybe, he'd get sloppy.

I asked him who he was, who he worked for, what he wanted with Sadira. Everything he expected. Then, out of nowhere, something he didn't.

"Where'd you get the tattoo?"

The beautiful, crazy, unpredictable thing about the human mind is that . . . well, it has a mind of its own. No matter how much you try to control your own thoughts and actions, there's simply no accounting for the occasional impulse or reflex.

It was the quickest of glances, a flinch of the eyeballs toward his right forearm. After his body got banged up in the van, his mind had no problem believing there was a tear in his black sweatshirt, exposing his skin.

Only there wasn't a tear. The sweatshirt was still intact.

I yanked back the sleeve. He went to stop me, but both cops stopped him even faster. On the inside of his forearm, just above the wrist, was a Jerusalem cross. It wasn't exactly a résumé, but it gave me something to work with. I suddenly had a hunch.

"You a fan of military history? Of course you are," I said, sounding as if I were back in my classroom. "You probably know that the Prince of Wales got that same tattoo while visiting the Holy Land in the early 1860s. It was right after your great British field marshal Earl Roberts reportedly said that every officer in the British Army should be tattooed with his regimental crest." I paused to make sure I had his undivided attention. "But you're more than British Army these days. So for the last time, who are you?"

And for the first time, he spoke. *"Who are you?"* he asked. But it wasn't a question. It was the answer to mine.

My hunch had made no sense and all the sense in the world, all at once. Foxx had only just shared the intel on Sadira with his counterparts at Vauxhall Cross, but our strongest of allies had already succumbed to their distrust. Rank nationalism may play well on our own soil, but it's a shit show overseas.

Foxx's driver, Briggs, was still alive because the men who took Sadira had no intention of killing him. They were skilled enough to stop him in his tracks without putting him in his grave. It may be a new world with new rules, but MI6 would never be in the business of killing CIA operatives. No matter who was in the White House.

Foxx returned. "He doesn't know anything, does he?"

I shook my head. "Nope."

"He's MI6, isn't he?"

"How did you know?"

"I didn't. But his director just called ours to apologize." Foxx turned to the agent and promptly made a very special relationship between his fist and the guy's jaw. "Apology not accepted," said Foxx, before walking away.

I followed him back to the Expedition for the drive to Grand Central. On the way, I had a call of my own to make.

Elizabeth picked up immediately. She'd been waiting on me.

CHAPTER 110

"BUCKLE UP, REINHART..."

It was another car chase. Only now against time.

Siren blaring, lights flashing, Foxx gunned it back toward midtown. He was driving the wrong way in the breakdown lane, aiming for the next exit south, while sideswiping any cars edging out to get a peek at what was making them late to work. At over a hundred miles an hour, we were easily the most effective PSA on record for *Stay in your lane*.

Along the way to Grand Central, we got the next best thing to direct updates from Pritchard. Foxx had a dedicated scanner with the live command channel that Pritchard was using to coordinate FBI, FBI SWAT, NYPD, and his own JTTF field unit. If we were lucky, they'd arrive before the attack. Unlucky? Any other scenario.

We were lucky. At least, so far. Grand Central was quiet. Well, as quiet as can be for a place that had thousands of rush-hour commuters funneling through it at that very moment.

Pritchard now had everyone in place. Within twenty minutes of getting the call from Foxx, and after a mad scramble from

Penn Station to Grand Central, it was now a waiting game. Those in uniform, mainly snipers, were in the ceiling and other hidden positions. Everyone undercover blended in throughout both concourses.

"Where the hell do you think you're going?" asked Foxx after he pulled up next to a hydrant at 42nd and Madison, a block west of Grand Central. I was halfway out to the curb before he'd even cut the engine.

"What do you mean?" I asked.

Only I knew exactly what he meant. The Mudir knew what I looked like. At this point, my image was probably seared into his brain. We couldn't risk having him see me. It could blow everything.

"Unless you've got a fake mustache and a wig stuffed in your pocket, you're staying right here," said Foxx.

"I can at least get closer."

"To do what?"

Good point. Even more so after he pointed to his scanner. At least I'd be able to hear everything by staying in the car.

"You win," I said, though I probably shouldn't have, at least not so quickly. Since when did I ever acquiesce to Foxx?

"I'm serious, Reinhart," he said, swinging his legs out to the street. He turned back to look me square in the eyes before shutting the door behind him. *Stay in the damn car.*

I pointed to the scanner. "I've got the play-by-play right here," I said. "No reason to go anywhere."

Foxx took off down 42nd Street, heading over to Grand Central. For the next ten minutes I sat twiddling my thumbs. It felt like an eternity. Pritchard had called for radio silence as everyone waited to see what the Mudir had planned. There was nothing to listen to. Everything was quiet.

Too quiet.

CHAPTER 111

"SHOTS FIRED!"

It wasn't Pritchard's voice, and by the sound of the actual shots, they weren't anywhere near him either. But they were definitely coming from somewhere inside the terminal. I could hear the echo.

"Move!"

That was Pritchard's voice for sure, and the second he said it, the echo gave way to a firestorm of shooting and screaming. People were literally running for their lives.

There was no way I was staying put.

I bolted out of my seat and sprinted toward the station without any game plan except getting there. Easier said than done.

Before I could even spot the doors to the station along 42nd Street, I could feel the rumbling beneath my feet. It was like an earthquake, the sidewalk shifting and sliding from the mass exodus. Faster, I told myself. *Run faster!*

Reaching the corner across from the station, I saw the pandemonium spilling out into the street. Every face had the same look. The wide eyes, the open mouths. Sheer terror. There was still gunfire behind them. Nothing was over.

Like a salmon with a death wish, I made my way against the current. There was no clear path; people were coming at me in droves.

Finally I reached the doors to the station, immediately cutting sideways to hug the wall. I was still fifty yards from the main concourse, but I could move quicker, free of the stampede. Amid the pounding of feet and continued screams, I didn't realize right away that the shooting had actually stopped.

The main concourse was up ahead and to the right, along with the ramp to the lower level. I hadn't seen any casualties, no lifeless bodies among the crowd, but I couldn't help the awful thought that everything was about to change when I made the turn. It was all I could see in my mind.

Maybe that's why I didn't spot him at first, even as he walked right past me only twenty feet away.

That should've been the first red flag. Everyone around him was running. He was *walking*.

And his face. There was no terror. Instead, an almost eerie calmness.

Still, to anyone else who might have noticed, he was surely just another commuter. He was wearing a suit and tie. Wing tips. He'd been on his way to work, like everyone else, when suddenly all hell broke loose.

But he was no commuter. He was the mastermind behind all this.

"Freeze!" I yelled at the top of my lungs.

The Mudir stopped. Everyone around him stopped. All heads turned. Then, just as fast, they all saw my gun and ran again, scrambling for cover. Everyone except the Mudir. He simply stared at me. And smiled.

"Back from the dead. I should've known," he said. "Never trust a woman."

I came off the wall, my Glock leading the way. He began to reach inside his suit jacket, his hand sliding across his chest and dipping beneath the lapel.

"Don't even think about it!" I barked.

His hand stopped, his fingers still tucked inside the jacket. He remained smiling, and all I wanted to do was wipe that grin off his face by slamming him headfirst to the ground.

"Take your hand off the gun and let me see both hands in the air," I said.

But there was something he wanted me to see first.

Something I didn't see coming.

CHAPTER 112

THE MUDIR shifted his dark eyes, his gaze moving behind me. He knew I wouldn't turn to look, so he did the next best thing to let me know what I was missing. What *he* was missing.

I was fixated on that hand still tucked in his jacket, but it was the other hand by his side that caught my eye for a split second, or about as long as it took for him to tuck his fingers into his palm as if he were holding something.

He was dressed as a commuter.

I now turned to look. I looked because I knew. He wasn't reaching for his gun. That hand inside his suit jacket was on a different kind of trigger. He'd been carrying a briefcase. It was sitting in the middle of the corridor, just where he'd placed it before seeing me.

I whipped my head back around to the Mudir, his smile now even wider. There was no time for me to get off a shot. No time to yell *Bomb!*

The explosion knocked me off my feet, the force of the blast throwing me through the air until I landed with a smack on the ground. I was burned and bloodied, but I was still alive. I'd even managed to hold on to my gun.

Staggering to my feet, I immediately turned to look for him. It was as if he knew the exact range of the blast, and he'd been standing on the edge of it. Now he wasn't standing anywhere. He was gone.

I ran back toward the doors, back outside. The sidewalk had cleared. Explosions have a way of doing that. I turned left. Nothing. I turned right. Nothing. What do they teach children to do before crossing the street?

I turned to my left again. He seemed to appear out of nowhere. The Mudir was standing ten yards away from me. He was no longer smiling. He was aiming. His suit jacket was pulled back, the empty holster hanging off his shoulder, and his MP-443 was aimed directly at my chest.

I raised my gun, but I knew I was outdrawn. He had me. All I could see was him squeezing the trigger. It was as if the entire world had collapsed around me. My world. And it was coming crashing down.

I felt the piercing, sharp pain in my ribs, the air leaving my lungs in an instant. I fell to the pavement, unable to brace my fall. It hurt like hell. My head was spinning, but even more so from the confusion.

What just happened?

The answer quickly peeled off me, rolling onto his side to squeeze off two rounds at the Mudir.

I hadn't been shot. I'd been tackled.

The Prophet. Eli. He'd hit my body like a linebacker, flying through the air and knocking me down in the nick of time.

I remembered. *You'll see me again,* the Prophet had said.

We both looked down the street at the Mudir running away. He was turning a corner.

"I think I clipped him," said Eli. "Don't know how bad, but—" He stopped and shook his head. "Ah, shit."

I looked back at him, following his eyeline down to his side. The hole in his shirt was an inch above the belt, the blood oozing out and spreading across his stomach. He'd taken the bullet for me. If I didn't stop the bleeding, he was going to die. But I also had to warn Elizabeth.

If I didn't, she was going to die, too.

CHAPTER 113

THE MUDIR was bleeding badly from his left shoulder, but he knew he would survive. He was sure of it. Martyrs die in an instant or they don't die at all.

He'd lost a battle today, but Sun Tzu didn't write *The Art of Battle*. This war was far from over. There were more attacks to come. Bigger attacks. Followed by the biggest one imaginable, the day to end all days in this godforsaken city.

As he continued running, weaving his way through the mayhem around the station, the Mudir looked back to see if he was being chased, but there was no sign of that son of a bitch Reinhart or whoever it was who saved the professor's life.

Ha! Some professor. You can put a tweed jacket on a CIA operative, but it will never change who they really are.

There wasn't a doubt in the Mudir's mind as he kept running that he would have his revenge and kill them both. Reinhart and his savior. All in due time.

What couldn't wait, the person who had to be taken care of

immediately, was the woman who'd betrayed him. How would he solve the problem of Sadira?

The Mudir knew exactly how.

Assuming he could find her. After her faking Reinhart's death, would she still be waiting for him in the white rental car as he instructed? There was a chance. A good chance, even. It all depended on her end game. How long did she want him to think she could be trusted?

The Mudir hadn't told her where she'd be taking him directly after the attack, his one errand before leaving the city to lie low, but he had to wonder if she'd somehow found out about his shipment from Viktor Alexandrov. It had finally arrived. Maybe her plan was to get her hands on the package before he did.

The Mudir could only hope.

It's so much easier to kill someone in cold blood when they have the courtesy of being where you want them to be.

Up ahead, at the corner of 46th Street and Third Avenue, the Mudir spotted a white Ford Taurus. He stopped running, craning his neck to peer through the horde of people that had filled the street.

Finally a path cleared for a moment, long enough for him to see her waiting behind the wheel. No, *arguing* behind the wheel. There was a cop standing by her door, angrily gesturing for her to move the car. Pulling down hard on a baseball cap, she was shaking her head vehemently, telling him no.

It was perfect. She was distracted.

They usually are before they die.

CHAPTER 114

ELIZABETH COULDN'T figure out what to do with her left hand. She kept meticulously adjusting the sideview mirror with it, then the rearview mirror, followed by tugging on the brim of her baseball cap. Lather, rinse, repeat. Over and over she kept doing this, funneling her nervous energy into keeping her left hand busy.

All the while her right hand sat perfectly still in her lap, her fingers wrapped tightly on the grip of her G19.

She knew this was a good plan. Dylan didn't have to sell her on it. She could play the role of Sadira Yavari. She could set the trap.

As her eyes darted between the mirrors in the white Ford Taurus, keeping a vigilant lookout for the Mudir amid all the pandemonium outside on the street, Elizabeth couldn't help playing the scene in her head. What she would do when he got into the car. What she would even say.

He would climb into the back seat, so distracted by the foiled attack and his rushing to reach his getaway car that he wouldn't even look at Sadira. *Drive!* he would bark at her.

That's when Elizabeth would turn back to him with the G19 in her right hand leading the way. *Think again, asshole!*

If everything went according to plan, that's how it would happen. She was sure of it. Right up until she heard her phone ring. Even before she looked to see that it was Dylan calling, she knew there was a problem.

"Get out of the car!" he said.

"Why?" she asked.

"Just do it," he said. "He knows I'm alive."

Dylan didn't need to connect the dots for her. If the Mudir knew he was alive, he would also know that Sadira couldn't be trusted.

The Mudir kills anyone he doesn't trust.

"Is he alone?" asked Elizabeth.

The question threw Dylan. She could tell in his voice, there was no time for a debate. All he wanted to hear was the sound of her getting out of the damn car and away from the Mudir.

"Yes. He's alone," said Dylan. "But—"

"If I get out of the car, we lose him."

"And if you don't . . ." He paused, frustrated. "I don't want to lose you, Lizzie."

Dylan never called her that. Not ever. She'd even told him that she didn't like *Lizzie* soon after they first met. But right then, in that moment, she really liked the sound of it.

But not enough to get out of the car.

"We can't let this guy get away," she said, before doing something she'd never done to Dylan. Not ever. She hung up on him.

Elizabeth checked the mirrors again. Now they really had to be perfect. There could be no blind spots. She needed to see everywhere around the car.

Oh, crap. You've got to be kidding me...

The cop was standing in front of the car, angrily waving at her to move it along. Yeah, he was just doing his job. Yeah, he needed to free up the street for ambulances and fellow law enforcement. But his timing couldn't be any worse.

Every second Elizabeth looked at him was a second she wasn't watching for the Mudir. Quickly, she flashed the cop her badge. Maybe it was the glare of the morning sun against the windshield. He kept waving at her. Now he was coming over to her window.

Again, she flashed her badge. Again, it was as if he couldn't see it. He was motioning for her to roll down her window, but she couldn't risk it—not if he wanted to look more closely at the badge. If the Mudir caught a glimpse of that, it was game over.

Elizabeth tugged even tighter on the brim of her cap, shaking her head no while holding her badge in her lap, hoping that he would finally see it. Maybe he did. But by then it was too late.

She saw him in the rearview mirror. The Mudir was coming toward the car, gun drawn. A moment's distraction. That's all it took for him to have the upper hand. The scene in her mind immediately changed. He would kill the cop and then kill her. She could see it so clearly.

Elizabeth reached for the door, pushing it open as hard as she could to knock the cop out of the line of fire. No sooner had he fallen backward to the pavement than the Mudir's first shot struck the sideview mirror, exactly where he'd been standing.

"Stay down!" Elizabeth yelled, as she peeled out of the driver's seat expecting to see the Mudir still coming right for them.

Only he wasn't. He wasn't anywhere. At least nowhere she could see.

Crouching as low as she could, she began edging her way

along the side of the car. Just as she reached the gas tank, she heard the voice behind her.

"Drop it!"

It was the cop. He'd drawn his gun, demanding Elizabeth drop hers. She had no choice. She had to turn back to him, and that's all it took. Another moment's distraction. The arm came out from behind the trunk, grabbing her around the neck.

The Mudir now had his gun to her head.

CHAPTER 115

"LIZZIE!" I YELLED.

But she was gone. She'd hung up on me. Damn it.

I had the phone wedged between my shoulder and ear as I kneeled on the sidewalk next to Eli, my hands frantically ripping his shirt to get a clear look at where the bullet had entered—and hopefully exited—above his hip.

No such luck. Sliding my hand around to his back, I couldn't feel a hole. He would need surgery. If he didn't bleed out first.

"The girl," he said, his voice beginning to falter. "She's in danger."

"Yes."

"Go help her."

"Not yet," I said.

I could hear the sirens only blocks away, the ambulances racing to the scene. All around us people were still running, desperate to get as far away from the station as possible. Could they even hear me?

It was a safe bet I would've gone my entire life without asking this question, let alone to a bunch of strangers. "Does anyone have a tampon?" I yelled.

I kept yelling it until finally a young woman in a jean jacket stopped. I could see her eyes dart back and forth between Eli and me before landing on the blood seeping between my fingers as I continued applying pressure against the wound.

With a quick nod, she dug into her purse and handed me a sealed tampon.

"What else can I do?" she asked.

"An ambulance," I said. "First one you see."

She took off as I tore open the wrapper and lodged the tampon into the bullet hole as tightly as I could. Eli winced from the pain but still managed a slight smile. "Smart," he said. "Now go help the girl."

"Not yet," I said.

Elizabeth was being so stubborn, so reckless. If the Mudir didn't kill her, I was going to.

"There!" I heard across the street. "They're over there!"

The young woman in the jean jacket was screaming and pointing with a couple of EMTs in tow. As soon as they saw Eli, they began to sprint.

I wanted to get the woman's name, get her number, and get the mayor to give her a key to the city and a ticker-tape parade. But all I had time for as the EMTs swooped in to treat Eli was a quick hug and a thanks. Superheroes don't always wear capes. Sometimes they wear a jean jacket.

I took off down the sidewalk, running as fast as I could to find Elizabeth. The closer I got, the more I could feel it. Not my legs aching. Not my lungs burning. It was the sense of dread, that something terrible had already happened.

I would've given anything to be wrong. *Anything.*

But I wasn't.

CHAPTER 116

I SAW the car first. Up ahead, glimpses of white in between an endless stream of bodies passing in front of it. People running. Scrambling. Then, a few people not moving at all.

A cop had his gun drawn by the driver's side door. He was young. Even from a distance he looked nervous. He kept shifting his feet.

I followed his aim, my eyes darting to the back of the car. Suddenly, I had a clear view.

The Mudir. He had her. One arm wrapped around Elizabeth's neck in a choke hold. The other arm raised up to her head, the barrel jammed against her temple.

"Let her go!" I yelled.

The Mudir yanked Elizabeth like a rag doll as he turned to see me walking toward him with my Glock leveled right between his eyes.

He smiled. He'd known I was coming. "What took you so long?" he asked.

"You don't want her," I said. "You want me."

I glanced over to see the cop's head on a swivel, back and forth from the Mudir to me. His forehead was scrunched. He couldn't stop blinking. It was bad enough he was nervous. Now throw in heavily confused. "Who the hell are you?" he asked me.

"Yes," said the Mudir. "Tell him who you really are, Professor."

Only I didn't have to. The cop heard *Professor,* and it suddenly clicked for him. "You're that guy with the book," he said. "The one the serial killer used."

"Yeah, that's me," I said. "Now I need you to lower your gun."

"Why?"

"Because we don't want any accidents," I said.

The cop shook his head. "I hear you, but I can't do that."

"Sure you can," said the Mudir. "Tell him, Agent Needham. We don't want any accidents."

Elizabeth winced in pain as the Mudir pressed his gun even harder against her head. "Please," she told the cop. "Just do it."

I kept watching the cop from the corner of my eye, his feet continuing to shift back and forth. It was a dance of indecision. Finally he lowered his gun, moving to the front of the car for cover. Perfect.

The Mudir and I now had each other's undivided attention.

"What's your plan, Professor?" he asked.

"That depends," I said. "What's yours?"

"I'm getting in that car with Agent Needham, and no one's going to follow us," he said.

I shook him off like a pitcher on the mound. "Not quite. You're getting in the car with me, not her."

Elizabeth wasn't buying either plan. She was scared. But she was also angry. "Take the shot, Dylan," she said. "Take it!"

She was serious. The Mudir knew it, too. He altered his stance a bit, tucking his head a little more behind hers.

But I wasn't taking the shot. I was doing the opposite. I was laying down my weapon.

"I told you," I said, kneeling. "You don't want her, you want me."

Slowly, I placed my gun on the pavement. Elizabeth screamed. "No! Don't do it!"

"It's okay," I said. *Trust me.*

Hatred is a human flaw unlike any other. It will make you do the unthinkable. Even worse, it will make you not think at all. My plan had been to outsmart the Mudir. But sometimes the only way to outsmart someone is to convince him that you're a fool.

I stood up and spread my arms wide. There was no way I could hurt him. "Now let her go and take me instead," I said.

The Mudir smiled again. I'd just committed suicide. He was sure of it.

So sure that as he pulled his gun away from Elizabeth's head in order to kill me, it never even occurred to him. He'd just made the biggest mistake of his soon-to-be-over life.

Take the shot, Dad.

My father fired from his perch in the scaffolding above the Duane Reade drugstore twenty yards away. As the blast echoed up and down the street, the Mudir's lifeless body collapsed to the ground.

Elizabeth had no idea she had backup. No one else would either. The .44-caliber bullet that exploded through the Mudir's brain would be as untraceable as the triggerman himself. This was old school. Off the books. The stuff that only ends up in one of those files stamped TOP SECRET.

"Are you okay?" I asked.

Elizabeth stood frozen for a few seconds with the Mudir at her feet, his blood fanning out across the asphalt. She didn't answer. Instead, she walked over and hugged me tighter than anyone ever has.

I took that as a yes.

EPILOGUE

IT GOES ON

CHAPTER 117

I'VE NEVER been a big fan of the expression *It could've been a lot worse*. But I understand why people say it. It's one of the ways we deal with grief. A coping mechanism. We can better process a tragedy if we allow ourselves to think—to believe—that, yes, it could've been a lot worse.

Had it played out as planned, hundreds would've died in Grand Central Station that morning. Instead, the attack was thwarted and the thirteen terrorists, including the Mudir, were killed—but not before they took the lives of eight innocent people while firing back at agents. So, yeah, it could've been a lot worse. But I highly doubt the families of those eight who perished will ever see much of a silver lining. For them, that day was as bad as it gets.

I made a point of mentioning those thoughts in the email I ultimately wrote to the students in my Abnormal Behavioral Analysis class. They hadn't heard from their professor since their final exam was abruptly cut short. I owed them closure, as well as some perspective.

They thought it was unfair that they couldn't prepare for their exam. Then the real world interceded and taught them a lesson better than I ever could. No matter how prepared we strive to be, life is always there to remind us that we're all sort of just winging it. On that note, I announced what I'd always intended—that they were each getting an A on the final exam. Even if that hadn't been my intention, I still would've done it. They had enough to worry about. We all did.

"How are you feeling?" I asked.

Sadira smiled from her hospital bed. "I feel like I was tied up, thrown in the back of a van, and then the van flipped over three times at a hundred miles an hour."

"I think it was actually four times," I said. "But who's counting, right?"

"So was it your idea?" she asked. "This so-called deal?"

"That depends. Did you accept it?"

"I told him I wanted to talk to you first," she said.

Yes, the deal was my idea. Landon Foxx was skeptical, right up until the intelligence report came in regarding the missing Pu-239, weapons-grade plutonium, from a nuclear power plant in Iran. Viktor Alexandrov's apartment had been turned upside down twice over in an effort to find out what package the Mudir had been expecting, but nothing had been found. Might it have been the plutonium? There was no way of knowing for sure.

But there was Sadira.

"You don't have to help us," I told her.

"Just like your Agency doesn't have to help me," she said. "At least, that's what your friend was suggesting."

It was somewhat jarring to hear her refer to Foxx as my friend. "He's bluffing," I said. "Trying you for murder requires too much discovery and cross-examination, two things the CIA avoid like the plague. Besides, the exculpatory evidence alone would probably get you a hung jury."

"For a professor, you sure do sound a lot like a lawyer."

"I should," I said. "I'm married to one, after all."

"Wait. *You're married?*" Sadira feigned heartbreak. "I thought you said you weren't before our first date."

"I know. It was all a ruse. Can you believe it?"

"Clearly, I did," she said. "So you have a wife, huh?"

I laughed. "Not exactly."

I told her about Tracy, as well as Annabelle.

"Sounds like you're a lucky man, Dylan Reinhart."

"I was," I said. "But then I blew it."

CHAPTER 118

THE VIDEO surfaced two days later. I should've known.

Among the slew of people escaping Grand Central Station, one of them managed to stop and film the Mudir after he'd taken Elizabeth hostage.

While the recording thankfully didn't capture the Mudir's head getting blown off, the shot from the "unknown gunman" at the precise moment I laid down my own gun raised a fair amount of questions among the news media. As they did with Elizabeth, they staked out where I lived in the hope of getting some answers. And as Elizabeth did, I stayed as far away from where I lived as possible.

But while the press didn't know how to find me, someone else who saw the video did.

The call came right after another hospital visit, this one to Eli. After two hours of surgery and one slug of lead removed from his abdomen, he continued to be recovering nicely.

"Give my regards to Eagle," he told me with a wink. He never asked if it was my father who delivered the kill shot to the Mudir. Nor did he have to.

"Is that really you?" I asked, answering the phone. It was Tracy calling.

"Meet me in the park in an hour," he said. "You know where."

I did. I knew exactly where.

An hour later, I arrived at Cleopatra's Needle in Central Park, Tracy's favorite place to think. He hugged me, but there was no smile.

"Where's Annabelle?" I asked.

"I dropped her off at Lucinda's," he said.

As much as I missed our little girl and was desperate to see her, I understood why Tracy had asked our babysitter to watch her while we talked.

"So you saw the video, huh?"

"Yes, and I read the Grimes article, too," he said. "If you're not careful, you're going to win that guy a Pulitzer."

I'd promised Allen Grimes that he'd look like a hero. Not only did he get to break the story of the bomb scare at Penn Station, he was able to detail his "patriotic role" in originally keeping the story under wraps. Forget the Pulitzer, though. If I knew Grimes, he was angling for his own cable show. *Grimes on Crimes*, only now on TV.

"When did you get back?" I asked Tracy.

I assumed he'd left the city with Annabelle, and I was right. He'd gone to visit his sister in Providence. I assumed, as well, that what brought him back was the video. But I was wrong.

"Before I left I checked the mail. There was a letter from Mosa," he said. "I took it with me, but I only just opened it yesterday."

The adoption agency had originally advised us not to be in contact with Annabelle's mother in South Africa, but Tracy and

I thought otherwise. Mosa should know that her daughter was well taken care of and loved, and that her decision to give Annabelle up for adoption, so she might have a better life, should never be regretted. Exchanging letters every few months was our way of doing that.

"What did she write?" I asked.

Tracy stared up for a moment at the large obelisk towering over us. "It's what she didn't write," he said. "It's what she never writes. Mosa never complains or even mentions how hard she has it. She's always just thankful that Annabelle is with us in America."

Tracy looked at me. I knew what he was trying to say.

"You had every right to be mad as hell at me," I said.

"Maybe at first. But without sounding too corny, I didn't stop to think about the danger you were obviously in, and how you weren't doing it for yourself. For that alone, I'm a fool if I can't forgive you."

I hugged Tracy. He was smiling now. "Thank you," I said.

"Shall we go get our daughter?"

"Absolutely."

We walked away from Cleopatra's Needle, the sun high over a beautiful June day. Our city had been rocked, once again the target of terrorism. People were on edge, fearful that there were more attacks to come. But no one was hiding. The park was bustling. There were joggers, bikers, sunbathers, couples on benches, parents and kids—anyone and everyone. They were all enjoying themselves. They were all busy living. Because that's what we do.

In three words, I can sum up everything I've learned about life: it goes on.

Well put, Robert Frost.

"It's pretty cool, in a way," said Tracy as we continued to walk.

"What is?"

"That I'm married to someone who once worked for the CIA. I mean, it sounds so wild. My husband, the ex-CIA guy."

Oh, boy. Here we go again. About that ex *part…*

"Funny you should mention that," I said.

ABOUT THE AUTHORS

JAMES PATTERSON is one of the best-known and biggest-selling writers of all time. His books have sold in excess of 385 million copies worldwide. He is the author of some of the most popular series of the past two decades – the Alex Cross, Women's Murder Club, Detective Michael Bennett, and Private novels – and he has written many other number one bestsellers including romance novels and stand-alone thrillers.

James is passionate about encouraging children to read. Inspired by his own son who was a reluctant reader, he also writes a range of books for young readers including the Middle School, I Funny, Treasure Hunters, Dog Diaries and Max Einstein series. James has donated millions in grants to independent bookshops and has been the most borrowed author of adult fiction in UK libraries for the past eleven years in a row. He lives in Florida with his wife and son.

HOWARD ROUGHAN has co-written several books with James Patterson and is the author of *The Promise of a Lie* and *The Up and Comer*. He lives in Florida with his wife and son.

Read on for a sneak preview of the next thrilling
instalment in the Women's Murder Club series

Coming October 2019

JULIAN LAMBERT was an ex-con in his midthirties, sweet faced, with thinning, light-colored hair, wearing a red down jacket.

As he sat on a bench in Union Square waiting for his phone call, he took in the view of the Christmas tree at the center of the square. The tree was really something: an eighty-three-foot-tall cone of green lights with a star on top, ringed by pots of pointy red flowers, surrounded by a red-painted picket fence.

That tree was *secure*. It wasn't going anywhere.

It was lunchtime, and all around him consumers hurried out of stores weighed down with shopping bags, evidence of money pissed away in an orgy of spending. Julian wondered idly how these dummies were going to pay for their commercially fabricated gifting spree. Almost catching him by surprise, Julian's phone vibrated.

He fished it out of his pocket, connected, and said his name, and Mr. Loman, the boss, said, "Hello."

Julian knew that he was meant only to listen, and that was fine with him. He felt both excited and soothed as Loman explained just enough of the plan to allow Julian to salivate at the possibilities.

A heist.

A huge one.

The plan had many moving parts, Loman said, but if it went off as designed, by this time next year Julian would be living in the Caribbean, or Medellín, or Saint-Tropez. He was picturing a life of blue skies and sunshine, with a side of leggy young things in string bikinis, when Loman asked if he had any questions.

"I'm good to go, boss."

"Then get moving. No slipups."

"You can bank on me," said Julian, glad that Loman barked back, "Twenty-two fake dive, slot right long, on one."

Julian cracked up. He had played ball in college, a very long time ago, but he still had moves. He clicked off the call, sized up the vehicular and foot traffic, and chose his route.

It was go time.

JULIAN SAW his run as a punt return.

He charged into an elderly man in a shearling coat, sending the man sprawling. He snatched up the old guy's shopping bag, saying, "Thanks very much, knucklehead."

What counted was that he had the ball.

With the bag tucked under his arm, Julian ran across Geary, dodging and weaving through the crowd, heading toward the intersection at Stockton. He waited for a break in traffic at the red light, and when it came, he sprinted across the street and charged along the broad, windowed side of Neiman Marcus. Revolving glass doors split a crowd of shoppers into long lines of colorful dots filing out onto the sidewalk, accompanied by Christmas music: "I played my drum for him, pa-rum-pum-pum-pum." It was all so crazy.

Julian was still running.

He yelled, "Coming through! No brakes!" He wove around the merry shoppers, sideswiped the UPS man loading his truck, and, with knees and elbows pumping, bag secured under his arm, dashed up the Geary Street straightaway and veered left to cross again.

Another crowd of shoppers spilled out of Valentino, and Julian shot out his left hand to stiff-arm a young dude, who fell against a woman in a fur coat. Bags and packages clattered to the sidewalk. Julian high-stepped around and over the obstacles, then broke back again into a sprint, turning left on Grant Avenue.

He chortled as oncoming pedestrians scattered. Giving the finger to someone who yelled at him, knocking slowpokes out of his way, Julian shouted, "Merry fucking Christmas, everybody!"

God, this was fun. He couldn't see the goalposts, but he knew that he was scoring, big-time.

Julian ate up the pavement with his long strides as he listened for sirens. He glanced behind him and saw, finally, two people who looked like cops running up from the rear.

He was winded, but he didn't stop. *Show me what you've got, suckers.* He put on another surge of speed as he headed toward Dragon's Gate and the Chinatown district. He slowed only when a lady cop's authoritative voice shouted, "Freeze or I'll shoot!"

MY PARTNER, Inspector Rich Conklin, was running out of time, and he needed my help.

He said desperately, "Would be nice if she told you what she wants."

"Where would be the fun in that?" I said, grinning. "You figuring it out is kind of the point."

"I guess. Make our own history."

"Sure. That's an idea."

We had slipped out of the Hall of Justice to do some lunchtime Christmas shopping in San Francisco's Union Square because of its concentration of high-end shops. Richie wanted to get something special for Cindy.

Rich had wanted to marry Cindy from pretty much the moment he met her. And she loved him fiercely. But. There's always a *but*, right?

Rich was from a big family, and while he was still in his thirties, he'd wanted kids. Lots of them. Cindy was an only child with a hot career—one that took her to murder scenes in bad places in the dead of night. And Rich wasn't the only crime fighter in the relationship; Cindy had solved more than one homicide, even shooting and being shot by a crafty female serial killer who became the subject of Cindy's bestselling true-crime book.

All this to say, Cindy was in no hurry to have a family.

It was a conflict of desires that in the past had broken up my two great friends, and it was tremendous that they were back together now. But as far as I knew, the conflict remained unsolved.

Rich pointed out an emerald pendant around the neck of a mannequin in a shop window.

"Do you like that?"

I said, "Beautiful. And very Christmassy," when I heard a scream behind us.

I turned to see a man in a red down jacket running past us, yelling, "Coming through! No brakes!" He nearly collided with a group of people coming out of Neiman's, clipped a UPS man, and just kept going.

An elderly man in a shearling coat was hobbling down the street in pursuit, with blood streaming out of his nose. He cried out, "Stop, thief! Someone stop him!"

Rich and I are homicide cops, and this was no murder. But we were there. We took off behind the man in the red jacket, who was running with all the power and determination of a pro tailback.

I yelled, "Stop! Police!" But the runner kept going.

I DIDN'T trust myself to run full out. My doctor had recently benched me for two months owing to a bout of anemia. So I slowed to a walk and yelled to Rich, "You go. I'll call it in."

I got on my phone and summed up the situation for dispatch in a few words: There had been a robbery, a grab-and-dash. Conklin was pursuing the suspect on foot, running east on Geary Street, turning north onto Grant Avenue.

"Suspect is wearing a red jacket, dark pants. We need backup and an ambulance," I said, and gave my location.

I trotted back to the elderly man with the bloody nose who was now on his feet, panting and leaning against a building.

He said, "You're a cop."

"Yes. Tell me what happened," I said.

He told me that he'd been minding his own business when "that guy" knocked him down and stole his shopping bag.

"What's your name, sir?"

"Maury King."

"Mr. King, an ambulance will be here in a minute."

He shook himself off. "No, no. I'm okay. Don't let that bastard get away."

"We won't. My partner is in pursuit. Stay right here," I said. "I'll be back."

Leabharlanna Fhine Gall

Also by James Patterson

ALEX CROSS NOVELS

Along Came a Spider • Kiss the Girls • Jack and Jill •
Cat and Mouse • Pop Goes the Weasel • Roses are Red •
Violets are Blue • Four Blind Mice • The Big Bad Wolf •
London Bridges • Mary, Mary • Cross • Double Cross •
Cross Country • Alex Cross's Trial (*with Richard DiLallo*) •
I, Alex Cross • Cross Fire • Kill Alex Cross • Merry
Christmas, Alex Cross • Alex Cross, Run • Cross My
Heart • Hope to Die • Cross Justice • Cross the Line •
The People vs. Alex Cross • Target: Alex Cross

THE WOMEN'S MURDER CLUB SERIES

1st to Die • 2nd Chance (*with Andrew Gross*) • 3rd Degree
(*with Andrew Gross*) • 4th of July (*with Maxine Paetro*) •
The 5th Horseman (*with Maxine Paetro*) • The 6th Target
(*with Maxine Paetro*) • 7th Heaven (*with Maxine Paetro*) •
8th Confession (*with Maxine Paetro*) • 9th Judgement (*with
Maxine Paetro*) • 10th Anniversary (*with Maxine Paetro*) •
11th Hour (*with Maxine Paetro*) • 12th of Never (*with Maxine
Paetro*) • Unlucky 13 (*with Maxine Paetro*) • 14th Deadly Sin
(*with Maxine Paetro*) • 15th Affair (*with Maxine Paetro*) •
16th Seduction (*with Maxine Paetro*) • 17th Suspect
(*with Maxine Paetro*) • 18th Abduction (*with Maxine Paetro*)

DETECTIVE MICHAEL BENNETT SERIES

Step on a Crack (*with Michael Ledwidge*) • Run for Your Life
(*with Michael Ledwidge*) • Worst Case (*with Michael Ledwidge*) •
Tick Tock (*with Michael Ledwidge*) • I, Michael Bennett
(*with Michael Ledwidge*) • Gone (*with Michael Ledwidge*) •
Burn (*with Michael Ledwidge*) • Alert (*with Michael Ledwidge*) •
Bullseye (*with Michael Ledwidge*) • Haunted (*with James
O. Born*) • Ambush (*with James O. Born*)

PRIVATE NOVELS

Private (*with Maxine Paetro*) • Private London (*with Mark Pearson*) • Private Games (*with Mark Sullivan*) • Private: No. 1 Suspect (*with Maxine Paetro*) • Private Berlin (*with Mark Sullivan*) • Private Down Under (*with Michael White*) • Private L.A. (*with Mark Sullivan*) • Private India (*with Ashwin Sanghi*) • Private Vegas (*with Maxine Paetro*) • Private Sydney (*with Kathryn Fox*) • Private Paris (*with Mark Sullivan*) • The Games (*with Mark Sullivan*) • Private Delhi (*with Ashwin Sanghi*) • Private Princess (*with Rees Jones*)

NYPD RED SERIES

NYPD Red (*with Marshall Karp*) • NYPD Red 2 (*with Marshall Karp*) • NYPD Red 3 (*with Marshall Karp*) • NYPD Red 4 (*with Marshall Karp*) • NYPD Red 5 (*with Marshall Karp*)

DETECTIVE HARRIET BLUE SERIES

Never Never (*with Candice Fox*) • Fifty Fifty (*with Candice Fox*) • Liar Liar (*with Candice Fox*) • Hush Hush (*with Candice Fox*)

STAND-ALONE THRILLERS

The Thomas Berryman Number • Hide and Seek • Black Market • The Midnight Club • Sail (*with Howard Roughan*) • Swimsuit (*with Maxine Paetro*) • Don't Blink (*with Howard Roughan*) • Postcard Killers (*with Liza Marklund*) • Toys (*with Neil McMahon*) • Now You See Her (*with Michael Ledwidge*) • Kill Me If You Can (*with Marshall Karp*) • Guilty Wives (*with David Ellis*) • Zoo (*with Michael Ledwidge*) • Second Honeymoon (*with Howard Roughan*) • Mistress (*with David Ellis*) • Invisible (*with David Ellis*) • Truth or Die (*with Howard Roughan*) • Murder House (*with David Ellis*) • Woman of God (*with Maxine Paetro*) • Humans, Bow Down (*with Emily Raymond*) • The Black Book (*with David Ellis*) • The Store (*with Richard DiLallo*) • Texas Ranger (*with Andrew Bourelle*) • The President is Missing (*with Bill Clinton*) • Revenge (*with Andrew Holmes*) • Juror No. 3 (*with Nancy Allen*) • The First Lady (*with Brendan DuBois*) • The Chef (*with Max DiLallo*) • Unsolved (*with David Ellis*) • The Inn (*with Candice Fox*) • The Warning (*with Robison Wells*)

NON-FICTION

Torn Apart (*with Hal and Cory Friedman*) • The Murder of King Tut (*with Martin Dugard*) • All-American Murder (*with Alex Abramovich and Mike Harvkey*)

MURDER IS FOREVER TRUE CRIME

Murder, Interrupted (*with Alex Abramovich and Christopher Charles*) • Home Sweet Murder (*with Andrew Bourelle and Scott Slaven*) • Murder Beyond the Grave (*with Andrew Bourelle and Christopher Charles*)

COLLECTIONS

Triple Threat (*with Max DiLallo and Andrew Bourelle*) • Kill or Be Killed (*with Maxine Paetro, Rees Jones, Shan Serafin and Emily Raymond*) • The Moores are Missing (*with Loren D. Estleman, Sam Hawken and Ed Chatterton*) • The Family Lawyer (*with Robert Rotstein, Christopher Charles and Rachel Howzell Hall*) • Murder in Paradise (*with Doug Allyn, Connor Hyde and Duane Swierczynski*) • The House Next Door (*with Susan DiLallo, Max DiLallo and Brendan DuBois*) • 13-Minute Murder (*with Shan Serafin, Christopher Farnsworth and Scott Slaven*)

For more information about James Patterson's novels, visit www.jamespatterson.co.uk